SUNRISE IN THE VALLEY

To Gary

With best wishes

for ~

Also by Fergus Smith

In the Shadow of the Mountain, published by Headsail Books 2013

> *"The British public sympathises with its army, but does not empathise with it... The army trumpets the ideals of leadership; this book explains what they are, and how they operate."*

Professor Sir Hew Strachan, Chichele Professor of the History of War at All Souls College Oxford

> *"...as thought-provoking as it is enthralling."*

James Clark, former Defence Editor, The Sunday Times

> *"Anyone with ambitions to lead should read this book. When the pressure is on, we learn, rank means little and the 'right to lead' is hard won and easily lost: 'command', it transpires, is an anxious and ever insecure place. Humility, sacrifice and integrity are every bit as essential as toughness, confidence and competence."*

Professor Chris Ivory, Deputy Director, Institute of International Management Practice, Anglia Ruskin University

SUNRISE IN THE VALLEY

Fergus Smith

Published by Headsail Books

Published by Headsail Books, 55 Westgate, LEEDS, LS20 8HH
www.headsailbooks.com

First published in the United Kingdom in 2016 by Headsail Books.

ISBN 978-0-9926872-3-6 (Paperback)
ISBN 978-0-9926872-4-3 (mobi)

Although this novel is based on true events, the characters are entirely fictitious and any similarity to real persons, alive or dead, is coincidental and not intended by the author.

Cover design: Claire Simpson claire@clairesimpsondesigns.co.uk

Cover photo: copyright © Alex Christian/500px. The person depicted is a model.

Cover photo of 'Microphone on air' ©Forest Run/Shutterstock

Cover portrait: Faye Kenny-Broom fkbphotography@gmail.com

Page design by Clare Brayshaw

This book has been produced by York Publishing Services Ltd, 64 Hallfield Road, Layerthorpe, York YO31 7ZQ
www.yps-publishing.co.uk

For all defenders of truth,
dhe për popullin e Kosovës

In wartime, truth is so precious that she must be attended by a bodyguard of lies.

Winston S Churchill

Kosovo, February 2001

Prologue

It was Zadunica, the Day of Souls. Anja's mother lifted the pogacha from the oven using a towel so she didn't burn her hands. She placed the bread on the wooden block and laid the towel over it before turning to close the oven door.

Steam rose through the fabric to fill the kitchen with the smell of sesame and melted butter. There would be slava for dinner, and maybe piglet if Tata could find it.

When her mother wasn't looking, Anja pinched the corner of the towel and teased it away from the loaf.

"Out," Mama scolded.

"I was just…"

"Don't lie. Go get some firewood. And bring in more water."

Anja pulled on her hat, mittens, and boots and stomped out into the cold. It wasn't fair. She had only wanted to try a tiny piece of the yellow crumb, where it swelled out between the oak coloured crusts. It was the bit she loved most, the bit that made her eyes close.

Her mother always knew when she was fibbing but Anja didn't know how. To find work, Tata had to say he was Albanian when actually he was Serbian. How was that different?

Anja ignored the woodpile and the well. The sky was the blue of goat bells, the blue of wind. The frost along the branches had melted in the weak sunlight. Small droplets of water dripped on her coat. Running along the track, she jumped on the puddles to crack the ice. She picked up a stick that had a good handle at one end, imagining it the hilt of a magical sword.

On the big rock, a crow picked at a piece of carrion held between its claws. As she got closer it lifted its head and flew away, wings clapping. There was a pink smear on the stone, but Anja climbed up anyway and looked back towards the wooden cottage hidden amongst the trees.

Her mother would not miss her.

She was not allowed beyond the rock, but the path looked too exciting to ignore. The mud had frozen into ruts where the tractors dragged logs out of the forest. Further along the ridge she came to a flat grassy field that overlooked the valley. It fascinated her that her feet could be at the same height as the very tops of the trees. The morning sun was unable to penetrate more than the upper branches. A cold wind swept up through the forest. It smelled of rotting pine needles. It made her nose wrinkle.

She was half Albanian and half Serbian. Tata said she should always assume strangers would do her harm. If she saw anyone along the track she must run home as quick as a mountain hare. But there was no one in sight, so Anja walked until the track twisted off the ridge to descend into the forest. She dare not go further, but if she cocked her head and stilled her breathing, she could hear the cars by the army gate on the safe side of the hill. Perhaps she'd see Tata and wave to him.

Not finding a way round the bushes, Anja squatted to peek underneath. There was a tunnel below the branches and she crawled along it. Twigs caught in her hair and she scraped her knee on a stone, but eventually she emerged onto a thin track that overlooked the road. A huge tree had fallen next to the path. Anja clambered up to sit astride the rough bark, finding it provided a commanding view down towards the gate.

Below her, the foreign soldiers had parked trucks by the side of the road. They were dark green and had enormous wheels. The front sloped up on the underside like a sledge. Tata said they weren't tanks as they didn't have a big gun on top, but they were still dangerous and Anja was not to go near them.

She studied the flags on the pole above the building. The one at the top was blue and white. On one side it said 'NATO' in the Latin alphabet, and on the other it said the same in Slavic letters. She was pleased she could read both and the blue was the same colour as the sky. The second flag was like a flash of red and blue exploding from the centre. She was sure it was the flag of *Tonyblair*, a tiny island in the distant ocean.

Just then, soldiers strode out of the building to climb into the green trucks. A man shouted and waved his arms. On the far side, where the road disappeared into the unfriendly forest, a soldier pressed down on a white block and the bar rose up. Three beautiful red buses appeared out of the forest and the shouting man directed them to halt side by side. Soldiers got on the buses and off again. A man with a dog walked up and down the bags. The soldier at the gate lifted the white block and the bar fell gracefully to bounce and settle across the road.

This much Anja knew: Tata was from Serbia, beyond the forest on the other side of the gate, but Mama was Albanian from this side. After the war, Tata could not get work. The girls at school pulled her hair because of her name, so Mama told Tata to teach her at home.

The red buses had the word *Express* written on the side in glorious Slavic letters. One of the green trucks roared into life, sputtering black smoke. It pulled out, all the wheels turning together.

The buses started their engines and closed the folding doors. It was Zadunica, the Day of Souls. These were

Serbian people going to the monastery in Gracanica to honour the dead. They were her people.

Anja jumped off the tree trunk and ran down the track to keep level with the convoy until it started to accelerate. She stopped as the front bus pulled away, her breath hot underneath her coat.

The third bus stalled right below her, crunching its gears.

A scalding wind flung her back against the trunk of a tree. Her head hit the sharp stump of a broken branch. It stung. There was blood on her mittens and she couldn't hear. All around, birds flapped in panic. She swallowed, and her head filled with the howling of people in agony.

The bus had exploded. The front section tilted forwards. Fire swirled and cursed inside it. A man with flames ripping round his body, his arms, his head, staggered a few steps then collapsed on his knees. He pressed flaming hands into his flaming face. The fire intensified around him. People had been strewn about like scalded corn. A woman hugged a bundle towards her belly, her screams silent. A man held his arm beside his body. The skin was charred and bloody. Dense, rubbery smoke rose furiously into the air. It made a popping sound. Soldiers ran towards the bus but were forced back by the heat. One tried to spray white foam but it had no effect. Another picked his way through the pools of blood and vomited.

Anja smelled cigarettes. A man appeared along the track, striding towards her. He frowned. She knew straight away he was to blame for the explosion. She raced up the track as fast as she could, skipping from stone to stone. She fell, grazing the palm of her hand, but pushed herself up. The man followed behind on long strides.

At the tree trunk, he nearly caught her. With a panicked yelp, she dived into the tunnel under the branches and scrabbled uphill on hands and knees. Pain was secondary. The man shouted in Albanian. He grabbed her boot, but she kicked herself free.

Branches caught her coat pocket. She twisted and slapped them off, tearing the silky pink fabric. She hurried along, heedless of the holes appearing in her stockings. Finally she found herself at the forest track that led home.

With two mittened hands on the frozen mud, she launched herself into open space. Fear clamped her chest. All she wanted was the woollen stretch of Tata's arms.

Her hood snagged. It pulled her backwards, strangling her.

"Come here!"

He lifted her off the ground and pressed her against the trunk of a tree. There was wood smoke on his clothing. His teeth were stained. He was dressed like a hunter, even though there would be no rabbits at this time of year.

"Who are you?" he said in Albanian.

Anja opened her mouth but her throat was too dry. He let her slump among the roots. She started crying. He towered above her. He had a shotgun slung over one shoulder. Lighting a cigarette, he looked round for where she came from. His cheeks tightened. He unslung the shotgun and it fell open in his hand. He took something shiny from a pocket and inserted it into the barrel.

"*Zotëri...*" she whimpered.

The man looked down, his eyes as dark as soot. "You are Albanian?"

Anja nodded.

He took a drag from the cigarette and dropped it by her foot. Slowly, he pressed the toe of his boot into the dirt to extinguish the butt. She watched the foot twist, the final wisp of smoke rise and vanish. He wiped tobacco from his lip, then closed the gun with a metallic snap. "Go home, little one," he whispered, and disappeared down the track into the dense forest.

Anja could not move for several minutes. Then the sky thundered. A vast helicopter blocked out the sun. Anja bolted home, screeching like a kit taken by a hawk.

NATO Strategy in Tatters as Balkan Peace Collapses
The Guardian, 20 February 2001
Nick Oakeshot, Balkans Correspondent

NATO strategy in the Balkans is yet again in disarray following the killing of twelve Serbians by dissident Albanian extremists yesterday. The Serbians were traveling by bus from the town of Nis in southern Serbia to the Monastery of the Holy Virgin in Gracanica, Kosovo.

The convoy of buses, escorted by British armoured vehicles, was destroyed by a two-hundred kilogram road-side bomb detonated by command wire. The blast was so powerful it left a three-metre deep crater in the road. Personal effects and body parts were scattered over a vast area.

One witness described the screaming: "It was like hell, the worst noise you can imagine."

Survivors were taken by British helicopters to military hospitals in Pristina and to the heavily fortified American base at Bondsteel. One was announced dead on arrival and a further two remain seriously ill.

The youngest victim, Danito Djuric, was only two years old. Both his mother and father were killed in the attack. His aunt, Jasna, 32, from Nis, described her anger: "My brother is gone, his wife, his son. Danito was our joy, our future. They have taken our dreams. NATO has betrayed us."

The Serbians were visiting the monastery for the All Soul's Day festival, a day of celebration in the Serbian

Orthodox calendar. Many had fled Kosovo during the 1999 war and were responding to the United Nation's invitation for refugees to return.

No British soldiers were injured in the attack but senior officers recognise that it was well executed. The Albanian insurgents allowed several NATO vehicles to pass over the bomb before exploding it underneath the Serbian bus. Privately, they admit to concerns about the rise in Albanian extremism across the troubled Balkan region. The bombers are thought to be hiding in the demilitarised buffer zone surrounding Kosovo, a five mile wide area known locally as the Presevo Valley.

"I doubt whether the Serbian population would trust NATO to protect them in the future," one officer said.

In 1999 British forces drove the Serbian army out of Kosovo in order to prevent the worst ethnic cleansing seen in Europe since the Second World War. The Prime Minister, Tony Blair, is seen as a hero by many Kosovo Albanians. The province remains part of the Serbian state, but the UN provides the police and civil administration under the protection of NATO military forces.

In a separate incident, the British forces spokesman in Pristina, Lieutenant-colonel Jasper Higgson, 38, was sent home following 'security concerns'.

PART ONE

Chapter 1

Located just off a motorway in northwest London, the command centre had been built to survive nuclear war. Known as *the Bunker*, it was where every military operation was supervised by Vice-admiral Sir John Hobbes, Chief of Joint Operations. More than anyone else, he was the man responsible for developing Britain's reputation as *the* global expert in counter insurgency warfare.

Paul hadn't liked the claustrophobic and insular feel of the place when he visited the first time. He liked it even less as he followed the Royal Marine out of the lift and along the narrow, curving corridor. It smelled of recycled air and carpet glue. The officers who passed him turned their shoulders and avoided his eyes. Dressed in baggy green combats, he was too obviously a *field man* summoned for a briefing. In his mind, by contrast, they were the sort of officer who didn't know a dossbag from a dachshund. The sooner he was on his way to Brize Norton the better.

"Message Command is down there on the right, Captain Illingworth," the escort said. "If you go too far, you'll hit the heads."

"Thanks, I remember now."

Paul continued in the direction indicated until he could hear Brassy talking on the telephone. Because the office door was open, his strident voice spilled out into the corridor. Paul stopped short of the doorway while the conversation finished. A plastic sign jutted out from the top corner of the door frame: *Lieutenant Colonel TJH Hampton-Brazel, Life Guards, Message Operations*.

"That's right, Sir," Brassy was saying. "That's far more consistent with the Five Themes. If we can get the Daily Telegraph to drop the story, I'll get the Defence Editor an interview with Vice-admiral Hobbes. Everyone's a winner."

Paul smiled to himself. When the conversation finished, Brassy thumped the receiver down on the cradle and his voice took on a more jovial tone. "Is that young Illingworth out there?"

Paul stepped forward, saluted, and smiled in greeting. Brassy pulled himself up to squeeze round the edge of his desk and proffer a pudgy hand. "How the devil, Paul? Wonderful to see you!"

"Good to see you too, Colonel. Thank you for your help last year."

Brassy made a dismissive gesture with his free hand. "After all that time you did in Oman, it would have been criminal to leave you. I told Flight Control: *I don't care if the man's only a captain; I want him home for Christmas. If first class is all there is, that's what he's flying.*"

Paul felt embarrassed to be indebted to a senior officer, but there was very little space for him to back off to a respectful distance.

"Do sit down," Brassy invited, indicating a chair. "I'll just nip out for a wiz if you don't mind. Can I get you a brew?"

Paul stammered. "I'll get them…"

"Certainly not. Coffee?"

"Please, NATO: white, two sugars."

The chair slotted between Brassy's desk and a rack of cables, laptops, and digital cameras. On the opposite wall, a magnetic planner had key dates marked for the following months: the anniversaries of historic campaigns, major exercises in Germany, Trooping the Colour. A long bar throughout the summer months was labelled *Purdah and General Election?* after which nothing else was marked. On the coffee table lay a pile of daily papers. An article had been neatly incised from the front page of the Daily Telegraph.

Behind a bronze of a cavalry horse on Brassy's desk, an internal envelope was labelled 'Kosovo – Illingworth'. Paul shook out the manila file and flicked through the maps and the dateline. He was reading the media assessment when Brassy returned with a mug in each hand.

"You found it! Good man. There's your coffee."

Paul closed the file and took out a notebook from the deep internal pockets of his arctic smock.

"You'll need that jacket where you're going," Brassy continued. "Bloody chilly at the moment. But it'll warm up pretty smartish. I hear the summers are lovely, and the fillies really quite special."

After shuffling sideways round his desk, Brassy heaved himself into his chair with a sigh. "So you made it back for Crimbo?"

"I did, Colonel; late on Christmas Eve. Like I said, I'm grateful for you pulling strings."

"No problem at all. I simply won't have the bean counters running the bloody army. We're a people business and that means shelling out every now and then. Was first class good?"

Paul nodded. "Yes, yes it was."

"Excellent. And family well? Is it Leeds you're from? Or Bradford?"

"Shipley."

"Good man. Dark satanic mills and all that. But you got to see the bird. Sasha was it? Or Sandra?"

The question had been innocuous, but Paul was not inclined to answer. The reason he was so keen to go to Kosovo was that Susan had dumped him in the brittle and uncertain period between Christmas and New Year's Eve.

"What do you need me to do in Pristina?" he said. "The incumbent was sent home?"

Brassy took the cue to cut the small talk. "Yes, the bloody fool. Jasper is a chum of mine as well. I was at his wedding, so it was something of a surprise to find he was shagging his Serb interpreter. The intelligence community had a field day, I can tell you!"

Paul frowned.

"Whatever she wheedled out of him went straight to Belgrade and I'm pretty certain went on to Moscow from there. Complicated business, the Balkans."

Paul patted the folder on his knee. "But all I need is here?"

Brassy leaned back in his chair to interlace fingers over his belly. "Pretty much. You weren't there with your regiment during the war?"

Paul shook his head. Despite all his entreaties to deploy, he had been serving with the Territorial Army and could not be released. "I'd been posted out of battalion."

Brassy studied him for a moment. "But you know the basics?"

"I think so. We went in to protect the Albanians from the Serbs. We established a buffer zone round the outside?"

"Exactly. Now the Albos are getting too big for their boots. There are pockets of them outside Kosovo, in southern Serbia and northern FYROM. That's the country formerly known as Macedonia, as I'm sure you know. They're making noises about a Greater Albania. You'll have to bring them under control."

Not only was a captain being sent out to replace a colonel, but Brassy was telling him to address big political issues. Paul beamed.

"This is perfectly within your powers, Paul. I can't tell you how glad I was to get you for this role. When you're out in the field there's a clear line of sight between what the journalists are being told, what we say here, and what Downing Street wants us to portray. It's seamless."

After taking a noisy sip of coffee, he waved a hand at the wall planner. "And you see that? There's an election this year. These New Labour people have proved quite keen to use the military. We've shown what we can do in Northern

Ireland, Sierra Leone, Iraq, the flooding up in Yorkshire and so on." He paused to clear his throat, then, "but if we want a decent defence budget after the election, we need to prove Britain still boxes above its weight on the world stage."

Paul did not want a lecture about foreign policy. He wanted to focus on the job at hand. "There was a bomb, Colonel? On a bus?"

Brassy placed his coffee down. "Yes, damn them. The bloody Albanians, like I said. They'd better be careful, Paul. This thing about NATO protecting them will only go so far. If they start murdering innocent women and children it gets harder for us to say we're neutral."

"But we're not calling them *murderers*? Or *terrorists*?"

Brassy shook his head. "Too strong at this stage. We're using the terms *extremists* or *insurgents* but we may have to up the rhetoric before long."

"Are the local media any good?"

Brassy took another sip of coffee. "Nothing like Sierra Leone. The Kosovans can read, for a start. There are TV stations and newspapers, but most of the work is done through the radio stations. You'll have a couple of hours of interviews every week."

He fixed Paul with his gaze. "Important, as always, that you don't deviate from the *Media Lines To Take*. We'll back you up from here, if you get asked anything difficult."

"Are there any internationals out there?"

Brassy nodded. "There are; two in particular we need you to get to grips with. Nick Oakeshot, who is BBC but also writes for The Grauniad, and a rather maverick freelancer called Aden Short who is the staff reporter for Reuters and writes for The Times. The locals ape them, so if you get them on message the job's halfway done."

Paul thought through the questions that had come to mind while he was driving down. "Who am I working for?"

"Me," Brassy said without pause. "In practical terms you'll be reporting to Commander British Forces Pristina, Brigadier Sandy Montrose. Or his Chief of Staff, Simon Easterby, another chum of mine. But we'll be talking on a daily basis."

There was another question Paul wanted to ask but didn't know how.

Brassy read his face. "You want to know who'll write your annual appraisal?"

Paul nodded. "I do, Colonel. I need a really strong recommendation if I'm ever to go to Staff College..."

Brassy laughed. "Of course, Paul! Goes without saying!" He leaned on his elbows. "You're going out as an acting major, not a captain, for a start. And people are waking up to what Message Operations can deliver. We're a force multiplier. We shape the environment. People like you, with extensive expertise, have a huge amount to offer."

He leaned back in his chair and opened his hands in a magnanimous gesture. "You do well in Kosovo, and your future is assured."

Even though this was what he wanted to hear, the exchange made Paul uncomfortable. Brassy's highly polished shoes poked out from under the front of his desk. His ankles were covered by a pair of mismatched socks, one red and one yellow. "You're off message there, Colonel," he said with a smile.

"Ha!" Brassy said. "Great, aren't they? Got them in Sloane Square. Need a bit of colour in a place like this, I can tell you. It never does to be too conformist, does it?"

Brassy thrust his hands deep into his pockets and snatched a glance at the clock above the door. "Listen Paul, I'm on a call in a few minutes with MoD Main Building. There's been another half-witted female getting her mammaries out for the tabloids. We'll have some dreadful Page 3 headlines about *Captain Crumpet* or *Lieutenant Lusty* unless I come up with ideas to deflect attention. Is there anything else you need?"

Paul patted the file on his knee and frowned. Slowly, he shook his head.

Brassy folded his arms. "After we got over that press conference in Sierra Leone, Paul, you proved yourself to be the best field man we have. You get me Kosovo on message before the election and I'll get you into Staff College next January."

* * *

The two Russian sentries slouched past the portacabin that constituted Pristina airport, their rifles slung low and fur hats pushed back on their heads. They regarded the British soldiers returning from leave with what looked like a mixture of envy and disdain.

Paul watched them saunter away, then clambered up the steps of the bus that would take him to the headquarters of British Forces in Kosovo. Taking a seat by himself at the front, he wiped the window with the sleeve of his jacket and peered out. The fields around the airport were edged by deep ditches brimming with litter. Scallops of snow snagged along lines of corn stalks. A boy in dirty clothing, seemingly impervious to the cold, carried a crate of chickens on his head.

The bus slowed behind a horse-drawn cart laden with agricultural containers. The driver wore a grey, conical hat and had the face of one who had laboured in the fields all his life.

They soon worked their way out of the narrow tracks and onto a two lane highway. Here, the passing cars were all high-end Mercedes and BMWs, considerably newer than the fourth-hand Vauxhall Paul had parked at Brize Norton.

Cresting a hill, Paul caught his first glimpse of Pristina, a town that had dominated the news only two years earlier. Pasted across the landscape, the regional capital at first appeared a wall of ugly, Soviet style tenements spotted with satellite dishes like the acne on a teenager's chin. Here at last, he thought.

As they slowed behind a traffic jam, he felt hemmed in and was surprised by the lack of an armed escort. Even in the ceasefire no one would have been unarmed in Belfast.

How different it must have been during the war. The television images had shown refugees fleeing south, the aftermath of a campaign of ethnic cleansing by the Serb army. The Prime Minister, Tony Blair, had convinced the United Nations that it must never allow genocide to go unchallenged in the backrooms of Europe. It had to enforce a peace between the warring nations.

It was a source of immense pride to Paul that Britain had led the world in committing troops to end the violence, and the root of a deep shame that he had not been one of them. All his friends had come home with medals and the glow of moral purpose, while Paul had been stuck in an office. He had watched the whole thing unfold on television with an increasing sense that his career was not taking the direction he desired.

But it would still be challenging now, he told himself. It may not be as militarily dangerous, or as thrilling, or as newsworthy, but it was still important. Lives were being lost. The balance of power between the Serbs and the Albanians had changed, but it was not yet stable. He saw a niche for himself in making it so. Whereas he had missed the cut and thrust of the war, the intellectual appeal of post-conflict reconstruction felt exciting.

Having cleared the choke point, the bus turned away from the city along an uneven mud track. After a few hundred uncomfortable metres, Paul recognised the gabion walls of a British base. The two signallers behind him roused themselves, stretched, and pulled on their berets. The approach to the main gate was lined with stalls selling CDs, the racks covered in sheets of see-through plastic. The stall owners clapped their hands in the cold.

"Music, Sir. Anything you can think of," said one of the signallers.

"And porn," sniggered the other.

"Any good?"

"They're great, Sir. Bought loads of them, me. And if you take them something they haven't got, they'll copy it and let you have one for free."

So business was booming under NATO. Paul ducked to read the sign behind the gate sentry. *Welcome to Slim Lines*, it read, *Headquarters British Forces and Multinational Brigade Centre*.

After clearing the security barrier, the bus turned in a wide arc. The door hissed and slapped open, allowing Paul to descend onto packed snow. Around him was a square of single storey portacabins joined by wooden walkways. The signallers slumped off towards their accommodation, bergens on their shoulders. One of them pointed towards a portacabin with a twenty-metre radio mast behind it. "The headquarters is that one, Sir," he said.

Inside, the Watchkeeper, a smart female captain from the Royal Artillery, escorted him through an empty briefing room to a door marked *Chief of Staff*. She knocked, peered round, then pushed it open.

The office was spartan, the walls covered with maps. Behind the desk sat a broad-chested, sandy-haired major in Black Watch uniform. He rose to shake Paul's hand and spoke with a gravelly Scottish accent. "Simon Easterby, Chief of Staff. It's very good to meet you."

Simon exuded the self-assurance of a man destined to command a battalion. The Watchkeeper excused herself and closed the door. Only then did Paul notice the two other people in the room: a very tall Brigadier wearing the belt of the Royal Engineers, and a plump, severe looking major from the Intelligence Corps.

The Brigadier jumped up as Paul hastily saluted. "Good gracious! Well done for getting here so quickly."

Paul smiled, keen to impress at their first meeting. "My pleasure, Sir. I've got rapid deployment down to a fine art after the last year or so."

The Brigadier laughed. "Well done you. I'm Sandy Montrose, Commander British Forces. You've met Simon, my Chief of Staff, and this is Blanche Henderson, Head of Intelligence and Security."

The woman didn't rise, but nodded in greeting. She studied Paul with tight lips.

"Have a seat," the Brigadier said. "So you've been away a good deal of late?"

Paul sat where he could face all three of them and tugged at his trousers to straighten the seam. "I was at home for Christmas, Sir. But before that I was in Oman, on Exercise Safe Sarea. Before that I was in Sierra Leone with the Joint Task Force."

The Brigadier frowned. "So how long have you been at home in the last year?"

Paul counted. "Six weeks."

The Brigadier folded his arms and turned to Simon, who shook his head as he clicked a pen. He made a note on a sheet of paper. "I'll put something together for the Bunker, Commander. This can't go on."

Paul looked from one to the other, uncertain of what he'd said.

"Paul, this is nothing against you," the Brigadier explained, extending a conciliatory palm, fingers splayed wide. "I'm sure you are robust enough to handle this sort of routine. But of late we've been sent a number of staff officers showing signs of what one might call *excessive wear*."

Paul nodded. If he was honest, he would have admitted to the utter exhaustion that had nagged him throughout January; the way even simple decisions assumed a turgid complexity. But he knew better than to be honest about such things.

Montrose continued. "This is a medium intensity operation in an increasingly fluid environment. I cannot afford to have people going off the boil."

"I'm sure," Paul nodded, his cheeks flushing.

Simon smiled, the recognition of one infantry officer to another. "I'm certain you'll be fine, Paul. You come highly recommended by a number of people."

"You've worked with the press before?" the Brigadier asked.

Paul toyed with the beret on his knee. "I instruct on the course, Sir. Journalists trust me because I'm infantry. If you're straight with them, they tend to give reasonable copy. There's no black art to it."

The Brigadier smiled, "what was it Napoleon said? He'd rather face a thousand bayonets than four hostile editors? That's certainly true here."

Simon waited for him to pause, then took up the cue. "How much do you know about Kosovo?"

Paul shrugged. "Just what was in the briefing pack I got from Colonel Hampton-Brazel – *Brassy?* – at Message Command. He was keen for me to focus on the international journalists."

"Why was that?" said Simon.

"He said the main effort was to ensure Tony Blair got re-elected this year. The army had to be constantly in the public eye as a force for good. It's one of the Five Themes. Then we could justify a decent budget at any future defence review."

"Fuck me," growled Simon, rolling his eyes. "Is that what they're saying?"

The Brigadier extended his legs into the centre of the room and folded his arms. "I think we might reset that expectation while we're here," he said, a smirk tickling the corner of his mouth. "I know there's an election coming back home, and New Labour's approach to media management is a highly polished affair, but the work here is somewhat more prosaic than you've been told." He straightened in his chair.

Paul, flushing for a second time, felt quickly for a pen and notebook in his jacket.

"First of all," the Brigadier said, "you do not work for the government's spin doctors in London. You work here, for me."

Paul wrote *dotted line to Brassy*, but said nothing.

"Secondly, this environment is getting ever more fractious by the day. You are not here to justify the next defence budget. You are here to set the conditions in which our ground forces and coalition partners can operate safely and effectively."

He indicated a map on the wall behind Simon. "In the next year or so the United Nations will have to decide whether Kosovo should become an independent nation or remain part of Serbia, as it is now. In the meantime we need to remove a significant proportion of the weaponry from the streets and reduce the Albanian extremism that's flowering throughout the region. That's where you come in."

Paul had wanted to sound self-assured, far-sighted, a safe pair of hands. Now he was afraid he had appeared disconnected from reality. "I'm sorry..."

"It's fine," the Brigadier said, raising his palm again. Paul was struck by how red it was, how deeply the lines etched into the skin. "But let's start off on the right foot. What I want from you is the trust of the local people, the Albanians particularly."

The room fell silent. Paul nodded. If he was reporting directly to Brigadier Montrose, this was the man who would write his appraisal.

"One more thing," said Blanche Henderson, her knees tucked to the side. "Your predecessor had to be removed because he was a security risk."

"I know," Paul said.

"Good. So I won't have to warn you to keep your cock in your trousers. We had to revoke the security vetting for the Serb interpreter and sack her. You've now only got Miss Xhaferi on your team. She's Albanian, but thankfully trilingual. I don't want to have to find a replacement."

Paul looked from Blanche to Simon to the Brigadier. "I'll do my best not to fuck her," he said.

Simon chuckled. "She's the best interpreter we've got, Paul. It's a mark of how much emphasis we place on Message Operations."

The Brigadier smiled expansively, then pulled in his legs as Paul stood to leave. "Good to have you with us," he said. "You are my voice on the ground, Paul, so I need you to be clear what you can say and do."

* * *

At least he had a room to himself, Paul thought. But the heating in the officers' accommodation was set so high that he had to lie on the duvet rather than climb underneath it. Footsteps echoed in the wooden walkway outside his door whenever anyone got up for a piss. A door banged in the distance. He had been awake since three the previous day but was still unable to sleep. The walls were bare, except for a single window facing out to another such room across a small gap.

When he'd gone for a shower, he found the ablutions were mixed. There was only a plastic curtain providing privacy in the cubicles.

Susan would have been mortified by how openly everyone lived. She wasn't prudish, but her ideal of beauty was best suggested by graceful clothing rather than flaunted. Paul, by comparison, could spend hours stroking his fingers down the valley between her hip bone and pubic mound.

Why had she left him? Was it simply because his appetite outpaced hers?

A memory came to mind: she had been cooking pasta and sent him to the corner shop for coriander. He'd returned with wine and, not knowing the difference, a bunch of flat leaf parsley. Because the door had locked behind him, he rang the bell.

"Is that you," she called out of the window of her flat.

"No," he joked. "It's someone else."

Again and again the scene played in his mind. And six long months stretched out before him like a vast and featureless ocean.

Chapter 2

The secure fax spooled pages that folded, backwards and forwards, into a cardboard box on the floor. Brassy had promised to send the updated media lines. Paul had been expecting a few pages relating to the latest events, but what was coming through dated back over twelve months. It even included the strategic messages in support of the Five Themes.

"You're taking the piss now," Paul muttered to himself.

Unlike the other staff officers who worked in the Operations Room, Paul's desk was located in the Press Office, a small portacabin between the camp gate and the Brigade headquarters. He was amazed by how cushty the deployment was. In Oman he'd slept in a tent for three months and had to hunch over a laptop in the back of a Landrover during a sandstorm. In Sierra Leone he'd spent the first four weeks kipping on the baggage carousel at Freetown airport, and the next four on the lobby floor of the Mammy Yoko hotel. In Pristina he not only had his own bedroom, he had an office with an internet connection, a secure fax, and a television. A plush red sofa with chrome arms occupied the space opposite his desk. A sagging Union Jack had been tacked to the wall behind the door.

"Is it good enough to give press conferences?" Brassy asked when Paul complained it looked tatty.

"This is a coalition operation in support of a United Nations declaration," he replied, keen to assert himself. "We should get a UN logo up, or paint the wall blue. At the moment it looks partisan and rather tawdry."

Brassy hummed for moment. "As long as there's a flag, that should be acceptable. Otherwise do what you want."

Once the fax stopped printing, Paul lifted the printout and spent the next half an hour separating the pages along the perforations with sharp flicks of his middle finger. He put them in order, then set about making notes. At eleven, he realised with some horror that he would very soon be on national radio for an interview scheduled to last an hour. And an hour, in interview terms, was an aeon.

The television could only play the BBC news channel. This alternated between domestic reports from the UK and a linking section of beeping and piping music over the image of an orange globe that disintegrated, rotated, and reformed. Paul ignored it. There seemed to be nothing more important than a story about sick cattle.

"Is that all they've got?" he said, clicking the remote.

Brassy wanted him to stick to the official lines. He had to *'emphasize the global leadership the UK was playing in the Balkans'*. But the Brigadier had been very clear that his focus was building trust with the Albanian population and getting them to disarm. The media lines, when he read them in detail, proved to be nothing more than vague statements in which the words 'peace and stability' were repeated ad nauseam.

"I can't fucking use these," he said aloud. He looked at the clock. If he was on air at two, he should be leaving at one so he had enough time to get to know the presenter. Before leaving, he should meet his interpreter – this Miss Xhaferi Simon said was so good – so she knew how he liked to work. But before that he needed enough material to fill an hour. All he had, really, were the peace and stability sections and an appeal for information about the bus bomb. Even with translation, it was no more than a few minutes' worth.

His stomach tightened. He liked being on air, sending his voice out to the world. He liked that his parents might hear him. But he didn't like being unprepared.

Journalists were bastards. They'd approach an issue from an angle that seemed irrelevant, only to twist the logic of his response. Or they'd be aggressive to throw him off balance. One guy in Sierra Leone, a greasy little BBC journalist, kept filling his glass to loosen his tongue. Getting them to tell the story correctly required planning, preparation, and a watertight knowledge of the media lines.

Shortly after half-twelve he knew he'd have to cancel. The media assessment in the briefing pack told him that Radio Black Eagle had originally been set up by NATO for public information broadcasts. After the funding had run out, the station had been sold to a local entrepreneur. He had renamed it to promote the interests of Albanian nationalism. Whereas young Kosovars were self-taught and intrinsically liberal, Radio Black Eagle catered for those who wanted to turn the map of Europe back to when the Ottomans ruled the region. Paul wasn't sufficiently comfortable with the media lines to know how to communicate with such an audience.

A confident knock on the door announced someone was coming in. She was young, perhaps in her early twenties, and stamped her boots on the mat to kick off the snow. She hung her coat on the hook on the wall, pulling out a small dictionary from an inside pocket.

Paul stood up. "You must be Miss Xhaferi? I'm Paul."

She was cute, long brown hair tumbling over her shoulders. Though she wore nothing glamorous, she had a feminine, youthful manner.

"*Zotëri Major*," she said, bowing very slightly. "Please call me Roza."

Paul shook her hand and invited her to his desk. He placed two fingers on the block of media lines. "I'm glad you're here. I need you to give Black Eagle a ring," he explained. "What would be most helpful is a chance to talk to them off air. Can you arrange that for tomorrow morning?"

Roza held the dictionary across her chest with both arms. A smile flashed across her face.

"What is it?" he asked.

She shook her head slightly. "They will want to hear from you, Zotëri Major. It is important for them to see you."

Paul placed his hands in his pockets. He had not expected this. "How do you know?"

"They tell me."

"You go every week?"

"Yes of course, with Colonel Jasper. And before him, Colonel Chris. They want to hear from NATO all the time."

Paul studied her. She met his eyes, the scent of imitation perfume permeating the space around them. He sneezed. "Sorry. But I don't like getting caught by a question I can't answer. I need another week to learn this stuff."

She glanced again at the pages under Paul's fingers. She placed a hand over her mouth to hide a slight cough. There was something ticklish about her.

"Is there a problem?" Paul asked.

"No," she said. "If this is what you want to say, I know it."

Paul sat, suddenly deflated. He looked forlornly at the notes he'd spent several hours making. "It's been said before?"

"Colonel Jasper? He say the same thing every week."

"Did he now?" said Paul.

"Yes," said Roza, nodding. "He did."

Paul was keen to differentiate himself from Jasper Higgson. "But it's not you being interviewed, Roza, it's me."

She shrugged. "Yes of course. But this is not what they want. You are new. They want to know about your home, your wife, your family…"

Perhaps this would be the opportunity he needed after all? "There's not much to say there, I'm afraid. But I'm sure I can chat about myself for an hour."

A smile appeared then vanished once again. "I will call them." she said. "Elire will introduce you to her audience."

"Elire?"

"She is interviewer. Very famous Kosova lady. Very clever. You will like her. All mens do."

He didn't correct her. "Can you promise she won't make me look stupid?"

"Yes, of course."

"So how do we get there? I have never been."

"We go with Landrover hard-top. It is outside, with driver, Aircraftswoman Jane Seagood."

Paul frowned. She was running his life. Lifting the blind and looking out of the window, there was indeed a hard-topped Landrover facing the main gate. The driver was barely visible but he could just make out the blue-grey of an RAF beret.

If there was one thing he wanted to develop, it was his fluency in front of the microphone. He might as well start now. "Ok, let's go," he said, and reached into his desk drawer to pull out his pistol and magazine.

In the Landrover, Roza sat in the back looking over the bulwark behind the driver's seat. Paul didn't talk to the driver, though he did notice how petite she was. She had to sit fully upright to see over the steering wheel and could only just reach the pedals. Even though Roza had said the interview would be gentle, he was not going to be caught out. It had happened once before, in Sierra Leone, and the experience had been painful. As they drove, he kept repeating the Five Themes to himself like a mantra: a force for good in the world, protecting peace and stability, democratisation, coalition operations, punching above its weight.

But the more he repeated them, the more muddled he became. Was it *'Britain has a role to play in ensuring stability in the Balkans'*, or was it that *'All Balkan states have an important contribution to regional security'*?

The thought of grasping for words on air was terrifying. To hide his fear he slid the window forward and tapped his palm arrhythmically on the sill to a vaguely imagined song.

Radio Black Eagle was not located in the city centre, but a ramshackle bungalow in one of the quieter suburbs. A ten-metre mast behind the house distinguished it from its neighbours. Roza had opened the back door by the time he got round, but he held out a hand anyway as she stepped down. She took it with an almost indiscernible touch, then let go. Paul slammed the rear door and patted the window to tell the driver to park up.

The wooden building had once been painted the same scarlet as the Albanian flag. The paint had since flaked off to reveal rotting timbers that crumbled under his fingers. The windows moaned in the wind, and a screen door constantly opened and slapped, echoing across the street.

Roza pulled at the screen door and Paul followed. The empty rooms smelled unused. A Madonna album was playing through speakers hanging from the ceiling. In the kitchen, a woman was sitting at the table eating slices of apple off the back of a paring knife. Roza greeted her in Albanian.

The woman pushed back her chair and swept a vast mop of wavy blonde hair from her face. "Hello Major! So you are the new Jasper?"

She reached out to shake Paul's hand. She had a strong grip, and grey eyes buried below thick eyebrows that almost joined in the middle.

Paul hid a sudden nervousness by thrusting his hands deep into the pockets of his smock. "Yes, I'm new. I hope we might…"

Elire didn't let him finish. "Yes, we talk about you today, not politics."

She was taller than Roza, and about five years older, but definitely under thirty. There was a slight hint of an American accent in the way she spoke.

"That would suit me very well," Paul said. "I need to understand what your listeners think."

Elire studied his face. Something told Paul he would like her. Her red, collarless jacket was very similar to his mess kit doublet.

"They think NATO very good for us." she said, nodding at Roza. "When we start, I speak in Albanian and she talk English. Some peoples only speak Albanian."

She led them to the studio. Below the square shoulders of the doublet, her tight skirt and black tights looked more rounded.

Inside the studio, a vinyl record spun on an ancient turntable. The windows had been blacked out with paint and the walls covered with egg boxes, some overlapping, some leaving oblong spaces. A blue bulb hung from the ceiling and two microphones, suspended by articulated arms, caught the light. Paul glanced at Elire and touched his lips. She shook her head. They were not on air just yet. In the corridor outside, the music had been quite audible. Inside, the room had the low mechanical hum of a lift. Paul shuffled along a wooden bench to sit just below the foam padding of a microphone. Roza sat next to him, their knees touching once.

"Sorry, *Major*."

When Paul fitted a pair of earphones on his head, he could hear his heart thumping. His palms were damp. Elire took her place at the microphone opposite, her nose and mouth just visible above the desk partition. She played with some dials and the music faded out, part way through *La Isla Bonita*. It was seven minutes past the hour when the bulb on the ceiling went out, and a red light on the wall came on. Elire read the news from a pad of lined paper.

Paul watched her lips almost kissing the microphone. Her voice was husky, and Albanian was an interesting language, part Latin and part something else. He recognised some words from the vowel sounds and her tone of voice. There had been a car crash on the motorway. Then she said something about the United Nations, as she definitely said the name *Hans Haekerrup*, the new Secretary General. Then there was something about NATO, except she pronounced it *Nahto*.

A telephone rang. The woman's voice was broadcast by holding the receiver towards the microphone. The caller spoke in bursts and then paused for long moments. She kept repeating one word which Paul jotted on the back of the notes he'd placed in front of him. It sounded like *oochaka*.

After the call had finished, Elire glanced at him from underneath the microphone and nodded. Her voice changed timbre as she introduced him. There was his name: *Zotëri Major Pol*.

Roza gently nudged his elbow. She said, "So welcome, Major, it is very good of you to come and talk to us today. We are very happy NATO should send you and we are very grateful. Please, tell us about yourself. Where do you come from? Where do you live? Do you have childrens? How do you find it here in Kosova?"

He gave a light laugh. If he smiled, it would sound as such. "Thank you Elire, I am delighted to be here."

He and Roza had not worked out a routine but after he'd said his name and where he was from, Roza tapped his elbow to indicate that was enough.

"And you have wife?" asked Elire.

Paul paused. No he didn't have a wife. He didn't even have a girlfriend. He was thirty-one years old and had never had a relationship lasting more than a couple of years. "No, I'm single," he said at last.

He thought briefly about joking that he had a dog instead, but ignored the idea. Albanians were Muslim, and Muslims don't like dogs. "My father is a politician in a city in the middle of England. Well, he's not a politician, but he works for a political party. He does fundraising, that sort of thing. My mother is a teacher. So a pretty ordinary upbringing really."

He didn't want to sound boring, but nor did he want to be arrogant. He had no idea how to connect to these people. Was he talking to an illiterate shepherd or a businessman in a beemer? It was half past. What they could possibly talk about for another half an hour?

"And you are British officer?"

"Yes," Paul said. "I joined the army in 1995, just as our Prime Minister Tony Blair was coming to power. I spent the first few years working in England and in Northern Ireland, where we too had an issue with separatism."

A flash of panic. If he wasn't careful it would sound like Britain occupied Ulster in the same way Serbia occupied Kosovo. He moved on quickly.

"And after that I was in Dover, Kenya, Borneo, and Belize. And last year I was in Sierra Leone and Oman."

Elire's face brightened. "So tell us, Major. Last year you were in Africa! Where your Prime Minister Tony Blair was helping other people?"

"Yes, I was there," Paul said, glad of something he could hold on to. "The best way I can describe it is to tell you about the first few days. The rebels in Sierra Leone were funded by the country next door, Liberia. They killed everybody as they closed in around the capital. If they didn't kill someone, they cut off their hands with a machete."

As he spoke Paul made a sawing action across his fore-arm. He recalled visiting the *Medecins Sans Frontieres* camp where he'd watched a four year-old girl lift a bucket between the stumps of her arms.

"On the first day the streets were empty. The rebels not only cut people, they raped the women and killed the men. They burned old people in their houses."

He didn't need to overplay the story. The audience would know what cruelty meant.

"On the second day, the rebels – the Revolutionary United Front – stopped advancing because we held Freetown. At that point we saw children peeking out of windows and waving. And the United Nations staff came back to the city."

He could talk more about how inept the UN staff had been, but it would not be helpful.

"And on the third day we'd see the men, running from hiding place to hiding place."

He paused, allowing Roza to translate and to build the drama. This was why he loved radio.

"And on the fourth day, we saw women. And when the women came out there was colour, the markets opened, and life returned. They had baskets on their heads full of yams and coconuts and bananas. There was noise. There was *commerce*."

He had his hands raised, as if balancing a basket. Elire smiled beautifully while Roza translated the end of the story.

"Well thank you, *Zotëri Major*, for telling us this story. We very much enjoy it and hope you will be coming here every week to tell us about what NATO is doing and what information you have for us."

The interview, it seemed, was over. Elire's voice changed back to being close and sultry against the microphone. Albanian music faded in as the red light went out and the overhead bulb came on. Paul pulled the headset from off his ears and hung it on the nail where he'd found it.

That was the first live broadcast of the tour. He was sweating and elated. On the ride back to camp he couldn't stop grinning despite a sudden wave of exhaustion.

From the back of the wagon Roza said, "She like you very much, Elire; she tell me after interview." She started laughing, her hands above her head balancing an imaginary basket as they wove through the traffic in the Landrover. "And I like it when you do this," she said. "Very funny."

Paul smiled back at her. No, the audience won't have seen his hand gestures, but the meaning had been conveyed.

The British are experts at counter insurgency warfare. You can trust us.

The path from the gate to the monastery had been brushed free of snow, but that made it even slipperier. Anja followed the shuffling crowd, but walked to the side of the flagstones through the deep drifts. She enjoyed how her new boots made a squeaking sound, and how she had to lift her knees really high.

As she got closer, the weatherworn wall of the monastery loomed over her. When she looked up, the main tower receded behind the bow of the roofline. Tata always said the building was magical.

After the hunter had left her by the tree, she had run home and flung herself at her mother.

"What have you done, girl? What was that noise?"

Anja could barely describe what she saw. The fire made a popping sound as it swirled like a hurricane. A soldier vomited. A man on fire pressed his flaming hands into his flaming face. The hunter had dark eyes, stained teeth. His boot pressed onto a cigarette.

Mama kept asking, "Who did this? Did they hurt you?"

Anja could not speak. The shivering would not stop. Mama gave her water, but she spewed it up all yellow and lumpy.

"Are they coming here?" she said, and Anja whimpered that she didn't know.

All afternoon Mama kept looking out from behind the curtains. She started packing. When Tata finally arrived home she said, "They will kill us all."

"In the market, people were cheering," he said.

Anja lay on a blanket by the fire, listening to her parents. Her stomach still heaved, but nothing came up.

"We must go to your sister," Tata said. "We will use your surname."

"No," Mama said. "The neighbours know I married you. It is better we go to the enclave at Gracanica, with Serbian people. Until you can get a passport. Then we go to France."

Tata had bought a chicken. The bird lay on the table, feet tied together, claws curling. Anja didn't feel hungry. They packed everything the car could carry and drove south in the night. Mama made her eat the pogacha and kept feeling her forehead. Eventually, she slept. Later, Tata carried her into a cold house. She cried at the dusty, sticky feel of the mattress; the cold smell of rust.

In the morning Tata said, "It is not finished, but we are safe. These are my people. They have given us shelter."

Whenever they went outside, Mama held her hand very tightly. She wore a black shawl over her head, something Anja had never seen her do. The other women looked at them, whispering. Young girls stared at her from behind their mother's skirts.

That had been five days ago. Today was Sunday. Tata had sent her ahead saying he would come along soon and they would pray together. "It is the most wonderful building in the world," he said. "It is a joy to worship there."

Anja did not believe him. The last time she had been to church the funny smoke made her sneeze. She liked the outside best; the cold blue of the sky and the snow.

A crowd of adults had gathered by a small door in the monastery wall. Some made strangled cries. Anja pushed through the forest of trousers and embroidered skirts to see what was happening.

At the centre, a man scrubbed the door with a stout wooden brush. Someone had painted large Albanian letters. Anja cocked her head to try and read them but she didn't know what the word might mean. The Bishop looked very sad with his head tilted forwards.

An old woman, bent at the waist like a sack of corn, pointed at her with a stick. "There will be more trouble," she said, and many in the crowd nodded.

Later, before dinner, Anja told Tata what the old woman said. He slammed the table with his palm, but then folded his arms to breathe heavily, staring at the fire.

Mama put down the potato she was peeling. "We must tell the police what she saw."

"No...!" Anja whimpered. The police were foreigners. If they made her talk it would be bad for everyone.

Tata's face was long. "We might invite trouble," he said. "Our welcome here is not without condition."

It was her fault. If she hadn't gone beyond the rock she wouldn't have seen the bus, wouldn't have met the hunter, wouldn't be living in this tiny shed.

"What are we to do?" Tata said, looking at the ceiling.

"Pray if you want to," Mama said. "But we need money. We need food. None of these women will employ me. You must teach."

Tata placed both hands flat on the edge of the table and breathed out into his beard. Mama finished peeling the potato, then cut it up into small squares and used the knife to slide them off the block into the pan.

"God will provide," Tata said, "but we must never admit what she knows."

* * *

It took Paul two weeks to even start understanding the complexity of competing political interests in Kosovo, and get to grips with the plethora of English, Albanian, and Serbian acronyms in use. In interviews he tried to present himself as neutral, but he could not help a deep sense that the Albanians had been the victims of a prolonged and uninhibited racism. NATO, therefore, was defending the weak against the tyrannical.

At the morning brief, Blanche Henderson stood by the map to give her security assessment to the assembled staff. She had rehearsed her pitch and delivered it in a taut, methodical style that Paul admired. Starting with Pristina city, she worked outwards to the wider Brigade area before finishing with events beyond the border.

"...and finally, Albanian extremism around the Presevo Valley is getting more volatile by the day." She indicated an area on the map with a laser pointer. "Last night, a Serb policeman was killed in Bujanovac, twenty miles from the buffer zone. This is the third time Albanian extremists have ventured so far out; an indication they are growing in confidence. We believe the leadership feud has finished. A front runner has emerged, but we don't yet know his name."

As she was about to sit, the Brigadier asked, "Blanche, have we had anything more about the bus bombers?"

She shook her head. "All avenues of investigation have gone quiet, Sir."

Afterwards, Paul kicked his way back to his office through the thick overnight snow. At his desk, he switched on the TV and watched the orange globe spin while the music chirped and beeped. A ticker tape of headlines across the bottom of the screen read, *Foot and Mouth epidemic spreads to third county: Minister of Agriculture.*

Shaking his head, he pressed the mute button and checked his watch. Brassy always called after the first rattle of headlines, so when his work mobile rang Paul was surprised to see that it wasn't him. *Aden Short,* the screen said, so he pressed the answer button. "British Press Office, Major Illingworth speaking."

The speaker had an educated London accent. "Is that the new media spokesman?"

"It is, Paul Illingworth."

"Aden Short. Reuters. Is there any truth in the rumour that a British helicopter has been shot down in the Presevo Valley?"

"None that I know of," Paul answered. "I've just come out of the morning brief."

"So you're sure?"

It was conceivable something had yet to filter through the convoluted NATO reporting structures.

"Aden, where are you?"

"Pristina."

"How did you hear...?"

The man chuckled. "I can't tell you that, my friend."

Paul said, "As you wish. I'll check, and ring you back, ok?"

It was the break he'd been waiting for, an opportunity to engage with one of the journalists describing Kosovo as chaotic. How could it be dangerous if his driver was an eighteen year-old girl who had to roll up the sleeves of the smallest available jacket?

He strode to the Chief of Staff's office. Knocking once, he pushed the door. "Simon, quick one: I've got the press telling me a chopper's crashed in the Presevo Valley. Is there something I don't know about?"

Simon studied him with an air of suspicion. "A helicopter, you say?"

Paul nodded.

"Nothing's come across my desk. Are you certain the man's not chancing his arm?"

"They don't do that. Should we check with NATO headquarters? It might not be ours."

Simon opened his mouth to answer but was silenced by the sound of several telephones ringing in the Operations Room at the same time. Then his phone rang as well. As he answered, the Watchkeeper knocked once and poked her head round the door. "Sirs, warning order: air incident along the boundary; a Puma, one of ours. I've dispatched the military police and a medical team to locate it."

She left, closing the door. Paul waited while Simon finished his call.

"...thank you. We have it in hand. I'll tell the Commander."

"I'll need to take them up there," Paul said. "I can't pretend it hasn't happened."

Simon sucked in a breath as he leaned back in his chair. "I don't want dead bodies on the news."

Paul shook his head. "Absolutely not. My job is to manage the flow of information so the families hear from us, not the telly. *If* there are casualties, that is."

Simon rose, picking up his tammy. "You obviously know what you're doing. Keep me informed. I'm popping next door to tell the boss."

Paul didn't know how Aden had found out, but he'd hear soon enough, when he'd earned his trust. The next hour was spent holding Aden off while the Watchkeeper collated snippets of information from various sources. Eventually she could list the missing men's names, blood groups, regimental numbers, and next of kin.

At nine-thirty the police commander radioed to say she had located the crash. Both pilots were dead.

Paul knew he should ring Brassy to clear his lines, but pushed the idea aside. Brassy would never take a risk. Instead, he rang Aden with an offer he hoped could not be refused.

"There are two dead. But we need time to tell the families." He paused to allow Aden time to think. "We don't know why it happened. There was one hell of a snowstorm last night. If you give me time to manage the casualty notification process, I'll take you up there this afternoon."

"I can't do it that late, Paul. How about one hour?"

"Two. And I'll need to take the BBC guy and Elire from the local radio station if she's free."

"All right, two hours. But I have to be back by file time."

"Done."

He wasn't sure how Aden would report the incident, but he could only influence it by establishing a good relationship and being coldly professional. He was unbothered by the deaths having not known either man. Shit happened in war. When the police commander returned to the headquarters, he followed her into Simon's office.

"We had to smash the front windows," she said. "The bodies had frozen stiff. The NCO was alive, but had broken both legs. A young soldier kept him conscious all night. The rest were just bruised."

"Well, there's a candidate for the Birthday Honours List," Simon said, turning to Paul. "So it's over to you. Make it look as good as you can."

Paul gritted his teeth as he buckled himself into the Landrover. The snow was starting again. Elire had said she would come later, weather permitting. Paul told her he couldn't wait. The drive up was too important; an opportunity to get to know Aden and Nick.

Once they were underway, he hooked his arm over the bulwark in the Landrover to introduce himself to the two journalists swaying in the back. "In Oman last year I worked with Sky News, Channel Four, and all the wire agencies. Before that I was in Sierra Leone. Nick, there was a big BBC party: Kate, Andrew, Mark, and so on. You know them?"

Nick was a taciturn, avuncular man in his late fifties, dressed in a zip-necked jumper. Hooded eyes gave the impression of war-weariness. The few words he spoke were delivered politely and quietly, but with a smoker's growl. He was accompanied everywhere by the smell of fruity tobacco.

"I remember your reports from Sarajevo," Paul said. "I was at Sandhurst at the time. Have you been in the Balkans ever since?"

Nick shrugged.

"Where were you before this?"

Aden chipped in on his behalf. "Nick's an old hand, Paul. He was in Africa during apartheid and the famines. He covered the Biafran War in Nigeria, Angola, and then Rhodesia-Zimbabwe. He started way back, didn't you, Nick? At Khe-San?"

"In Viet Nam?" said Paul. "Christ, I was only..."

"Yeah," laughed Aden, "me too. I remember Nick's reporting when I first wanted to be a journalist. He even interviewed General Giap, the man who led the NVA, didn't you, Nick?"

"You're joking!" said Paul.

Aden was sitting directly behind him and he had to turn more to make eye contact. The two of them were of a similar age, although Aden's hair hung down to his shoulders. With Nick being so uncommunicative, Paul said, "And what about you? I'm guessing you're no less experienced?"

Aden was certainly not shy of talking about himself. "I covered the Gulf in ninety-one, and the First Chechen War from ninety-four to ninety-five. I was in Afghanistan for the siege of Kabul in ninety-six. I wanted to go back to Chechnya for the second war, but they'd started kidnapping for ransom and no news agency could get insurance. I got sent here in ninety-nine." He indicated the badges on Paul's arm. "You weren't here yourself?"

Paul glanced out of the windscreen to hide the flushing in his cheeks. "No, I was posted to a training job in England."

These two men had more war experience than he'd ever have. All Paul had done, if he was honest, was a ceasefire tour of Northern Ireland, and a humanitarian operation in West Africa.

Nick shouted above the road noise. "Were you on Operation Barras, the rescue of the Royal Irish in Sierra Leone?"

Paul shook his head. "I was in the country, but wasn't part of that operation."

Nick gave a disappointed nod. Not knowing what to say next, Paul checked the map. The driver was the young girl with the rolled-up sleeves. She was enjoying the power of the Landrover, racing the executive cars along the motorway. His phone rang, and he knew it was Brassy before he slid it out of his pocket.

"Paul, what's this I hear about you taking journalists up to the crash site?"

"That's correct," Paul said in an assertive manner. He couldn't discuss the matter with Nick and Aden in the back. "ETA in about forty-five minutes."

"Are you mad?"

"I'll call you back," Paul said, and ended the call. He hoped the two journalists had not heard Brassy's voice. He pointed at a road sign and the driver nodded.

An hour later, the afternoon light gently fading, they were skidding along a gravel track that became increasingly narrow at every turn. The two journalists had to grasp the bulwark for security.

"Take it easy," Paul whispered to the driver. "If you kill them, I'll get bad copy."

"I'll try," she giggled. "That'll be it there."

The route would have made a superb cycle path, if tourists were ever to come. Snow floated down from tall pine trees guarding over the road. Although there had been considerable traffic in the past few hours, the tyre tracks were already covered. Ahead of them stood a parked Landrover and a nine-by-nine tent. A yellow light shone through the plastic window. The sentry, well wrapped up against the cold, approached them as they slowed.

Paul leaped out and spoke to the soldier. He pointed into the woods. Paul then opened the back door of the Landrover, spilling warmth. "It's two-hundred metres up the hill. Bring what you need."

Aden passed out a TV camera and a heavy, folding tripod. "Watch it. They cost a fortune."

Paul took it in one hand and started off, following a line of mine tape strung between the trees. The initial section was steep, with footholds cut into the mud bank. They were a little too far apart for comfort and partially covered with snow. He had not expected such a trek and so had not briefed the journalists to come better shod. He balanced the tripod behind a tree and went back down to haul Nick up by the hand.

In the trees the light had an ethereal, churchlike calmness. Petals of snow drifted down from the gently swaying upper branches. The Puma lay on its side. The rotors were buckled and twisted but still attached to the engine. The tail section was bent upwards. The fuselage had been protected by a tarpaulin and was already covered in snow. The two journalists surveyed the scene with critical eyes.

"I'll need to be quick before we lose the light," Aden said. Nick walked off in a wide arc with the deliberation of one in a graveyard.

The mobile rang again. It was Brassy. Paul was surprised that he got a signal and took the call, retreating to where he could talk.

Brassy was seething. "Don't ever cut me off like that again."

"Sorry, Colonel, but I had Nick Oakeshot and Aden Short in the back."

Brassy hissed, "Why are you taking them up in the first place?"

His anger punctured Paul's confidence in what he was doing. "I need to gain their trust. They knew about it before we did. I couldn't lie."

"I didn't say *lie*, Paul. For God's sake! This could go utterly strategic! It could be on the nine o'clock fucking news!"

"But..."

"Listen, Paul. Remember that Chinook that crashed in the Mull of Kintyre in ninety-four?"

Paul grunted.

"One media spokesman said it was pilot error, and another said equipment failure. We had two blasted investigations, and both drew different conclusions. Utter cockup. And the families! The pilots' wives have still to get compo, even today."

The parallel was sharp. The shock of having misjudged the situation iced through Paul. He had seen an opportunity to make friends with the two journalists, but if they wrote it up in a negative light, his plan would backfire.

"If this goes badly, I'll be pulling you out quicker than that fuckwit Higgson. We can wear the odd shagging story, but I'm not having complete systemic failure. Not while I run Message Command. Do you fucking understand?"

"Yes, Sir."

Paul's hands shook as he slipped the phone back in his pocket. He was on his own now.

Nick sidled up to him. "Any special forces involved?"

Paul shook his head. "There's no SAS in theatre and I couldn't talk about them even if there were. The passengers were Duke of Wellington's Regiment and the pilots Army Air Corps."

"Names?"

"I can't give them yet," Paul said. "But when I can, I'll give them to both of you."

The sight of two of them together quickly brought Aden over. "Paul, can we do a piece to camera with the chopper in the background?"

"Let's do it on the road," Paul said, looking up at the trees. Brassy's anger had shaken him. "The light's better down there."

Thankfully Aden didn't force the issue. Although having the crash as a backdrop would make good TV, Brassy would hate it.

What could he say that would hit the buttons he had been told to press and still keep everyone happy?

The journalists kept slipping as the ground steepened so Paul eventually took the tripod down, then climbed back up for the camera. Once out of the trees, he found it was snowing again. He checked his beret in the wing mirror of the Landrover while Aden set up the shot with the sentry, two Landrovers, and a snow covered tent as the backdrop. It would convey an image of being an all-weather organisation, Paul thought.

The flakes made Paul blink as Aden clicked his fingers and lifted the eye piece of the camera.

Paul cleared his throat to speak with a deep, slow voice. "We regret to announce that a Puma helicopter crashed this morning in the British Sector of Kosovo, about twenty miles from the city of Podojevo.

"The casualties were taken to the British military hospital as soon as possible after the crash. Both pilots were killed in the accident and I believe that their selflessness in the final moments saved the lives of their passengers."

For the next part, he allowed an inflection of anger to give the impression that he had been personally affected.

"We do not know the exact cause of the crash. An investigation will take place when the time is right. But all British Forces working here to establish peace and security in the region would like to pass on their condolences to the families and loved ones of the men concerned. We know they believed fully in what they were doing."

Standing by the camera, Aden had a microphone in his hand. He was nodding. "Could the crash be the result of Albanian extremism?"

Paul changed his voice to make the clip less usable. "We don't know. And I'm not going to speculate. But we do not believe at this stage that hostile action was to blame."

"What about the names of those killed, can you give them?"

There was something about a camera that made people talk. Aden knew this. The names of the pilots were in the notebook in Paul's pocket, but he had yet to be told that their families had been informed. He stepped out of shot.

"If you don't mind, Aden, I'd prefer it if they heard the news from us. We have a process."

"We can hold onto the clip until you say we can use it. You have my word on that."

"No," Paul said. "Now let's go home."

Aden and Nick glanced at each other, then started folding away the camera.

"That was great," said Aden, "can you get us back for five? I'll tell my desk something's coming in."

As they were packing up, a car sped into view along the route they had come. It was low and light, skidding and correcting in the deepening snow. The sentry dropped on one knee to study the car through the sight of his rifle.

"That's another journalist," Paul said. "Hold fire."

It was a Volkswagen Beetle, the bonnet a much lighter colour than the remainder. It stopped behind Paul's Landrover, the headlights making him shield his eyes. The engine moaned, whirred, and went quiet. The door opened then closed again. The woman inside gave a loud expletive then kicked the door harder. A mane of wavy hair appeared.

Paul smiled. "Thank you for coming, Elire. I know it's a long way."

She was wearing sneakers, tight blue jeans, and a black puffer jacket. She hopped from foot to foot in the snow. "I need interview for news programme," she said. "Then I go. It is cold."

Reaching into her coat, she pulled out a digital recorder with a microphone coiled round it. The other two were quickly clambering into the Landrover to keep warm.

"How would you like to see it, now you're here?" Paul said.

She looked down to her shoes.

"You'll be fine," he said, and took her by the hand. "Come."

He was surprised by how easily she allowed herself to be led, and how much nimbler she was than the others. She only put a hand down once. At the top, Paul offered his handkerchief to wipe her fingers. She took it without looking, silenced by the solemnity of the scene.

When she held out her recorder, Paul provided a spiel slightly different from what he'd said before.

"We are working to make Kosovo peaceful and stable, Elire," he whispered. "We are sorry to say that two British pilots lost their lives in the pursuit of that goal today. We don't know how it happened, but we do know that they believed in what they were doing. More than anything they want Kosovo to be a stable and peaceful place for all the population, Albanian and Serbian, to bring up their children and enjoy prosperity."

Elire stood open-mouthed, looking up at the snow falling through the trees.

"You are very brave mens, all of you," she whispered, the ghost of her breath rising and disappearing into the fading light.

Two killed in Kosovo helicopter crash
Reuters: 15 March 22.05 CET

Two British soldiers were killed in a helicopter crash in the mountains along the Kosovo-Serbian border early yesterday morning.

One of those killed was the pilot. He has been named as Captain Glen Jones, 28, of the Army Air Corps. The other fatality, the co-pilot, has not been named at the wishes of the family.

The six passengers were taken to the British hospital in Pristina for treatment. One had broken both legs. The spokesman for British Forces in Kosovo, Major Paul Illingworth, said: "Our thoughts are with the families at this very difficult time. These men died doing what they loved. They believed in a stable and peaceful Kosovo."

The deaths come at a time of increasing tension in the troubled Balkan region. Ethnic Albanian extremism has been on the rise for some months and though the presence of the SAS is denied, it remains a necessity that NATO controls the movement of arms and explosives across Kosovo's notoriously porous borders.

Well-armed militias are forming in the Albanian dominated regions of Southern Serbia and the Former Yugoslav Republic of Macedonia (FYROM). It is not believed, however, that the crash is the result of military action. An investigation into the causes of the crash is expected to be announced soon.

PART TWO

Chapter 3

As Paul unlocked the door, the sound of spooling paper from the fax machine made his stomach tighten. The press coverage of the crash was being faxed through and he'd soon find out whether his gamble had worked or not. When he pulled the pages out of the cardboard box he found Brassy had written "TO BE DISCUSSED" in thick pen on the cover sheet. He didn't have long to wait for the call.

"What the fuck were you thinking? Those pictures make us look like fucking amateurs, not a first world army."

"Colonel, I..."

"I told the Chief you and I were close, Paul. I told him that once you got your act in order, you could be trusted implicitly. What am I going to say now?"

"Look, that's..."

"And imagine opening your paper to find your son died in some arctic wasteland."

"Utter nonsense," Paul snapped. Even if Brassy was a colonel, he was not going to be treated like an idiot. "The photos show the chopper landed intact. The text says an investigation will follow. And from the cuttings you've sent, only the BBC Online and The Sun printed the story anyway."

"Doesn't matter. It's the principle."

"The principle," Paul said after an intense pause, "was to get Short and Oakeshot to trust me."

"And did that work?"

"Yes, it did. They're veteran war reporters, not lobby journalists."

Brassy grumbled. "They're out of control, that's what they are."

Paul shook his head. "Not at all. But there's no point spouting official lines at them. They need to be shown evidence, not read a strapline. What they've said is accurate. Albanian extremism is an issue."

Brassy said, "It's not the line we're pressing."

"Of course it's not," Paul said with a click of his tongue. "But I can't deny what's in front of their noses!"

Brassy sniffed. Paul became conscious of the rank divide between them. He must be more astute about how he expressed himself.

"So why did you release the names of the dead? I did not give you permission," Brassy said.

Paul smacked his lips. "I was withholding them until we spoke. But Aden rang to confirm the spelling of the co-pilot. He'd got both names from the NATO press office in town."

"Who?"

"There's a NATO press office bolted on to the United Nations headquarters. It's run by an American, Major Breitman."

"Since when?"

"This week. NATO's trying to demonstrate they can work effectively with the UN. Breitman is number two to the UN spokesperson, a Spanish civvy."

Brassy became incandescent. "Work effectively with the UN? They can't even... You're going to have to grip him. Yanks don't understand counter insurgency warfare and reporting deaths is a national issue. It's not for sodding NATO to do, never has been."

Paul was happy to deflect his rage. "I'm lining up that conversation today, Colonel," he said. "But you should realise that Aden didn't print the name of the co-pilot for one reason: out of a favour to me. I explained his mother was a Jehovah's Witness and didn't want his name in the press."

Silence on the line.

"It's give and take, Colonel. Not just parroting the official lines. Can't be too conformist in a place like this."

Brassy grumbled. "I hear what you're saying. But now you've got them onside, I want to see 'safe and stable' in the first paragraph, every time."

Paul would have to let him win a point or the call would ramble on. "I'll speak to them," he said.

"You'd better, and quickly," said Brassy. "Getting them to report accurately is going to be more important from now on."

Paul frowned. "How do you mean?"

"You haven't had the gypsy's wink from your Brigadier?"

"No. What's happening?"

Brassy cleared his throat. "Plans have been agreed here overnight. Very soon we'll be giving the Ground Safety Zone back to the Serb army."

"The buffer zone?"

"Yes. It was always part of the original ceasefire agreement. After the war we insisted on keeping the Serb army away from the border. They only agreed if it would be returned within two years. That time is up."

Paul grabbed a notebook and started jotting thoughts. "If there's one thing that will stoke the fires of instability, this is it."

"That's why you need to bring Short and Oakeshot under control. Kosovo is, ultimately, pretty stable and fundamentally secure."

* * *

Anja was excited. It was her first day at school and she was desperate to meet girls she could play with. While Mama locked up the cottage, Anja ran through the radio station and unlocked the heavy metal door that led to the street. When she pulled it open, the chains rattled.

45

"Let's go," she said, pulling Mama's hand. "I want to be early."

Mama was wearing a shawl again. She felt heavy. "Slow down, Anja. Girls here do not behave like this."

The school was on the far side of the monastery. In the market square, other mothers were walking with their children towards the gate.

Anja looked forward to having a race. Or a game of tig. Or slap hands. She had even spent the whole of yesterday evening doing her multiplications with Tata. He had said she was very clever, and she was keen to prove it.

She knew she was different. But that difference made her special. This time, the girls would not pull her hair because of her name.

Mama let go of her hand some way short of the gate where a crowd of mothers were funnelling through the narrow gap. Anja ran on but then looked back.

Mama gestured her to go inside. Then she pulled her shawl round her face and turned away.

Inside the playground, a few boys stared at her, but she ignored them. She was wearing jeans and a torn pink jacket. The boys wore shorts and the girls, skirts. As she was waiting for someone to start a game, a tall boy with a satchel pulled the pigtail of a girl she had seen at the monastery. The girl turned and told him to go away, but he tugged at the other pigtail instead. He laughed. The girl pushed him but he avoided her. It looked to Anja like she was not trying hard enough.

Using the inside of her boot to scrape up some compressed snow, Anja bent over to mould a small, icy snowball in her hands. She spent time compressing it so it would fly further.

Two young boys stood nearby. They watched her and could tell who she was going to aim at.

Anja wound up the throw like the Americans she had seen on the television, canted over on one leg. The snowball left her hand cleanly and in a perfectly straight

46

line. The target was turning when it struck him just above one eye. He buckled, one leg going before the other, a hand over his face.

Just as she was about to smile at the girl with the pigtails, a teacher grabbed her shoulder.

"Don't you ever do that again, young lady," she said. Then she looked down at Anja with her hands in front of her tummy. She had a face like a mouldy turnip. Anja thought about kicking her shins, but knew it would be a bad idea.

"You are the Cokic girl, aren't you?" the teacher said.

Anja nodded. That was her.

"You have a lot to learn," the woman said.

* * *

As he approached down Mother Teresa Street, the Grand Hotel reminded Paul of a 1970s shopping precinct in Bradford. The concrete façade, half covered in scaffolding, disappeared into the low cloud. The 'e' of 'Hotel' was missing from the ironwork bolted above the lobby entrance. As he got out of the Landrover, a race of crisp packets jolted along the pavement to swirl in a vortex. He shuddered, patted his smock for his pistol, and entered through the glass doors.

Inside the lobby, his boots squeaked on the black marble floor. Barrel-chested men in grey suits talked in low voices. After sizing him up, they ignored him. Paul hastily walked to the far wall, where a square of deep-seated sofas enabled him to keep his back protected while observing the main door. Had he forgotten to sign out in the book in the Operations Room?

A grey light filtering through the chiffon curtains reflected off the floor. Paul checked his watch and tried to catch the eye of a rake-thin waiter wearing a red waistcoat. When he raised a hand, the man swiftly lifted his chin and strutted out of sight.

"Paul, how are you?"

Nick looked tired as he placed a worn leather satchel on the floor and sank into a chair.

"Hi," Paul said, leaning forward to shake his hand. "I didn't see you come in. Are you staying here?"

"Oh no," Nick replied, pursing his lips and shaking his head in a way that made Paul chuckle. "This place is famous for incapacitating more journalists than Slobodan Milosevic."

As if by some unseen magic, the waiter in the red waistcoat appeared at Nick's shoulder. He ordered a coffee, making sure Paul got one too.

"I've been here half an hour. That man's been avoiding me," Paul said.

Nick smiled. "I do a lot of meetings here. You have to tip them."

"And you've learned Albanian?"

"*Natyrisht*, my friend. Naturally."

Paul hoped small talk would ease the messages he had to deliver. "I didn't know Mother Teresa had a street named after her."

"She was Kosova Albanian."

"I didn't know that."

Nick's phone beeped. He excused himself to listen to his messages. Paul sat with his legs crossed and one arm extended along the back of the sofa until the waiter returned with two small cups on a steel tray.

Sliding his phone into the chest pocket of his shirt, Nick continued where they'd left off. "Be careful about Mother Teresa, Paul. She died a week after Diana Spencer, so the world never paid her sufficient attention."

Paul thought this was an opportunity to understand Nick better. "Well you obviously know the people here. What are you working on at the moment?"

Nick shrugged. "I'm driving up to Belgrade this afternoon. I'm interviewing Kostunica in the morning."

"*President* Kostunica? The President of Serbia?"

"Yes."

"Wow. I guess that's the reach of the BBC. And then what?"

Nick's face seemed to harden. He picked up his coffee and made a show of stirring it before balancing the spoon on the saucer and downing the drink with one graceful tilt of the head.

"Paul, what did you want to talk about?" he said. His hooded eyes and quiet demeanour seemed suddenly cold.

Taken aback by the change, Paul said, "I want to talk about how we work together. But I want to wait for Aden, is that ok?"

"Since he's not here, why don't we start?"

A sudden clap of thunder was followed by a heavy rumbling of rain loud enough for everyone to turn towards the windows. If Aden arrived at that moment, he'd be soaked.

"Very well," Paul said. "I want to talk about what you report."

He realised immediately this would sound wrong, so backtracked. "I'm not coming at this with a censorship agenda. But you should realise that my masters in London will pressurise me if you don't…"

Nick's face was implacable. "You want me to spout the government's messages?"

"Not at all," Paul said, his voice rising in pitch. "But is the BBC not obliged to represent all sides in an argument?"

Paul had thought this would be his ace, but it only served to make Nick scowl. With slow deliberation, he placed his coffee cup on the table and lit a cigarette. His eyes remained focused on the wall above Paul's head.

As Nick blew smoke into the air, Aden appeared from near the lifts. He waved, but was then accosted by a fat man whom he obviously recognised. They shook hands and exchanged words while Paul and Nick waited. When he joined them, Aden's face was flushed. He swigged from a plastic bottle of imitation Kosovo coke and spoke very quickly.

"Sorry. Had a meeting. Overran. Have I missed anything?" He raised a finger for the waiter, who nodded from the far side of the room.

Nick said, "Paul was asking if we would parrot the official lines."

"I didn't say that," Paul interjected. "I asked if you would report the NATO point of view. That's not the same thing."

Nick and Aden exchanged glances. Aden was jittery, his hair held out of his face by a head band.

Nick took another slow draw on his cigarette. It was difficult to tell what he was thinking. He looked at Paul with a steady gaze. "Paul, the official line on Jumping Jasper is that he was sent home following *security concerns*. Was he intimately involved with his Serbian interpreter?"

"I don't know," Paul stammered.

Aden laughed as he took a swig of coke. "So he did! She was sweet! He was only here a couple of months and got laid more often than I do in a year. Good chap, Jasper, a good laugh."

Nick leaned forward to tap his cigarette into a plastic ashtray. He drew out his words slowly, "Paul, how do you think the NATO involvement has changed traditional alliances across southern Europe?"

Tendrils of smoke made Nick blink. He leaned back and re-crossed his legs.

Paul rested his elbows on his knees. "Come on. I'm a soldier. That's way outside my scope. Our mission is to…"

"Ok, let's stick to military matters," Nick said. "I'm not trying to catch you out. I just want to know what you think. Do you suppose NATO was over-optimistic in the use of airpower prior to the ground war?"

Paul tried to recall a lecture from his dreadful promotion course, but Nick did not give him space to answer.

"Or how about this… can you explain to the Serbian population of Belgrade why they were bombed? Because I can tell you they really have no idea at all."

"The air campaign was two years ago," Paul replied. "We've moved on since then. We're no longer in the peace *enforcement* stage. The policy is peace *building*."

"Ok, good. So if we are now in a phase of peace building, can you explain why the European Union committed to spend fifty billion deutschmarks over five years, but none of it has been forthcoming? Not one pfennig?"

The placid, forgettable face had gone.

Aden chuckled. "I want to know if you think President Kostunica should extradite Slobodan Milosevic to the International Criminal Tribunal?"

Paul found himself looking from one to the other like a cornered schoolboy.

"And if Kosovo becomes independent, what flag should adopt? The Albanian eagle, or another?"

"Paul, would you say this was a 'moral war', to quote Tony Blair?"

The questions came so fast that Paul sat back on the sofa and raised his hands. "Gentlemen, it's easy to sit on the sidelines and criticise. It's much harder to act on your convictions."

He looked at his watch, then at each journalist in turn. "I can get answers, if you want. But I think you just want to poke me for the fun of it."

He picked up his notebook and patted his jacket to check the pistol was secure. "If that's all you've got to do, I'm afraid I have other people to see."

Placing two photocopied business cards on the coffee table, he stood up and fitted his beret.

"Thank you for the coffee. But let me say that things are going to get more exciting very soon. So please have a think about how we can help each other."

* * *

The snow had melted everywhere except for between the houses. The sky was no longer the rich blue of winter. It was diluted, almost green.

Today was market day and the girls were expected to help their mothers rather than go to school. Anja waited while Mama came out of the cottage, locked the door, and placed the key in the pocket of her apron. She muttered as she walked down the path between the rows of cabbages, listing the things she needed to buy. She adjusted the shawl over her hair and retied the knot under her chin.

Anja said, "I can go on my own, if you want."

Mama's face blossomed into a sad smile. "Hold my hand, my darling," she said, "you can be brave enough for both of us."

They descended the stone steps and pushed open the door to the radio station. Inside, the scrawny man was smoking and drinking coffee. He waved, without smiling. The smell of his body was so strong that Mama hastily unlocked the heavy metal door to the front of the building and stepped outside.

"That boy needs a woman," she sighed.

Anja held her nose between two fingers. A smothered titter exploded into a giggle, which infected her mother's face. The two laughed as they walked hand in hand towards the central square.

By the monastery gate, three handcarts stood in a row; one laden with vegetables, one with plastic kitchenware, and the other bearing round, white cheeses and loops of dried sausage. A group of women accompanied by their daughters stood chatting in a huddle. As they turned to face them, Anja felt her mother's hand tighten.

"*Zdravo*," Mama said, "*dobro jutro*." Her accent was not as good as Anja's.

The women nodded back, but did not reply. In their faces, Anja read pity, though she did not understand why they should feel that. One of the young girls, quite tall and with a cute pink nose, was the one with the pigtails. Anja wondered if she would spurn her, but she didn't.

"Happy market day," she said.

Anja did not know how to react. Even after a week at school, very few children had played with her.

"Come," the girl said. "Let me show you something."

She wore a traditional dress and a beautiful lace shawl, while Anja sported a heavy fur hat that Tata had got in Belgrade. It had a Russian army badge on the front.

"Be careful, Sveta..." a woman called, and the girl made a cursory glance back to show that she was listening. Holding her hand, she led Anja at a run round the corner to where a bench sat beneath the dripping bows of a sycamore tree. Then they walked, keeping step.

Something shiny flashed in the grass and Anja immediately saw an opportunity. "Gold!" she cried, landing on two feet to crouch and pick up a slim pen. She wiped it on the legs of her dungarees and held it up for inspection. Light dripped down the side. Her reflection seemed stumpy and disjointed by the fluting on the shaft.

Sveta stood close, their shoulders touching. Anja thrust the pen towards her with a firm extension of her arm. "I want you to have it," she said.

Sveta gasped. The shaft did not pull off the nib, it unscrewed. The cartridge had green ink inside and the two girls took turns to squirt it at the bench, giggling as they did so. Then Sveta's face clouded and she screwed the pen back together.

"I should give it to my mother," she said, brushing a strand of hair underneath her shawl. A smear of green ink from her fingers stained the lace.

Anja couldn't understand. It had been lost. She had found it and had given it to Sveta. "Why?"

Sveta didn't answer. Spinning on the heel of her boot, she followed the wall back to the stalls, holding the pen before her like a candle. Her mother took it from her fingers and examined it.

"I found it," Anja said in an excited manner. "I gave it to Sveta."

The woman straightened. "This pen belongs to Father Longin," she said. "Well done, Sveta, for returning it." Then she saw the green smudge on her shawl. "What have you been doing!"

Anja felt the smile fading from her lips. Her fingers were stained green. Sveta would not meet her eyes. The other women twisted to stare silently at her mother as she placed a turnip into a deep cotton bag.

"We return what is not ours in this village," one said.

Mama lifted the cotton bag off the cart. The weight of it made her shoulder droop. She faced the women. "Come, Anja," she said in Albanian. "Let's go home."

Anja looked round, but no one wanted to be with her. She was alone again, as she had been in the mountains. She reached out to take her mother's hand and walked with her in silence across the main square.

Just before the corner, she looked back. The women were watching them with their arms folded. The girls were huddled in a circle, giggling and whispering to each other behind their hands.

Chapter 4

At least his fatigue was no longer a problem. The fear of fucking up and the adrenaline rush of having to stay one step ahead of the journalists, Brassy, and even Simon surged through his body. Unable to sleep, he'd got up and gone to the gym.

Paul didn't like cycling as a rule, but the camp was too small to run round so he used the exercise bikes to burn off aggression. The more he pedalled, the more his mind could focus and the gym, at five o'clock in the morning, was one of the few places where he could get some privacy.

The day before, he had walked out on two international journalists. It was what every PR spokesman wanted to do, but never dared. Had it been wise, or the dumbest thing ever? As Aden told him on the way back from the crash site, the Russians in Chechnya banned journalists from the front, so they just went round the other side and reported the war from the Chechen perspective. Would the same happen here? Neither Simon nor the Brigadier knew enough about Message Operations to provide guidance. Brassy, by contrast, was explicit, but his judgement was flawed.

The trust of the Albanian community. Disarming. Elections. Tony Blair. Trust.

It all came down to trust.

Why did Susan leave him? What had come between them? He mulled over this question every night, replaying in his mind the deliciously happy evenings they had spent together.

After he had finally got away from Brize Norton after six months in Sierra Leone, Paul had driven through the night. It was raining. He found a place to park, then trudged the few blocks to Susan's flat, the bergen heavy on his shoulders and a large wooden carving under one arm. A couple in their twenties walked by him, their footsteps in almost perfect unison. They reacted with surprise at the sight of someone in uniform.

He felt self-conscious in public. At the flat, no one answered the door. After pressing the doorbell a third time, he craned back to shout up to the second floor window.

"Susan?" he called, but too quietly. He did so again, much louder, "Susan!"

Nothing.

He leaned the carving against the doorframe, turned, and unhooked the straps of the bergen from his shoulders. It thunked heavily onto the doorstep. He sat on it, reaching into a pocket for his mobile phone. He called her, but it went through to voicemail. He called again and the same happened.

He had wanted to surprise her. He wanted her to run into his arms, wrap herself around him, envelop him in the tumble of her hair. She was probably at the minimarket buying milk.

After an hour, the rain had soaked through his smock and he started shivering. It had been in the high twenties when he left Freetown. He had an old fleece in the top of his bergen, but for some reason didn't want to get it out. Instead, he shivered on the front doorstep, rubbing his hands and hoping time would pass.

A taxi turned the corner of the street, the engine slowing as it came nearer. This is it, he thought, but it stopped at the house next door and Paul remained stationary, hoping the brightly voiced woman who got out wouldn't see him below the hedge.

"Here's a tenner, have a great evening. *Tatah.*"

Perhaps people would think he was in the TA, he thought.

Why else would someone be sitting on the doorstep of a London house in full military uniform on a Wednesday night?

Then, noises in the hallway behind him. He jumped up and banged on the door.

A man's voice: "Who's there?"

Paul knocked again. "My name's Paul. I'm with Susan, in flat 4. I don't have my keys. Could you open the door?" He tried not to sound desperate but there was something embarrassing about his position.

"What did you say your name was?"

"Paul Illingworth. Susan in flat 4 is my girlfriend. Could you..."

The bolt was drawn. The door opened, snagging on the coir mat and a pile of white mail.

"Thank you."

The man blocked his path, "Listen, I don't know you..."

Now there was light he was not going to be thrown back into the darkness. Paul coiled. The man sensed his intentions and braced behind the door.

"Could you at least take this?" Paul said, changing tack, his voice more of a demand than a request. "I've just come back from Sierra Leone. "I've got 24 hours before I have to be up in Catterick. I don't want to carry this round all night as I try and find her."

The man was tall, thinly built, and had an expansive afro that the hall light shone through. He was afraid.

"Just put it behind the bikes," Paul said, and backed up. "Is the doorbell working, by the way?" he added.

The man nodded as he took the carving. "I'll look after this for you, but I still can't let you in unless Susan's at home. I'm sorry, but you know..."

"Would you check?"

The man seemed nervous and yet wanted to be accommodating. The Sierra Leone war had been on the news. Surely he knew what a noble thing the army was doing out there?

Paul planted his feet and folded his arms. The rain dripped off the front of his beret. The man leaned over on one foot to peer up the stairs. Just as he did so, a pair of slender legs came down. It was Susan, carrying a bin bag.

"Susan."

She stopped at the bottom of the stairs, one hand on the snail-shell finial of the oak banister. Placing the bag on the floor she walked towards him, high heels striking the tiles. The man behind the door pressed himself against the wall to let her by.

"Hello Paul," Susan said from the doorway. "If I'd known it was really you, I'd have answered."

In the gym, Paul lowered his head and pedalled faster. Another kilometre, then another, and he'd rest.

The fucking bitch.

* * *

The mood in the briefing room was terse. Every seat was occupied and every unit and sub-unit under command was represented. Paul noted that even the Italian Carabinieri and the woman from DfID were on time. On the far side of the room, the colonel commanding the training team, and a detective inspector from the UN police wearing a Royal Ulster Constabulary uniform, were having a laugh. The only unit not represented was the Russian company guarding the airport. Since they never communicated with anyone, there was little point inviting them. At the Chief of Staff's order, the room fell silent, braced for the Brigadier's entrance.

"Ladies, Gentlemen, sit easy." The Brigadier said. He stood in front of a large map on the wall, long limbs filling the space.

"In a few weeks' time, we are going to honour a commitment made to the Serb military when they agreed to withdraw their forces from the province of Kosovo."

Paul started making notes. *How do we ensure this appears balanced?* he wrote.

"The original purpose of the buffer zone has been abused," the Brigadier continued. "It has become a haven for Albanian extremism and the locus of criminal smuggling throughout Europe. This smuggling funds, we now know, the expansion of Albanian militarism into Serbia to the East, FYROM to the South, and Montenegro to the west."

He hooked his thumbs into his stable belt.

"What you are going to be told now is how we plan to return the buffer zone, especially the disputed Presevo Valley, to Serb control."

He paused to let the information sink in.

"It must be done in such a way that minimises the risk of bloodshed; either on the part of the Serb security forces, or to the Albanian rebel groups in the forest. I suggest we all pin back our ears and listen in."

Paul's heart raced. This was it.

* * *

Paul held the phone to his ear with his shoulder while he typed an email to Elire. "This is not a press conference, Nick, it's an informal briefing. I want to talk off the record about what's going to happen."

"The UN have called a press conference tomorrow morning," Nick said. "They'll announce the hand back of the buffer zone."

"That's right," Paul said. "I told you things are going to get exciting. And in the afternoon, if you come here, I'll tell you how it's going to work so that there won't be any more ethnic cleansing."

Nick was smoking. He sucked in air. "You'll need answers. The NATO spokesman will be crucified if he handles the conference badly."

Paul knew. He'd seen what happened when the press got wind of an unpopular decision.

"That's why this is an informal briefing. I'm going to tell you stuff, and if you've got a legitimate concern, tell me what it is and I'll get an answer."

Nick cleared his throat. "Ok, I'll be there."

Paul put the phone down. He felt pleased with himself. Roza and Seagood, his driver, had taken down the tatty Union Jack and were painting the wall UN blue, joking as they did so. Dressed in white crime-scene suits blagged from the Camp Quartermaster, they looked like students decorating a flat. Both of them had dabs of blue paint on their elbows.

"And Roza, tomorrow morning, we should go through the wording of the statement."

"Yes of course, *Zotëri Major*," Roza replied with a smile.

It was good of her to help with the painting, but she had volunteered since the alternative was to sit in the interpreters' hut drinking endless cups of coffee. Paul thought the decorating would serve to bond his little team ever closer together. The driver pulled a step ladder away from the wall, knocking a tray of paint onto the floor.

"I need it to look good, Seagood. These are international journalists coming tomorrow."

His driver turned, revealing glasses speckled with paint. "It'll be brill, Sir," she chuckled. "You wait and see."

Paul smiled. Their levity was welcome. "And you'll pick up the flags later, including the Czech one?"

"Yes of course, *Zootery Maiyor*," said Seagood, making both of them collapse into fits of laughter.

Paul left them to it. The next port of call was the Brigadier, who was sitting in the Chief of Staff's office. Paul saluted.

"Sir, we were going to talk about the press briefing tomorrow. Is now a good time?"

The Brigadier lounged, hands in pockets, in one of the chairs facing Simon's desk. It was the thing about Montrose that everyone warmed to: his consultative, relaxed manner. It was a critical skill in a coalition operation, Paul had come to realise.

"I've had a bit of a rethink, actually. I know we said I would play a central role in the briefing, but Simon and I have been summoned to a command conference at NATO headquarters. You're going to have to do it alone."

Paul sat heavily. He sucked his teeth. "It won't be as effective, coming from me," he said. "If they ask a question and I get the answer wrong..."

Actually, the more he thought about it the more it felt like he was being dropped into very deep water. "What if I say something that jeopardises the operation?"

"You know very well what you can and cannot say," the Brigadier replied. "And you know what we want the Albanian insurgents to do?"

Paul nodded.

"Well then, I trust you to make the right decisions."

An array of emotions swept through him. On the one hand he was being trusted to give a press briefing to international journalists on his own, the impacts of which could be on the news the following evening. And on the other hand, the thought of Brassy bollocking him, and the fear of getting ambushed by a hostile press, filled him with dread. It had happened once before, and once was enough.

"I got pilloried once, in Sierra Leone," Paul said. "These things work best when I facilitate, and the senior commander presents the message."

The Brigadier and Simon studied him, then looked at each other. "You learned from that experience?" the Brigadier asked.

"Oh yes," Paul said, nodding. "It's not something I want to repeat."

"Then I'm sure you won't," the Brigadier replied, leaving Paul in no doubt that the ball was very firmly in his court.

He spent the rest of the afternoon going through his statement and any number of possible follow up challenges. He would brief Roza in the morning. Though he needed her to be fluent with the answers, it would be wrong to burden her with too much classified information too early on.

The repainting was finished, and a Royal Engineer corporal had fitted a bracket to support a splay of flags representing all eight countries in the British brigade. To the left of the flags was a poster of the UN logo and to the right, a NATO compass above the wording *Multinational Brigade (Centre)*. The impression Paul wanted to convey was one of international solidarity behind a UN Security Council Resolution. With such unified alignment, what could possibly go wrong?

He sat in the chairs that the press would use and looked critically at the display, imagining himself standing behind the lectern. He checked his notes, and mentally ran through the official media lines, testing his recall.

That night he lay in bed staring at the ceiling, haunted by the first press conference he'd run. With the usual spokesman, a colonel, incapacitated by malaria, he had been obliged to take over, and the press pack contained every household name he could think of.

It had been a very simple statement. *Operation Palliser was shortly to end because the rebels had been repulsed and Sierra Leone was now safe and stable. The British forces were leaving.*

It sparked panic. No sooner than his voice had been broadcast, the local press were printing news sheets to be sold by hawkers at the Cotton Tree Roundabout. *Stock up on yams and flour – rebels certain to return* ran one headline. *What Now Queenie? You leave us to die?* ran another.

Within two hours, a crowd of three thousand men were at the gates of the British High Commission, chanting and waving placards. The BBC reported that the British Army was abandoning the very people they had promised to save. What sort of demonstration of political will was this?

The impact was immediate. The Prime Minister had gone on the Today Programme the following morning to announce that British troops would not return home until Sierra Leone was safe from rebel incursion. There would be a training team established, which would support a re-armed Sierra Leone army. There would be a governmental advisory panel. There would be ten million pounds of aid for those recovering from the "dreadful and shocking" after effects of the civil war.

Having got the message wrong, Paul had been side-lined. Brassy even told him never to give a news conference again. A colonel was flown out to replace him as spokesman, while he remained in country for continuity. It didn't matter that the statement had been agreed, or that what he said was true. What mattered was that he was no longer considered credible.

He'd been used as a pawn, and burned. How could he stop that happening again?

* * *

The UN press conference proved as brutal as Nick predicted.

The United Nations Mission in Kosovo, UNMIK, was headquartered in a building that looked like a university, all polished concrete and heavy bronze doors. The Albanian security guard waved Paul through the metal detectors and directed him to an auditorium that could have seated several thousand.

In the front rows were groups of young women, their digital recorders on the desks in front of them. They laughed like students deconstructing the escapades of a previous night.

Scattered around the room Paul noted the uniforms: two French, one American, three Norwegians, and one Finn, a woman with phenomenally blonde hair.

The people representing the many charities that Kosovo attracted sat in small huddles, identifiable by their earnest expressions and drab clothing.

Walking up and down the steps was a team of two men, one with a television camera on his shoulder and the other with an extendable sound boom. Paul smiled when the camera focused on him, then picked a row of chairs with almost nobody on it and shuffled sideways to take a place in the centre. He nodded at Aden and Nick, sitting at the end of the row just below him.

The chatter quietened when a woman in a brown suit entered the room. She was followed by an American major with square shoulders and a square head. The woman hobbled in a pair of high heels and clambered onto the dais by pulling on a rope banister. Taking a seat at the desk, she laid out a sheaf of papers and shuffled them to check the order. The American major sat to her right and tapped the microphone to elicit a dull thudding through the sound system. He nodded at the woman, who pulled the microphone towards her. She spoke in a lisping Spanish accent.

"Good morning. For those who don't know me, I am Carla Alvarez, the UN spokesperson. Today we are going to talk about civil reconstruction and regeneration projects in the Pristina area. Then Major Breitman will have some messages from NATO for those of you concerned with security issues."

She read from a prepared script, her glasses balanced on her nose. To the front of the dais, two women translated the speech into Serbian and Albanian. They spoke into small microphones, although no one appeared to be wearing headphones to listen. To the right of the podium, a large man in a bulky puffer jacket constantly changed the slides on an overhead projector. On the acetates were the key points in English, Albanian, and Serbian. The writing was too small for anyone to read.

Despite the murmuring to her front, Carla spoke very clearly: there were to be road closures throughout March; the incidence of daylight power outages had been reduced by a further seven per cent. The name of the next Special Representative of the Secretary General would be announced soon.

When she had finished a page, she placed it ceremoniously face down to her right before starting the next. The young journalists at the front scribbled every word. The old hacks, Nick and Aden among them, watched with a look of tired ambivalence.

After twenty minutes, Aden Short raised his hand and clicked his fingers to attract the man with the sound boom. The audience turned to look at him.

Carla tapped the microphone with her pen. "Excuse me! If you don't mind we have a protocol for questions…"

Aden grabbed the sound boom and held it low in front of his face. "Carla, could you tell us please what has been done to arrest those responsible for the bombing of the bus last month?"

Carla shook her head. "I'll pick up that with you later, Aden."

The audience responded noisily to this exchange.

Aden retained possession of the sound boom. "Is it true that those responsible are hiding in the Presevo Valley outside the agreed boundaries of Kosovo?"

Carla leaned forward and peered over the top of her glasses. "If you don't mind, Aden, I will take questions at the end…"

The sound operator tried to lift the boom, but Aden refused to let go.

"One for Major Breitman: if the ethnic violence spreads into Serbia when you hand back the buffer zone, will NATO extend its mandate to protect the Albanian populations of Southern Serbia?"

A wave of gasps swept across the room. Hands poked up everywhere. The local journalists started making calls once they saw how Aden's line of argument was developing.

Aden released the sound boom as others started calling for it. The camera operator didn't know who to focus on, so trotted down the steps to film the audience. Aden folded his arms.

On the podium, Carla placed a hand over the microphone to whisper to the American major. The audience shouted questions in both English and Albanian. The Albanian translator pointed at people as she could not manage everyone at once. The operator of the overhead projector got his acetates in a muddle and was busy shuffling them.

As he did so, the one projected against the wall was clearly titled *Future of the Presevo Valley*. When people noticed it, a chorus of shouts erupted. The American major hissed for the machine to be turned off, but the operator did nothing except fold his arms.

A German captain, posted by the door to keep order, started banging a gavel onto his lectern. A group of Albanian journalists started singing.

Carla raised her hands, "Excuse me, excuse me," but it was obvious she'd lost control.

Paul gathered his notebook and sidled towards the door.

* * *

"I hope this isn't going to be like the UN conference," Paul chuckled, as he waited for Aden, Nick, and Elire to take their places on the red sofa.

"So do we," said Aden, lifting a camera case onto Paul's desk. "Am I setting this up?"

Paul leaned on one elbow on the lectern, the clicker for the slide carousel in his other hand. "I'd rather just have a chat to start with."

Sitting at one end of the sofa, Elire sniffed the air.

"We've been decorating, just for you," Paul said. She was wearing a tight skirt that stopped above stockinged knees. Because of the angle of the sofa and where he was standing, the dark shadows drew his eyes. He looked away when he saw she'd noticed.

Seagood and Roza stood attentively at the back of the room. Nick stroked tobacco off his trousers with sharp sweeps of his hand. Aden stepped over his legs to sit in the middle of the sofa and swept hair out of his eyes.

"I invited the Editors of Koha Ditore and Radio Rilindja, but they're not here," Paul said, looking at his watch. "How long shall we give them?"

Nick pulled a notebook out of his shirt pocket. "Let's start," he said. "They can catch up."

Paul nodded at Seagood, who flicked the lights. He pressed the button on the slide controller and the carousel clacked mechanically to project a map of Kosovo against a mobile screen. Paul talked them through the essence of the Brigade plan, less the classified details.

"So in essence the buffer zone, or Ground Safety Zone as we call it, extends all the way round the Kosovo-Serbia border. Some areas of it have a greater Albanian population than others."

Elire had a digital recorder with the microphone pointed his way. Nick took a few notes, Aden none.

Paul continued, "We've broken it down into risk areas, the highest risk being Sector D to the east of Kosovo, along the Presevo Valley. We will manage the Serbs' occupation sector by sector, and control their rate of advance as they move in."

He reached up using a plastic ruler to indicate the areas he meant.

"And at the bottom of each sector we will erect a gate through which anyone can enter Kosovo. We will disarm them, but they will not be imprisoned or questioned."

He looked directly at Elire. Her station had access to these people. If she repeated this, lives could be saved.

"What I want you to realise is that we've planned this so the Albanian extremists living in the buffer zone have time, between now and the day when the reoccupation takes place, to move out."

Nick raised a hand. "When will that take place?"

Paul stepped round the lectern and pulled out a chair to sit close in front of the three of them. "That's classified. I won't be able to give you the exact time until it is happening. Otherwise we risk setting up the Serb army to be ambushed."

There was a lull while his words were digested. He'd said them more harshly than intended, but wanted the journalists to understand the plan clearly. He nodded for Seagood to turn the lights back on. Roza was smiling at him. Elire glanced across at the two men. Aden started twiddling his thumbs.

"You don't seem convinced," Paul said.

Aden pulled a face. "It's not that I'm not convinced. It's that you don't understand what you're dealing with."

"How do you mean?"

"You know how I knew that helicopter had crashed?"

Paul shook his head. "You wouldn't tell me."

"I know people there. I've interviewed the leader of the National Liberation Army in the Presevo Valley. Dragusha, he's called, Shefket Dragusha. He will not hand in his weapons."

During the morning brief Blanche had said the same name. This was the man who had turned a gang of smugglers into a coherent military force.

"They may be calling themselves the National Liberation Army, Aden, but we do not recognise that term. We're calling them a militia. The Presevo Valley was never part of Kosovo."

A long "No," emanated from Elire, accompanied by a steady shake of her head. "Not true, Major Pol. Back in Tito time, Yugoslavia time, Presevo part of Kosova."

"Was it?" Paul's cheeks reddened.

"Yes. Tito, very clever man. He know too many Albanian people give him problem. So he divide them. How you say?"

"Divide and rule."

"Like this. He take little bit of Serbia, and give to it to Kosova to manage. This Mitrovica, where French army living. Many more Serbian peoples than Albanian. Then he take Presevo, with many Albanian mens, and give it to Serbian province to manage. He is keeping everybody down this way."

Paul was flummoxed. "That may be true. But I'm referring to the current borders of Kosovo, the ones agreed during the ceasefire two years ago."

Nick placed a hand on his chin. "Well actually, Paul, this is precisely the issue. The Albanians are a nation divided between several states. That's why they are rebelling. Not only in Serbia, but also in Macedonia."

"The former Yugoslav Republic of Macedonia," Paul corrected. "We call it FYROM."

"You can call it what you like. The people in the north are ethnic Albanians, as are the people in the Presevo Valley, as are the people here in Pristina."

Aden nodded. "I've seen their base. They're the same men who fought against the Serbians for the Kosovo Liberation Army two years ago. When NATO came in, they moved over the border."

Why did journalists always make life so complicated? Paul thought. He stood up and indicated the map with the ruler. With the lights on the image was difficult to see.

"I'm not talking about the historic position," he insisted. "This bit is Kosovo. That bit is Serbia. NATO are giving back what was never theirs. That is all."

"Paul, you're not listening," Aden said. "You haven't met these people. This is their land, where their families are buried. They will fight for it."

Paul looked from one to the other. "What can I say? I'm telling you our plan. If they stay and fight, NATO will be forced to take action."

"So you're going to turn against the Albanians?" Nick said.

Elire's eyes widened. She held out the recorder. Paul realised he was falling into a trap. Either he had to accept that the imposed borders were wrong, or that NATO would be drawn further into conflict. He spoke slowly, testing his words as he said them.

"No. We are not turning against anybody. The support of the Albanian population of Kosovo is crucial to NATO's success. But the UN mandate, resolution 1244, does not extend into Serb territory."

Nick shook his head. "Paul, it doesn't sound like you have a firm grasp of the local conditions. Your plan is flawed."

***

After he'd finally waved the three journalists off at the gate, Paul went straight to see Simon. Luckily, Blanche was in his office as well, sitting with her hands on her lap and her knees folded to the side. When he arrived, they were discussing what had come out of the NATO command conference. He took a seat, but felt what he knew was too important to wait. "The journalists are certain the Albanians will stand their ground," he said.

"What makes them so sure?" Blanche asked, her lips zipping tight after she'd spoken.

His comment had riled her, something he had not intended. "I'm not stepping on your shoes, Blanche," he said. "You should look at them as another source of intelligence…"

"They're another source of *opinion*," she corrected. "Only when information is verified does it become *intelligence*."

Simon interlaced his fingers behind his head. "Will they tell us anything more specific: locations? numbers?"

Paul shook his head. "Pointless asking."

"Even if it's the right thing to do?"

Paul shook his head again. "Journalists have gone to prison rather than reveal a source."

"Which is what makes their statements unreliable," Blanche said with an air of finality.

She seemed to enjoy scoring points. Paul could not help his hackles rising. "How could they ever go places where people thought they were snouts?" he said. "They have their lives at stake all the time."

Blanche was stumped by this. To break the silence, Simon asked, "Could you ask them to indicate the general area? So we could drop leaflets?"

"Paul's not trained in tactical inquiry…" Blanche said.

The thing about intelligence people was they couldn't see the wood for the trees. "I know how to ask a question," Paul said, not trying to hide his irritation. "The issue is not that they know more than we do. It's that they're convinced the rebels will fight. That's the message they're putting round, no matter what I say or do. And that message will boost the rebels' confidence."

Blanche looked away. Simon folded his arms and thought for a while. "You've done what you could, Paul," he said. "You won't be able to change the course of events just by talking to the press."

Paul did not agree. Actually, he was becoming convinced that was exactly what he could do. As long as he could get the press to report in a certain way.

"It's just a shame…" Blanche said, but Simon raised a hand to cut her off.

"Our business is risk," he said. "If the press are amplifying it, and Message Operations have done everything possible to mitigate it, then we have to prepare accordingly." He looked at Paul. "That, in itself, is highly useful. We'll have to go in hard. Helmets rather than berets."

"I didn't tell them we will be sending reconnaissance parties ahead of the Serb forces," Paul said.

"And that's fine," Simon said. "But our main failing in all of this is that we're not talking to the Serb civilians. We need to keep them informed too."

Paul frowned. That was very true.

Simon continued, "What do you know about a radio station in the Gracanica enclave?"

"Nothing."

"Apparently there's one somewhere down there. The Serbs living near the monastery have set it up. It was mentioned at the command conference."

Paul's mouth opened and closed. "First I've heard of it."

"Me too," said Simon. "I thought you might like to see whether it's a channel you could use?"

He was right, and Paul felt annoyed not to have known about it. He roused himself from the chair, fitted his beret, and saluted. "I'll go and visit them right away."

Blanche had a smirk on her thin lips. Paul winked at her as he pulled the door closed behind him.

***

Lying awake in bed, Paul listened to the sound of footsteps in the corridor. He'd tried reading, but his eyes wouldn't focus on the words, and the fantasy novel he'd picked out of the box at the back of the scoff hall was too far from his experience to be meaningful.

He was exhausted. Masturbating only served to amplify his fatigue without enabling him to sleep. The most annoying thing was that he didn't know what was keeping him awake. What was making his mind go round in circles?

Blanche's nettling had been irksome. He had thought at first, watching her present at the morning brief, that she was very impressive. But since then he had come to see her as narrow minded. She did not have the imagination to see what Message Operations could deliver. And yet she was going on the next Staff College course! No wonder she treated him with such disdain.

But there was something else, something deeper. When Susan kept asking *"Is that you?"* was she making a joke, or a point? When he was with her, was he being himself, or was he pretending to be someone he thought she'd like?

Paul opened his eyes. He had the horrible feeling that the reason his relationship had failed was not due to Susan, but was down to him.

And yet to make the press behave as he wanted them to, he'd have to stop being so honest.

BBC Online, 23 April 2001
NATO unprepared for bloodshed as buffer zone is handed back to Serbian control
Nicholas Oakeshot, Balkan Editor

NATO plans to hand back the buffer zone surrounding the troubled Balkan region of Kosovo are doomed to fail, according to experts.

The demilitarised area runs through the disputed Presevo Valley region, home to a high percentage of Serbia's ethnic Albanians who are opposed to the Belgrade government. Major Paul Illingworth, spokesman for British Forces, said that NATO would not extend its mandate. "If there is more fighting, NATO will not get involved," he said.

In contrast, the leader of the National Liberation Army, Shefket Dragusha, has vowed to fight "to the last man, to the last bullet!" if the Serbian army attempts to reassert control over the area. Speaking from his forest hideout deep in the Presevo Valley, he claimed to have 17,000 seasoned fighters, all of whom saw action against the Serbian army in 1999.

Meanwhile, Serbia's President Vojislav Kostunica is walking a very fine line. He has promised that the Serbian security forces will act "with impartiality and professionalism," and yet he must also satisfy those on the right wing of his government. The Minister of the Interior and former supporter of Slobodan Milosevic, Dragan Vucic, has described ethnic Albanians as "cockroaches who should be stamped on."

The exact date of the transfer of the buffer zone is not yet known, but throughout the region, political and military leaders are waiting to see who blinks first.

Chapter 5

It was dark outside. Paul had done two radio interviews that day, one with Radio Rilindja and the other with Black Eagle. In both he'd stressed how important it was that the Albanians in the Presevo Valley think about leaving prior to the Serb reoccupation. The phone lines had gone mad. He'd done his best to answer every question in a calm manner, but nothing mitigated the fact that the sectarian enmity in the Balkans made Northern Ireland look like a playground tiff.

Exhausted, he watched the words 'Message Operations' written in red, three dimensional letters, bounce between the corners of the computer monitor. He should reply to an email from his mother, he thought. He should drop a note to Becky, his sister, and ask how she was coping with university. But he was too tired.

The door opened and he looked over his shoulder. Roza entered, ran across the floor and flung herself onto the sofa. She was crying, her hands shredding a paper tissue. Flecks of it fell on her jeans and the floor. She blew her nose on the little that remained, tears rolling down her cheeks. She wiped them away with the sleeve of her jumper.

"What's the matter?" Paul said. When she did not respond, he said, "Roza, what is it?"

She turned her face away, unable to stop crying. There was something forced in the action. Paul rolled his chair towards the sofa and placed a hand on her knee.

"Has someone said something?"

Roza buried her face in her hands, her breathing jagged. Paul put his hand on her shoulder. "I can't help unless you tell me."

The sobbing continued. Paul sat back and folded his arms to watch her, wondering if she was either immature or just a bad actor. Her nails were bitten short and the skin around them raged with eczema. When she looked up, her face framed by a cascade of mahogany-coloured hair, he saw panic in her eyes.

"Major Henderson," she said at last, shaking her head. "She ask me if I go to the bed with Colonel Jasper. I said no, but she keep asking. I said no, I am not that sort of girl. But she keep doing it. She keep saying I was seen. That people say on me."

She broke down again, letting out a low wail. Paul tried not to smirk at the display.

"They say he was with me in the night but it is not true." Hiding her face, she started sobbing again.

Paul did not reach out. She sounded like a child swearing she had not taken a biscuit from the tin. "They asked you and you said no. So why are you crying?"

"Because they keep asking me!" she said, banging her hands on her knees. "I need ticket for to work. I need for the money. They have to make assessment. We all do it, every year. But never this hard."

She turned to him, begging. "I never did anything, Zotëri Major. Jasper too much interested in Irena, Serbian interpreter. I swear it."

Paul was angry that Blanche hadn't warned him of this investigation. "Have you been sacked?"

"They will check something. They will let me know." Then suddenly, "If they call you in, they just say go. You don't get time to say bye-bye or collect your things. I need money for my family. My brother is working but my father is injured."

She shuffled forward until she was almost kneeling. "Major Paul, please help me. I don't know what to do."

She reached out a hand towards his knee but when he didn't take it, she withdrew it. Paul pushed his chair back a little, and crossed his feet at the ankles. Despite this demonstration, he didn't want to lose her. Jasper must have been quite a guy to be shagging two girls in their early twenties. A colonel would be in his late thirties at the earliest.

"I can help you, Roza, now you mention it. But we have to do something we haven't done before."

She looked up at him and sniffed.

"You speak Serbo-Croat?"

She nodded.

"Good. All I've done so far is focus on the Albanian stations. I need to go and see a radio station in Gracanica."

Roza wiped her nose on her finger. "You want me to go with you to Gracanica?"

"Yes."

"You want me to speak to Serbian people?"

"Yes."

She paused. Her face clouded as she bit her lip. She moved back on the sofa.

Paul said, "They won't harm you. It's just another radio interview."

She blinked, the wheels of her mind turning before his eyes. "You will protect me?"

"Of course."

She twisted the tattered tissue in her hands, folding it over and over.

"And I will put in a word with Blanche Henderson," he said.

"Okey-dokey," she said. "Then I do it."

* * *

Seagood halted the Landrover next to the chain-link fence surrounding Radio Black Eagle, disengaged the gear stick, and pulled on the handbrake. "There you go, Sir. I have to take this wagon back to camp to be serviced, but I'll pick you up in an hour and a half."

77

"You'll be here?" said Paul.

"They'll give me another wagon if this one isn't ready," she said, and Paul had little choice but to believe her.

He made sure he had his weapon in its holster, then shouldered the passenger door open. At the back, Roza was looking out through the dirty window over the rim of the spare wheel. He offered his hand as she reached out with the toe of her sneakers for the step. She took it, and only let go when she had both feet on the floor. He slammed the door. Seagood engaged the gear and disappeared along the lane.

The winter had been quickly replaced by a vibrant spring. What had been snow covered mounds only a week before were now recognisable plants in the radio station's front garden.

"It's an oak!" said Paul, pulling a leaf from one of the stunted trees by the steps. As he studied it, movement caught his eye. "Look at that!"

Underneath the building, a nervous, wall-eyed dog peeked out from behind a concrete pillar. Paul knew better than to approach it – there could be pups with her – but he knelt and held out his hand, rubbing his fingers. "There you go, good girl."

Roza climbed the steps to the screen door. She held her notebook in front of her chest and shook her head.

"These animals are dirty," she said. "Why are you British so friendly with them?"

The dog glared up at Roza out of the corner of her eyes. She looked back at Paul and wagged her tail. When he pulled himself upright, she retreated into the shadows.

"I have a dog like this," Paul said. "Well, not exactly like this. Black and white, not grey and white. They are for herding sheep."

"You have sheep?" Roza asked, frowning.

"No," Paul replied, "but sheepdogs are very faithful."

"Yes. Loyalty very important," she said, then turned to open the screen door. Following her, Paul couldn't help tracing the lovely outline of her hips, the way her buttocks neatly filled a pair of faded blue jeans. He was becoming used to her perfume and welcomed it when they were squeezed together for an interview in the small studio.

Elire met them in the corridor. She was eating a pastry, pressing stray crumbs into her mouth with long, manicured fingers.

"How are you?" said Paul in an exaggerated Yorkshire accent. "You look lovely today."

"You are gentleman, Major Pol," said Elire, guiding them through to the kitchen. She offered them coffee and the last slice of Danish.

"I've eaten, thanks," said Paul, but Roza accepted the cake and sat down, one hand underneath her chin.

"Major Pol," Elire began, "my listeners are unhappy. They want to know why NATO not help the Albanian people in Presevo. You know Serbian army do very bad things to them."

Paul sat on a wooden chair and crossed his legs. He waited for Elire to sit as well, then checked his watch. He had come early especially to have this discussion.

"Elire, I know what you're going to say. And I understand what your listeners want. But I'm not going to say NATO will support the Albanian cause in the Presevo Valley. It won't."

Elire swept a hand through her hair. She looked angry.

Paul continued, "I'm also certain that the Serb army will not start evicting people from their houses in Presevo like they did here," he said.

"How you know?"

Paul counted points on his fingers. "Milosevic is no longer in power. There are sanctions. President Kostunica wants to join the European Union. He can only modernise Serbia if he runs an effective democracy. The EU won't take him if he is killing his own population."

"They do it here, Major Pol. They do it for many years."

Paul felt like saying the Albanians were doing the same thing to the few Serbs who remained after the war, but he didn't. "That was when Milosevic was in power," he said. "Kostunica will arrest him and give him up to the International Criminal Tribunal before too long."

Elire crossed her legs and leaned her elbows on the upper knee. "I don't think so. Serb people cannot be trusted."

Paul shrugged. "My question would be: how do we help Serbia down the path of democratisation and responsibility?" She was no fool, and he hoped his plan would work. "This is going to be hard for people to get, Elire," he said, "but we have to tell them the truth. The fighters in the Valley must either become peaceful residents of the Serbian state, or move across the border to Kosovo and hand in their weapons. There is no future in violence."

Elire said nothing.

Paul continued. "If you fight, they will fight harder. That is the nature of governments."

"But here, we win. We make them leave!" she said defiantly.

Paul shook his head. "No Elire, you didn't. I know that's a popular standpoint, but it isn't true, is it?"

She said nothing.

Paul continued. "The Kosovo Liberation Army fought very bravely to protect the Albanian people. But the Serb army left Kosovo after a two month air campaign and the deployment of an international NATO coalition. There are forty thousand troops here."

"Ok, so NATO help."

Paul laughed. "Well yeah! And just because we helped last time does not mean we are going to start a war every time an Albanian feels his honour has been affronted."

Elire frowned. "Fronted?"

"Insulted," Paul corrected himself. "We are not here just for the Albanians. We are here for peace and stability on all sides."

He took a careful glance at Roza. She sat straight backed, her hands curled on her lap, looking at him with wide eyes. He winked.

Elire swept a hand through her mop of hair. "But what you think, Major Pol? You know what Serbian peoples do to us."

Paul folded his arms. It was now or never. "Elire, if the Albanians want Kosovo to become independent, they must think cleverly. A European state does not export terrorism."

He'd chosen his words carefully. Elire's reaction was immediate. "You think we are terrorists?"

She expected a denial, but he didn't provide one. "Peaceful people do not live in camps in the forest, Elire. They do not bomb buses or shoot at the women cutting the corn."

"This is nothing!" Elire snapped. "Serb people kill thousands of women. Thousands of mens…"

In the background, the station was playing the theme to the film *Titanic*. Paul spoke as quietly as possible. "Repeating such things will only turn others against you." He held her eyes. "Think about it, Elire. You are a very clever woman. If Kosovo becomes independent, who will it trade with?"

"We have Albania. We have ourselves."

"Oh come on! Think what independence could mean!"

It was the third time he had suggested it. Had she heard him? Would she bite?

She looked away. The light from the window made her features strong. "You want us to abandon our brothers in Presevo for our own independence?"

Paul coughed. He was so far off the media lines he had no choice but to keep going. But she could see straight through him.

"You won't say this, Major Pol, will you, on air?" she said.

Paul shook his head. "No, Elire, I can't. But you can. You enjoy saying something contentious and getting people to call in."

Elire smiled as she slid her hands down the front of one shin. He'd hit the nail on the head.

"Ok, I think about it," she said. "But we do interview now."

She shook the collection of bangles down her forearm to pull them off her hand and place them in a pile on the table.

"But none of this, about independence," Paul said as they rose.

She nodded, great ripples of movement flowing through her hair. "I know. You must ask about bus. And tell people to leave Presevo." She stepped towards the door into the corridor. "But tell me, Major Pol. You really think Kosovo can be independent?"

"It all depends on you," Paul replied.

* * *

Seagood was late, but Paul wasn't disappointed. The discussion prior to the radio interview had left him elated. If he was given free rein to say what he wanted, he would pave the way for almost any outcome. If he could get the press to say something was going to happen, anything, it inevitably would. And if the Albanians would only stop killing Serb civilians, there was no telling what they could achieve. Kosovo was beautiful. With such welcoming people and rich arable land, it could be the next Czech Republic. There could be thousands of tourists flocking to Pristina every year. But not if the ethnic slaughter continued.

Standing outside the chain-link fence, Paul held up his hand to protect his eyes from the sunlight. The afternoon was much warmer than he'd expected. He unzipped his smock and laid it on a wooden bench facing the car park. "Let's wait, Roza. Seagood'll come soon."

"Okey-dokey," said Roza, ensuring her bottom was on his smock and not the mossy slats of the bench.

"What you say is true," she said after a while. "If we want to be newborn, we must be good people."

The sentiment seemed uncommonly astute from one so young. Was she saying it because she believed it, or because that was what she knew he wanted her to say?

She had her eyes closed and face tilted up to the sun. The skin of her throat was spattered with freckles. Her perfume seemed even more floral in the open air.

"It will be a difficult message," Paul said. "Violence helped last time, so they will try it again."

He had to be careful. She was, after all, Albanian. She squinted at him, one hand shielding her eyes.

"Did you have to flee? During the war?" he asked.

"Yes," she said. Then her face contracted. She said nothing for a few moments. "We are lucky. We have a place in Albania, in the mountains. My father is, how you say, business man? He has many houses."

"So you weren't in one of the refugee camps?"

She blinked a few times. Paul became afraid, suddenly, to hear her experience. He said, "I'm sorry. If this is something…"

Behind them, the screen door creaked open and slammed. Elire stepped noisily in high heels down the concrete steps, watching carefully where to place her feet. Paul stood up.

"You need a lift Major Pol? I take you?" She looked at Roza. "You can both come. But Pol, we put you in front seat."

She rattled her car keys and opened the door of her beetle, which was parked against the chain-link fence.

"My driver is coming, thank you Elire. I will wait here."

From behind the driver's door, she leaned on the roof. "There is big demonstration in Mother Teresa Street. If she come that way, maybe long time."

Paul shrugged, indicating the tatty lane where the station was located. "It's kind, but I don't want her to come here and waste the journey. She's a young girl."

Elire smiled, casting a sly glance at Roza. "Ok," she said. "See you."

Paul waved her off as she swung the car round. Roza raised a hand as well and Paul wondered for a moment if the two women were mouthing words to each other.

"She likes you," Roza said after the car had gone. "She always likes army mens."

"She's a very engaging lady," Paul retorted.

They sat in silence for a while, her shoulder occasionally touching his arm, their faces towards the sun. The light burned through his eyelids so much that he could tell when a distant and inaudible helicopter blocked out the light.

"Tell me what happened," he said. "I want to know."

She shivered, then folded her arms. "During the war, my family leave Pristina. We think Serbian soldiers would take our money so we go in the night, all of us. We drive. We hide the money and lock the house."

Her voice became a whisper.

"But the roads were full with refugees. Many, many people, all looking to find somewhere safe. Serbian soldiers, they know this. They have photos. We had to leave the car and walk. For eighty kilometres, we walk. Even my grandmother…"

Roza's mouth distorted. She paused, gathering herself. "When they see my father, they recognise him and take him to the side. They beat him here, two little things…"

"Kidneys?"

"Yes. They beat him in the kidneys. My brother was not there. If he was, he would fight them and they would kill him. They had guns and we had nothing."

She was silent again for a while, using her hand as a visor along the line of her eyebrows.

"My little cousin… she was only nine years old. Mimi, my little Mimi. She took the bag with my mother's jewellery. She ran into the fields. The soldiers, they chase her…"

Roza spluttered. Fat tears streamed over her cheeks. "There was minefield," she said at last. The sobs became uncontrollable. "They make my father go in…"

Paul placed an arm round her shoulder and hugged her to him. She let herself be drawn. "I'm sorry," he said. "I'm asking because I want to know what you experienced."

Roza swallowed, and dug into the pockets of her jeans for a tissue. "I know," she said. "And I like it very much."

When she stopped crying, she wiped her nose and straightened herself. He took his arm off her shoulder and rested it along the back of the bench. She tucked away the tissue she had used to wipe her nose, then leaned her head back to rest upon his bicep. He ought to move in case they were seen, but he didn't. She was in his team and he wanted her to trust him.

Closing his eyes, he enjoyed her delicious proximity and the sensation of blood pumping along his arm.

* * *

Anja pulled on her Russian hat. Tata said it was wrong to wear it for church; she should wear the new leather boots, her good dress with the flowers on it, and the apron that was once his mother's.

"I don't want to," Anja said, sticking out her lower lip.

Tata brought his face down and his eyes were sad. "Please Anja; put on your clothes and I will bring you back quickly. I promise."

But after the service, the men gathered in the market square. Someone had been given a child so there was slivovic to pass round, and discussions about what was happening in the homeland.

"I hear they are going to send Milosevic to face trial."

"Trial for what?"

"He killed his opponents, we all know that."

"He killed his own people, too."

The talk was urgent. Every opinion was immediately challenged. In the centre of the throng, Tata was too distant for Anja to summon and yet too near to walk away from. It was a few hundred paces to her door, but she was afraid of going alone.

A man said, "In the spring, when we are planting, the Muslims will shoot at us. They only need a few more attacks and they know we will leave."

"Who is leaving? This is where I pray. This is where my family are buried."

Something hard and small hit Anja on the shoulder. She turned. Five little boys were darting up behind her to lob pebbles at her back, giggling as they did so.

"*Albanski, Albanski!*" they teased.

She bolted for them, joking at first, to make them scatter. But then they threw the stones harder.

"I'll get you," she said.

She wasn't like other girls. She had been brought up in the mountains; she could chop wood, trap rabbits, build fires. But the little boys were nimble. They dodged and weaved and when she was chasing one, another picked up a pebble and threw it at her back.

So instead of scattering them, Anja picked on one, the biggest, and chased him down. He ducked and spun, but his smile faded when he realised how angry she was. She reached out to grab his coat. "I'm going to…"

But at that moment the toe of her unfamiliar boots caught the edge of a cobble. She stumbled and fell flat on her front. Stones scraped her palms. Now she was not only angry, she was embarrassed. She looked at the boy with venom. She was going to hurt him. This was not about being teased, this was about being her.

Something hit her then, but it wasn't a stone. It was soft and sludgy and slipped off when she turned.

"*Albanski, Albanski!*" the boys chanted.

Then another splat of horse manure hit her right in the face, hard enough to sting.

"Stop that!" she screamed. "Stop that!"

But the boys didn't know how. They had already collected the small balls of dung and had dirty hands.

* * *

Gracanica was forty minutes south of Pristina. A single sign, written in Cyrillic and sprayed with graffiti, indicated the turning from the main road. The fields were not bordered by rusting cars or discarded tubs; they were pregnant with green wheat and dense, gnarled vines that skirted the hillside in orderly rows. The houses were painted in pastel colours, each doorway decorated with hanging baskets dripping with water.

"Where are we going, Sir?" Seagood asked.

"I'm afraid I don't know," Paul said, looking from side to side. "I thought it would be obvious when we got here."

It hadn't been easy to track down Radio Gracanica. Paul had needed to talk to Carla Alvarez, the UN spokeswoman, and a number of NGO intermediaries, before finding the number of a man said to be the owner. But in his haste to set up a meeting he had forgotten to ask where the station was.

"I'm hoping there'll be a radio mast," Paul said, craning forward. "She said if we get to the monastery, we've gone too far."

They passed a line of sycamore trees masking a square building covered in domes. Seagood giggled.

"Turn round. Let's ask someone," Paul said.

Seagood obliged, raking the gears. The market square was empty, reminding Paul of his first days in Freetown. They pulled up by a wooden gate and looked down a vista of trees to admire the monastery. The windows seemed mismatched, squares of glass set amid heavy pillars, a curious blend of art deco and baroque. A two-wheeled tractor pulling a box trailer chugged past, the driver bouncing up and down on a sprung seat. He scowled at them, then looked away.

"Sir, look," said Seagood.

An old woman appeared from the side of the monastery hobbling at a glacial pace, each placement of her stick a deliberate act.

Opening the door Paul said, "I'll ask her. Roza could you help?"

The woman was dressed entirely in black, a shawl covering a thin sweep of grey hair. Paul waited by the covered gate, then saluted.

"Excuse me? Scusi? Madame?"

She craned backwards to look at him but shook her head and touched her ear with a shaking, arthritic hand. She hobbled past. Roza spoke to her and Paul only recognised the words *Radio Gracanica*.

The old woman studied Roza with stern, unblinking eyes.

"What is the name," Roza whispered. "What is the name of the man you come to see?"

"Stefan," Paul said, pointing to his chest. "I have come to speak to Stefan Savic. I come from NATO."

The old woman mumbled something, waving her stick back the way they had come. She continued on her way.

"Did she just tell us politely to leave?"

"No," Roza said. "We drive past it."

Paul called out his thanks to the old woman as he helped Roza climb back into the Landrover.

The radio station was inconspicuous. When they saw it, they noticed a man with greasy hair and bony features leaning against the wall, smoking. He seemed nervous, frequently glancing up and down the street.

"Stefan? I'm Paul. Paul Illingworth."

The man studied him before scrubbing out the remains of his cigarette between his fingers.

"You speak English?"

Stefan shrugged, twisting his wrist.

"That's ok, I have an interpreter," Paul said and Stefan nodded, smiling at Roza. She smiled back, standing close to Paul's shoulder.

"*Molim*," Stefan said, indicating the entrance. After telling Seagood to park up, Paul obliged.

Once inside the building, a heavy door slammed behind them. It was reinforced on the inside by an iron plate. Chains clattered against the jamb for a few moments before stilling. The floorboards were bare, narrow strips of darkness voiding beneath them. Stefan led the way through to what had once been a kitchen. The remnants of cupboards adorned peeling yellow walls. He emptied a conical coffee pot and refilled it from the single tap. Spillage from the sink tinkled onto a tiled floor that sloped towards a drain. He placed the coffee pot on a gas ring and pressed the clicker until a flame poffed alight. Then he set the dial.

"I wash..." he said, collecting three glasses and making the hand signal of one scrubbing. He was thin necked, thin shouldered, and thin waisted underneath a grey sleeveless jumper. An acrid body odour followed him wherever he went, overpowering the smell of cigarettes.

Paul took one of the chairs to sit at the table, inviting Roza to do the same. He whispered, "Translate exactly what is said. Let me keep eye contact."

"Okey-dokey." She shivered, clasping her hands between her knees. Her mouth formed a taut line.

"Are you all right?"

She nodded.

Stefan turned, holding up two glasses. He spoke in Serbian, looking at Roza. She nodded, indicating Paul. Stefan turned back to the cooker and drummed his fingers on the worktop as he waited for the pot to boil. Music came through the wall, harmonious chanting backed by chiming bells.

"What sort of programmes do you do here, Stefan?" Paul asked. "Just religious? Or current affairs?"

Stefan turned, eyebrows arching. Smiling, he shook his head and looked to Roza for explanation. She said nothing, knitting her fingers together and hunching forwards. Glancing at Paul, she translated.

The effect was immediate. Stefan grabbed the coffee pot off the gas ring and swept the glasses off the worktop. They skittered to the floor and shattered. Spoons cascaded off the walls. He looked round for something heavier, shouting hysterically.

"Albanski!"

He put the pot down and grabbed a chair, holding it as if taming a lion, then kicked the table towards Roza.

Roza yelped and leaped backwards towards the door. Paul jumped up to protect her. She grabbed the back of his shirt. It was like having a terrier and a rat in the same cage.

"Fucking whoa," snapped Paul, shaking Roza off him.

"Why you do this?" Stefan yelled in English. "Why you bring Albanski to my home."

Roza moaned, keeping hidden behind Paul's shoulder.

"Both of you sit down," ordered Paul. "No one is going to get hurt and no one is going to fight."

Nobody moved. Turning to Stefan, Paul placed the fingers of his right hand over his heart, something he had seen people do.

"Stefan, I mean no insult by bringing this girl. She is my interpreter. I do not have another. She is no harm to you, you have my word."

He stopped. Stefan did not understand him. He looked round at Roza, "Tell him exactly what I said. Speak of yourself in the third person." She did so, and Paul continued. "Stefan, I ask that you welcome us. She is necessary for me to understand what you say."

Stefan's face dripped with sweat. He spoke again in faltering English. "How I trust her? Last night, men drive here shooting guns. They not kill. But they not have to."

"Men were driving through Gracanica? Last night?" Paul demanded.

Stefan nodded.

"Did you get the number plate? Could you describe them?"

There was a pause, then Stefan shook his head. He spoke in Serbian. Roza translated, "When men with guns come to your town, you do not open the door to look at their cars."

There was a long pause. Stefan lowered the chair. Paul righted the table then sat down, pulling at Roza's sleeve to bring her beside him. After a while, Stefan sat as well.

Spilled water tinkled down the drain. The gas ring hissed. Stefan switched it off, then poured what coffee he could from the pot and passed a cup to Paul and another to Roza.

Paul sipped his and nudged Roza with his knee to do the same.

"Keep translating," he whispered, then, "How can we help you, Stefan? What can we do?"

"You protect us," he replied. "We have no guards. Only one or two times men come through in tanks. We have no one to guard our monastery."

"I know it is important," Paul said. "And it is very beautiful."

"It is the most beautiful church in all of Yugoslavia," Stefan replied. "More wonderful than the church in Rome, Michelangelo."

"The Sistine Chapel?" said Paul.

Roza stammered at the name.

Stefan frowned at her translation, then laughed. "Not 'sixteen'," he chided. "*Sistine*." Then in English, "Is good you look. I show you."

Paul nodded. "I would like that very much, but not now. There is work to do. I can't promise you guards."

"But the French," Stefan said, "in Mitrovica, on every street they have men. And there is no shooting. They do not kill us, the Albanski."

"The French do things differently," Paul replied. "We have less people. But we cover the same ground by doing random patrols."

"French way is better," Stefan said, nodding for emphasis. "Is good you bring more people."

"I cannot do that," Paul said. "I am not the Brigadier. I'm just a major."

"But major is important," Stefan insisted. "Please protect us."

"You do not see what we do outside of Gracanica, I think," Paul said after a pause. "We are doing many things to make life better. Peace is not for one people. Peace is for both people or it is not peace at all."

Roza translated. Stefan kept his eyes on Paul.

Paul continued, "How about we take you to the UN press conference? That way you get to hear what is happening in the rest of Kosovo and you can tell your friends in Gracanica. We will protect you."

Stefan snorted. "How can you protect me outside of village? Even with your guns and tanks, you cannot do this."

"Meaning?"

Stefan started gesticulating. "Were you born in a field? Have your apples gone bad?"

He shook his head, then spoke in English. "One man. That is all. One man killed twelve of my people. Twelve! And a two year-old boy. Do you know what that means to us? Do you understand the insult? The people on the bus are innocent. They are coming to visit their dead."

His face crumpled. Returning to his own language he said, "You are a military man. You understand honour, yes? In war, you understand honour? Is it not true that you can collect your dead and your injured? You stop fighting to do this? If you have honour, if you have pride?"

Roza translated and Paul had to nod. Stefan made a dismissive gesture towards Roza.

"Then how can you say you can protect me. These people are vermin. They are…" He stopped, his hands gesticulating. He seemed suddenly embarrassed to have insulted Roza to her face.

Paul frowned. "Stefan," he said, "how do you know there was only one man?"

* * *

Stefan led them out of the back of the radio station to a small courtyard. They had chosen a place from which they could run if they were attacked, Paul noted. The building was an outhouse, perhaps once a chicken shed, at the very back of the garden. It was surrounded by trellises of fruit trees and a patch of winter cabbages. A red-faced woman in a long black skirt and an apron sat on the concrete step peeling carrots. She looked up at the sound of footsteps and Stefan quickly greeted her, holding up his thumb and first two fingers. The woman shook her head angrily. Words were exchanged.

Paul and Roza stood off until introduced. Stefan shook his head. Then the woman snapped at him like a snake, making him raise his hands.

"She is Albanian!" whispered Roza. "Her daughter saw the bombing."

"Really?"

"She is from Pristina, I am certain of this. The way she talks."

"Help me speak to her," Paul said, stepping forward.

The woman leaped up holding the peeling knife in stiff wrists.

Quickly, Paul saluted, "My name is Major Paul Illingworth..."

Roza translated into Albanian, *"Une jam Zotëri Major Paul Illingworth, Brigade Multinacionale I Cendre..."*

Paul explained that if she knew someone who saw the bombing incident, or if she could help identify those responsible, then justice could be done.

The woman did not change her hold of the peeler. At the sound of a helicopter, she turned to look at it. Paul fell silent. The woman glanced at Roza and exchanged words in Albanian. Roza nodded.

"She said she knows nothing," Roza said.

Paul put his hands into his pockets. Behind her, the door to the shack was partly open and a small face was looking at him from the shadows.

"It cannot be easy for her to be here, among the Serb people," Paul said. "It must be hard to raise a child, living like this."

Roza looked at him, and he told her to translate word for word.

The woman lowered the peeling knife. "*Pasaportë,*" she said. "*Unë dua një pasaportë!*"

Her eyes were small and insistent. She could only have been in her thirties if she was the girl's mother, but her face and body looked older.

"Yes," said Paul, nodding. "If you want, I'll get you a passport."

Her expression changed, but she did not move. What else could he do to persuade her?

Behind her, the shed door creaked. Inside was a girl of around nine years old. The woman turned. Seeing her, the woman snapped and gestured for her to stay inside.

The girl shook her head slowly. She had a Russian army hat in one hand.

Paul took a step forward, but this only made the woman lift the peeling knife again. He opened his arms wide. "Roza, keep translating what I say. I mean her no harm..."

But Roza had knelt on the floor. "She looks just like my cousin," she said. "Just like my little Mimi."

Looking past the mother, she smiled at the little girl. "*Përshëndetje, Mimi,*" she said.

"*Unë nuk jam i Mimi,*" the girl replied. "*Emri im është* Anja."

* * *

Simon's mouth hung open. "Fuck me," he drawled. "Are you really suggesting we put a full-time guard on the church in Gracanica?"

"Yes, I am," Paul said. "Of platoon strength."

Simon shook his head slowly, then glanced at the Brigadier, whose face was unreadable. It was Blanche Henderson who spoke next.

"You're certain? There's a nine year-old girl who could identify the bus bomber?"

Paul nodded. "I had to promise the mother we'd help to get her a passport. And I've committed to taking Stefan to the UN press conference every week. It's like a medieval siege down there. They're eating rats."

"What?" said Simon.

"I'm joking. But also I'm not," Paul said. He hooked his thumbs in his belt and faced the Brigadier.

"They're totally isolated. There's no internet, and no phone signal for the Serb networks. They get no radio or TV. If we want to build their confidence, two things need to happen: we need to give them a better perception of security. They don't feel it, especially after the bombing. And we need to get them to understand what else is happening. At the moment their ears and eyes are closed to the world."

The Brigadier nodded. Slumped low in a chair to the side of Simon's desk, he steepled his fingers in front of his face.

Simon said, "Paul, I'll need to discuss this with the Commander. I'm not sure the infantry battalions will want another fixed guard commitment."

Paul nodded but did not move. He did not want to go back on what he'd promised. That would make him feel a fool.

The Brigadier toyed with his lips. "Did you really tell her we'd get her a passport?"

Paul swallowed. "Yes, Sir. I had to promise something, or else she'd never have agreed to help."

The Brigadier pulled a face and lifted himself up in his chair. "Not good, Paul. You don't have that authority and I have no idea what the process is for such things."

Paul coloured and straightened his back. "I'm sorry. I thought..."

"You thought what?"

"I thought it something we'd be able to help with. Perhaps the Political Advisor..."

"The POLAD will do what I ask her to do. But she's not here to process refugees. You must never promise something like that again."

Paul bowed his head. "I'm sorry, I..."

Shaking his head, the Brigadier waved a broad palm in Paul's direction. "Leave it with me. But remember, the higher the risk, the more important your integrity becomes."

This was his dismissal, but Paul had still not finished. "I'm very sorry, Sir, but one more thing?"

The three others looked at him with surprised expressions.

"I had to take my Albanian interpreter with me. They were hostile to her at first; recognised the accent, I guess. But she was brilliant with Anja because she's half Albanian and half Serbian. It was really Roza that convinced her to help us."

With a quick glance at Blanche Henderson, he concluded, "Just thought you'd like to know."

Chapter 6

"It's next week," Paul said. "The easy areas first, and the Presevo Valley last, in one twenty-four hour period."

Sitting in a chair in the Grand Hotel, his back to the lobby, he looked from Aden to Nick and then to Elire. He had their attention.

Nick leaned forward to extinguish a cigarette. "What day?"

"I can't tell you yet, but I will, in time."

Aden said, "Are you going to hold a press conference after it's done?"

Paul hoped to surprise them. "I want you to come and watch it happening."

Aden's mouth hung open. "From where?" he said.

"From high ground overlooking the Presevo Valley. You'll watch, or at least hear the Serbs passing through below."

"How do you mean?" asked Nick.

"The area's heavily wooded. But there's an escarpment that sits above one of the last sections."

"You won't take us into the valley itself?"

Paul chuckled. "No. It could be dangerous."

"How's that?" said Aden.

How could he put this? "I don't want to risk mixing up non-combatants and combatants in an already busy environment."

The three journalists looked at each other, frowning like panellists on a quiz show.

"Truth is," Paul said, "your presence will only encourage people to fight. I'd rather keep you hidden. That's the deal."

"I'm very happy with what you're proposing, Paul," Nick said. "It's just the logistics. How do we file?"

"I'll take you up there and bring you back to the land of phone signals. Bring some camping clothes and a dossbag. I'll provide a tent and food."

Elire had said very little. She had her fingers interlaced over one knee. Oversized earrings followed the movement of her jawline. "Pol, when this happen? I have to make schedule for disk jockey."

"I can't say yet. And I'll only be able to give you two hours' notice of when we are going."

Aden clapped his hands. "I love a bit of military camping!"

Nick pulled out another cigarette, but didn't light it. "You seem confident this won't become a gun battle."

Here was the question. "I can never be one-hundred per cent confident, Nick. But we've taken every possible action to mitigate the risk. We've leafleted them from the air. We've told other people to tell them. But the reoccupation is going to happen. The Serb government must be allowed to manage its own territory."

Elire didn't meet his eye, but pursed her lips and looked somewhere over his shoulder.

All he needed was for this operation to go well and he'd have them singing his songs.

* * *

Their house had been burned to the ground. Anja held Tata's hand as they looked at what was left of the place where she was born. The stone chimney stood erect above the charred remains of the walls. One blackened roof beam leaned at an angle. A pile of rusting mattress springs and the buckled oven lay on what had once been the floor of the kitchen.

"Is this your house?" said the lady she liked. She spoke in Albanian.

Anja nodded. There was a muddle inside her. She felt guilty. She wanted to be somewhere else, but didn't know where. In Gracanica the children bullied her. Here, the forest was full of hunters and thinking about the bomb made her feel sick. There was a man with flaming hands and a flaming face. The smoke popped.

Tata squeezed her hand. His face was long. He pulled at his beard. The fat British woman in the green hat spoke to him, but he shook his head and she went away again. Anja didn't want to go along the track. She could see the big rock. Beyond that point it was dangerous.

The soldiers faded back to form a wide circle. They were starting to fidget. The tall man in the red hat talked to each of them in a quiet voice.

The Albanian lady squatted down at eye level. She smiled, and spoke in Serbian this time, as if telling her a secret.

"Do you know why I called you Mimi?" she said.

Anja shook her head.

"You remind me of my little cousin. She looked very much like you. Same hair. Same eyes. Same nose."

The lady touched her gently on the tip of her nose. Anja smiled at the touch and wriggled her shoulders.

"She was very brave. Just like you," she said.

There was something in the way she talked that made Anja feel special. She wanted to show her that she could be brave, as brave as she said she was.

"Roza?"

The lady smiled. "Yes, Anja?"

"Will she play with me?"

"Who?"

"Your cousin, Mimi."

The woman's face changed. There was a smile, and then a cough of surprise. She covered her nose as tears popped out of her eyes. Anja felt sorry. She had not meant to make her cry.

"One day," Roza said. "One day, for sure, you can play together."

Anja smiled. She was happy again.

Roza stroked her cheek with a finger. It was warm. "I will make sure they do not hurt you," she said. "But will you show me the place where the man held you against a tree?"

Anja nodded. It was beyond the rock. Turning along the track, she tugged her hand free of Tata's grasp, and took hold of Roza's. She started to walk.

"This way," she said.

The clay soil had baked hard. Her boots kicked up dust. The plants had grown so much that she did not recognise everything. Would she know the tree when she got there? It had been a long time.

Two soldiers strode ahead of her, the straps of their rifle slings dangling down by their elbows. Anja wanted to tug one, but it seemed wrong. The men were even bigger than Tata. She looked for the gully that led down to the road, but everywhere was blocked by nettles.

On her right the valley opened up. The tops of the trees now had fresh green leaves. The air smelled of pine.

"Up here," she said, letting go of Roza's hand to run between the soldiers. A lizard skittered across the path. A track appeared on the left that she didn't recall.

Where was she?

Tata had taught her to locate her traps by looking in three directions and noting what she saw. There was the place where the track disappeared into the forest. Behind her was the route she had come.

"There!" she said, pointing to a tree. She ran up to it, just to check.

On the ground, covered in dust, was one of her mittens. And next to it, the bent, discarded butt of a cigarette.

* * *

"You've told them?" Brassy asked when they spoke on the phone.

"Yep. I'm taking them up late morning."

Brassy grunted. "Good. But make damn sure it's not like Willy Howard Russell watching the charge of the Light Brigade. I want a good score on this one."

Paul tutted, perhaps a little too loudly. Of course he would deliver.

"It's important, Paul," Brassy insisted. "We're facing the largest foot and mouth crisis since the sixties. There are dead animals lining the motorways and now the fucking French have banned our exports!"

"What's that got to do...?"

"It's the news, Paul! We're losing the news agenda!" Brassy sucked in air. "The Ministry of Agriculture is being pilloried. The Chief Vet looks like a puppet without strings, and the government sounds untrustworthy. They can't even manage a meat market without fucking it up. We need *good news*."

Paul put the phone to his other ear so he could make notes. "I'm a diversion?"

"No, Paul. You're the centre of attention! We want to see something working well."

The realisation of where he fitted into Brassy's plans made Paul shudder.

"Paul, if this goes well, we'll get you on the Today Programme in the eight-ten slot."

"Christ."

"Exactly. It's *that* important. Get this right, Paul, and you'll become a household name."

* * *

The Operations Room hummed with the purposeful, urgent chatter of staff officers preparing for a major operation. Paul stood by the desk marked 'G1 – Medical' and listened to the captain, a friend from Sandhurst, talking to her counterpart in the Bunker.

"We've got the body bags. If it escalates, we may take more casualties than the British hospital can handle, so we've booked places with the American one in Bondsteel just in case."

Paul gave her a thumbs-up and moved along the aisle. The fresh-faced liaison officer from the RAF winked at him.

"How's it going?" Paul said.

"It's good. We'll have top-cover from a Lynx, and a Chinook on standby in case of casualties, but I can't get a Puma to move the Quick Reaction Force. They've been grounded after the crash."

His eyes were wide with the thrill of it all. Their conversation was interrupted by a shout from the Watchkeeper at the front of the room.

"Ladies and Gentlemen, listen in!"

Phone calls were ended as heads turned to face Brigadier Montrose. He strode into the room clapping one fist against the other palm. The Watchkeeper saluted. "Good morning, Brigadier."

"It's Tuesday," the Brigadier announced without further explanation. "At the moment this information is classified and is not be repeated."

He looked from face to face, settling his gaze on Paul. "I expect everyone to have their plans in place by Monday afternoon."

Paul started to speak, but the Brigadier silenced him with a raised finger as he strode down the central aisle to the back of the room. Everyone turned to face him. Reaching the fire door, he spun round.

"Handing back the buffer zone is the most important thing British Forces have done since we came to Kosovo two years ago. We have to ensure all possible risks have been considered."

Making eye contact with those nearest him, he walked slowly back up the central aisle. "I know many of you are surviving on very little sleep. I know that we've been at this for what seems like an age. But don't stop. Unpick everything. Ask questions. If an extra minute, or an extra hour, saves a life, it is an hour worth your effort."

Looking round the room, he gave a cursory nod. Raising one finger, he said, "We have four days to get this right!" then strode out on long legs through the briefing room door.

The murmur of conversation rose as the officers looked at one another, smiling nervously.

Paul had sweat beading in his armpits. This was what made life real.

* * *

On Sunday night, Paul was at his desk in the Press Office waiting for the evening news. Seagood was lying on the red sofa looking up at the television, her tiny feet on the chrome armrest. Roza entered without saying anything. Seagood moved her legs to let her sit down. Roza perched on the edge of the sofa with her hands between her knees. Her perfume floated through the room.

The piping music on the television had begun to irritate Paul, so he turned it off. Headlines ran on ticker tape along the bottom of the screen. *Army should assist with foot and mouth epidemic: Leader of the Opposition*, ran the main item, then something about an actor who had been photographed with a prostitute.

"Seems so silly, don't it," said Seagood.

"How so?" said Paul.

"Some actor's been caught shagging; how's that important?" She pushed her glasses up her nose. "I really like what we do, Sir. I tell me nan I'm working for you, and she sees your name in the papers."

Paul liked that. He imagined people back home telling others they knew him. But what if he got something wrong? What if he looked a fool? His throat constricted and stomach tightened at the thought of it.

When the news started, he put the volume back on. The first few items were boringly predictable: a scientific analysis of the spread of foot and mouth disease throughout England and Scotland; a display of graphics highlighting affected counties. Yorkshire was coloured the deepest shade of orange, but some areas were not affected at all.

"That's me there, Roza," Seagood said, getting up to point at Essex. "We ain't got it."

"Yet," said Paul gruffly.

The next item was the Minister of Agriculture holding a press conference in Downing Street, a policeman and the black door of Number 10 out of focus in the background. He stammered and stumbled through his speech. Camera flashes made him blink. He couldn't say when the disease would be controlled.

"Fucking idiot," Paul mumbled, shaking his head. "By holding it there it looks like the government can't even control their own spin."

The two women looked at him, but he didn't explain. They wouldn't understand. No one understood what he was capable of.

"Look at that!" Seagood said, giggling at the next item on the news.

On the screen was a parliamentary chamber, rows of seats in concentric arcs around a central podium. Men in suits shouted at each other. Someone threw a wad of papers, scattering them. A fight broke out.

Seagood and Roza laughed at a man falling over a desk as he threw punches. Paul reached for the remote to turn up the volume.

"Amid violent exchanges, the Macedonian government…"

The next camera angle showed a hilly rural community with the minaret of a mosque poking out above a verdant treescape. Then a convoy of police cars.

"Macedonia," said Roza. "They are moving more police to press down Albanian uprising by Kosovo border."

"You know this?"

"I hear it before I come in for night shift. Albanian people are making a riot in town of Tetovo."

Paul nodded. He was about to turn the volume off again when Seagood burst into another fit of giggles.

"I love it when you see important people fighting," she said. "They never do that back home."

"We are passionate people," Roza said. She smiled at Paul.

I bet you are, he thought.

* * *

"Is your house in order, Paul?" said Brassy down the phone.

"Yes. We got the NATO commander, an Italian general, to write an open letter to the rebels asking them to leave the buffer zone. It was published in all the Albanian papers."

"Good. Anything else?"

Paul spoke confidently. "There's a gate, an escape hatch, established towards the south of the valley. As the Serbs occupy the valley from the north, escaping Albanian fighters can enter Kosovo at the bottom end. All they have to do is hand in their weapons. About forty men have already done so. And we're sending a reconnaissance team through the valley ahead of the Serb forces, to check it's clear."

"A bullet magnet?"

"Not really," Paul said. "The vehicle's white. It'll have more Union Jacks than Ginger Spice's underwear and will be broadcasting through loudspeakers. The guy commanding it is a gunner from the training team. He's known, and speaks Albanian. His job is to roll up any snipers or stragglers left behind and persuade them to leave."

"Yes, that's been approved from here. Just remember, though, the journalists may not get what that vehicle's doing. No matter what they tell you, the press don't really understand the nuances of counter insurgency warfare."

"That's why I'm going with them," Paul said.

From his desk, telephone in hand, he watched the images on the television screen. There was heavy rain somewhere in northern England. A road though a village had collapsed into a hole. A single traffic light had partially fallen over, but still changed from green to amber to red as if loyal to some fallen master.

It gave Paul an idea. "We're as sorted as we can be, Colonel," he said.

"Good. Because if the fighting does kick off, the press will say we are victims of our own rhetoric."

"Trust me," Paul said quietly. "By Wednesday morning, I'll have them eating out of my hands."

Chapter 7

For once, Paul slept long and dreamlessly. He woke, muttering, to wonder where he was. It was still dark. Then he remembered. He snatched a towel and went for a shower.

The operational orders had already been given, so the morning brief was snappy and functional. Each officer presented his activities for the day in a curt, precise manner.

When it came to him, Paul said, "Today I will take three journalists up to observe the Serb occupation of Sector D of the Presevo Valley. My intended effect is positive reporting on the whole concept of NATO operations in order to reduce Albanian extremism throughout the region."

The other officers held their breath to see how the Brigadier would respond to such a boast.

"You do that, Paul," the Brigadier said at last.

They were beginning, Paul thought, to understand the power he had at his fingertips.

* * *

It was eleven. In the press office, Paul watched the news with the sound off to make sure he didn't miss anything before they left. The tickertape of headlines was tracking on a continuous loop along the bottom of the screen. Every agricultural market in the country had been closed. A footballer had beaten up his celebrity girlfriend. The Spice Girls were either splitting up or reforming, Paul could not tell.

What tawdry, inconsequential dross. Kosovo was where the real news was. He, Paul, was at the centre of world events, and directing how they were to be perceived.

"Are you ready, Sir?" Seagood said from the doorway.

Paul nodded. "Where's Roza?"

"In the wagon."

"It's loaded?"

"Just your kit to go."

Paul turned the television off. "Let's do it," he said.

* * *

The track was too muddy for Seagood's driving ability. The Landrover choked and skidded sideways. She panicked, pressing the brake and the accelerator by turns. The wheels spun. Mud spattered the windows and stones clanged underneath the wheel arches.

"Stop!" Paul said, slicing his palm down.

Seagood froze. The vehicle slithered backwards to an angled halt.

"Perhaps I should drive," Paul suggested. The relief on her face was immediate.

"Do you want us to get out?" Nick shouted from the back. He was looking out of the rear window. The four of them were covered in bags and bits of each other.

"Let me try first, but if it doesn't work we'll have to rethink," Paul said. "The problem is we've put tanks up here as overwatch. They've churned up the mud."

Paul backed up as far as he could, following a thin edge of firm soil between the mud and a terrifying precipice that fell for a hundred metres through dense trees. "Best I don't drop you over the side, eh? Guaranteed way to get bad copy!"

Revving the engine and keeping in low gear, he took a direct line up the hill, changing up a little too early. The Landrover slowed just short of the brow and started slipping. Paul kept his foot down, gritting his teeth. "Come on… come on!"

Elire bounced up and down, urging the vehicle on. One wheel bit. The car lurched. With a cry, everyone was thrown backwards and then suddenly forwards. Nick banged his head against the door hinge. His laptop fell between his legs and made an unpleasant crunch. There was blood on his palm when he looked at his hand. Paul watched his face in the rear view mirror. "War wound!" he shouted.

"Compared to some drivers I've had, you're one of the better ones," he said.

Paul was pleased with this. The next section, jolting along between dusky hardwoods, was reasonably level. "Only six miles to go!" he shouted, then laughed at the groans that erupted in response.

Nick and Aden traded stories of journeys through the Congo and Namibia, Afghanistan and Rwanda. Elire listened attentively, her mouth open. After half an hour, the Landrover crested a plateau that broadened onto a wide and grassy ledge. On the right stood the remains of a burned out cottage, a stone chimney the only thing still erect.

Paul slowed to look at it. Roza leaned forwards to see over the bulwark. Paul winked. They could not say anything about Anja just yet.

Further on, beyond a large stone that had been pushed aside by a tank, they found the escarpment overlooking the treetops. Beyond that, where the path twisted down into the valley, the area had been cleared of scrub and levelled with hard core.

"You have reached your destination, punk," said Paul, imitating Clint Eastwood.

The ridge ran for miles in either direction, a precipice of rock overlooking the feathery pinnacles of a mixed forest that fell and rose to a hillside about five miles away. Clambering out of the Landrover, they stretched.

"The famous Presevo Valley," Paul said. Behind him, the late afternoon sun cast long, indistinct shadows across the tops of the trees.

"We can't be far from where the bus was blown up," Aden said.

Paul pointed west. "Gate 3's just over that ridge. It's only a few hundred yards away."

Nick nodded. "You can see why they hid here," he said, pointing to a track that descended into the forest.

A little way along from where they stood, a huge British tank was parked up. On the far side of it was a much smaller Czech armoured personnel carrier. The commanders of each sat in their respective turrets, taking occasional peeks into their weapon sights. Paul clambered onto the tank to speak to the sergeant, and took a look through the gunsights. On the far side of the valley, above the tree line, a Serb army camp had been fortified with a wooden balustrade. Inside this perimeter, perfect lines of white tents were set around a flag pole and a parade square, which the Serb soldiers were running across, carrying logs.

"Fuck me!" Paul laughed. "National Service circa 1950!"

The cavalry sergeant smiled. "Bless 'em, eh, Sir!"

Paul asked him to inform his Squadron Commander that they'd arrived and was pleased that the officer, someone he knew from Sandhurst, immediately gave permission for the sergeant to let the journalists see inside the tank. Neither sergeant nor journalist needed telling twice. Nick soon had his eyes glued to the weapon sight, watching the Serb army doing their evening drills, while the driver talked Aden through how the transmission worked.

If he'd learned anything, it was that little things like this produced better copy than any sound-bite. He didn't even bother briefing the sergeant what subjects to avoid or stress. Soldiers had an innate ability to make complex ideas simple and refer difficult questions up the chain. It was officers, actually, who needed to be watched.

Paul set about erecting the tent. After ten minutes of struggling alone with the heavy canvas, Aden came to help.

"Cheers mate," Paul said.

"No worries," Aden replied, the sun glinting off his hair band. "Happy to help."

When the pegs were finally banged in and the guy ropes tightened, Aden's face glowed. He nodded towards the Czech personnel carrier. "Do you know why the Soviets lost so many of those in Afghanistan?"

Paul shook his head.

"It's a Russian BMP-1. The gun only elevates to sixty degrees, and the fuel tank is inside the rear doors."

Aden conjured a scene of steep gorges and tribal fighters. "The mujahedeen used to fire at them from the hillsides knowing they couldn't shoot back. And when the convoys stopped, they fired an RPG up its arse. The fuel tank did the rest."

He looked like a boy at a funfair, his face radiant. "You get off on it," Paul said.

Aden shook his head. "It's real, Paul, that's all. There's no artifice in war, no lies. You cut away all the pap that people think is important."

Paul met his eyes. They understood one another.

Aden nodded, then went back to the tank. Paul beckoned for Roza.

"You want me to cook?" she said.

Paul nodded. "That would be good. Feed them before they get tired. It will be dark in two hours."

Afterwards, he made up the camp beds while Roza washed the mess tins in water from a jerry can. The three journalists sat on a folding bench, smoking and watching the sky fade to crimson.

Paul said, "The tent's only big enough for three. Nick, Aden, and Roza should sleep inside. Elire and Seagood can doss in the Landrover."

"And you, Pol?" Elire said.

"I'll doss out," he said. It had been years since he had kipped with his head on his bergen, feeling the pattering of morning rain on his bivvy bag. The idea exhilarated him.

"Are you sure?" Nick asked.

"Absolutely!" he said.

Elire laughed, smiling at the two men she was squeezed between. "When I am little, my father take us camping, my sister and me." She made a boy-scout salute with her thumb and little finger. They all laughed.

As the sun set, the air became moist and cold. Paul dug out a battery powered lantern and turned it on. Elire produced a small spray of insect repellent and passed it round. Aden told a joke. Nick started humming *Scarborough Fair* as he blew smoke into the midgy air.

For Paul, it was heaven to be away from the baked, dusty city. His lungs felt fresh and a cigarette blagged from Nick tasted smooth and chocolaty. In the distance, they could hear what sounded like music. Gradually, it got closer.

"This is it. This is the final section of the occupation," Paul said. "Only the last few miles to go, then Serbia has control of the entire buffer zone."

They walked to the edge of the escarpment to stand with their hands in pockets. They could see very little except for the headlights of a vehicle between the distant trees. The beam rose and fell, twisted and faded. It had a ghostly beauty of its own. Behind it, and out of sight, was the much heavier sound of armoured vehicles.

Paul explained, "The car in front is British. In this section, to make sure no one fights, we're sending through a reconnaissance patrol."

"And that's the Serbian army behind?" asked Nick.

"It should be, yes."

Nick pulled a face, nodding. Aden was leaning over, his hair falling sideways.

The vehicles' progress was tediously slow. After fifteen minutes Paul left the journalists and went to put on a fleece. Standing next to the tank to keep warm, he listened to the radio chatter coming out of the turret.

"This is Juliet-three-one. We've reached report line HAMISH, I say again HAMISH. No evidence of combatants, out."

Ten minutes later the same voice came up. "This is Juliet-three-one. Now at report line ANGUS. Nothing seen, out."

The sudden crump of an explosion made Paul feel for the pistol under his armpit. The tank turret spun and the barrel lowered as the crew brought their thermal sights into effect.

The radio sputtered into life. "Contact, wait out."

Paul went to find the journalists. They were standing closer together than before.

"Come away from the edge," Paul said, "while we find out what's happened."

They didn't move. The tank's radio was silent. About a mile away, lit from below, a thin column of grey smoke rose through the trees.

"Sounded like a mortar," Paul said.

"That was a landmine," said Nick.

* * *

Brassy would be at home, but the absence of a phone signal meant Paul couldn't warn him. Having got the details of the incident from the tank commander, he felt exposed. He was on his own now, and only his charm and wit would prevent the journalists saying they were right all along.

Nick and Aden had tried to find a phone signal but both had failed. They returned to the tent. Roza, Seagood, and Elire were sitting on the bench, coats round their shoulders. The explosion had taken the joy out of their mood. Without speaking, Roza cracked open some chocolate and passed it round.

"Has anybody been killed?" Nick asked.

"The driver of the reconnaissance vehicle is dead, but the passenger's being casevacced, probably by helicopter. I don't know anything more."

Thankfully it was past the file time for the next day's papers, but the wire services were always on duty. As information filtered over the radio it was broadcast by the speaker inside the tank turret.

The men from the tank seemed drawn and angry at the same time. The sergeant dismounted and took each of them round the back to have a personal word. In the smothered light of a pen torch, he placed a hand on their shoulders.

"You gonna be all right, Crofty? I need you to stay focused."

"I'll be ok. Just one of them things, isn't it?"

The Czech crew withdrew inside their vehicle and closed the hatches. Then the commander opened the top hatch and presented the British sergeant with a bottle of vodka. He saluted, bowed, and withdrew once again. All the while, the sound of heavy machinery advanced through the trees in the valley below.

Nick and Aden watched everything with their arms folded against the cold. After the tank commander had spoken to his team, he got back inside his turret.

"The dead man's from the same troop," Paul whispered to the journalists. "You've probably heard his name over the radio, but I cannot officially release it until his family have been informed."

Both Nick and Aden looked saddened rather than vindicated.

Paul added, "If you know what it's like to lose a friend, I would ask you to be respectful. Right now, these men..."

Nick and Aden responded in unison, "Of course not..."

Paul sucked his cheeks. "If you want to write this up, I'll take you back to Pristina now. It will take time to collapse the tent and get down the hill, but we could be there by around Zero-three-hundred?"

He made it sound like a reasonable offer, but to be truthful, he was not keen to negotiate the mud in the dark.

"Or else we can watch the rest of the operation and head back in daylight. This is my preference, but if you agree, I'm going to ask you not to report anything until I say so. You could jeopardise everything, and I don't want anyone else to get killed."

He looked from one to the other in the lamplight. "If there are rebels down there, and if they find out you're here, they might lay on an ambush or a snipe for your sake. That'll mean more casualties: ours, theirs, or Serb. I can't allow that to happen."

Nick spoke for them all. "Paul, it's fine. We'll stay. My laptop's broken anyway."

"Yeah," said Aden, "might as well see the morning through. Look, you can have my phone…"

Elire shrugged. "I stay," she said.

"Your word is good enough," Paul said. "But the Serbs will finish moving through at zero-four-hundred. If you want to watch them do so, we should get our heads down until then."

* * *

Unable to sleep, Paul sat on the bonnet of the Landrover. A faint orange glow flared up inside the tank turret and illuminated the sergeant's headphones. A thin plume of cigarette smoke rose between the radio antennae, silhouetted against a magnificently starry sky. In the distance, the oddly familiar bark of a fox.

He shivered as he lit a cigarette. The snoring in the tent had started again. The canvas gently puffed in and out in the breeze as if the tent itself was breathing.

Another death. How could he portray this one? The nobility angle was wearing thin.

At around midnight, a Chinook had flown in to winch out the casualties. Paul had sat on the edge of the precipice as the blaze of lights moved noisily and clumsily through the trees below, their progress even slower due to the need to sweep for mines.

After the machines and the tannoy had passed, the night became so peaceful, so utterly lovely, that he did not want the harmony disturbed.

When had he last known such serenity? When had he become so unmoved by death?

He turned at a whiff of perfume incongruous in the forest. Roza appeared next to the wing of the Landrover, her skin almost translucent in the lamplight. Placing one foot on the fender, she offered a hand for him to pull her up. She sat next to him, her thighs unashamedly touching his, her body warm.

Paul threw the fag away and made a snorting sound. She chuckled, nudging him gently with her elbow.

Her hand sought out the space between his arm and his body. He took her hand. Her skin was soft and warm underneath his fingers.

"You've been wonderful," he said. "Not just here. But with Anja."

"It is a pleasure to work for you," she whispered. "I will do anything you want."

There was a long pause while Paul held her hand, stroking the skin on her knuckles. He wondered what the last comment meant. The feeling of her thumb gently moving over the back of his hand made him sad.

He was on the limits of how far he could go. He was an officer in the British Army, and an officer always had integrity. It was the word they had drilled into him at Sandhurst. An officer had integrity.

"If I was not in the army, would you... I mean do you understand that I can't..."

His voice crackled in his throat.

She leaned towards him to make a gentle nudge with her shoulder. "Yes," she whispered.

At that moment, she felt small and beautiful, delicate in his hands. Being so close made him confused.

"But you know I have... I mean you know I had a girl..."

She placed a hand on his thigh and squeezed his leg. "I know," she said.

He should stop her, but the sensation of touch was so wonderful that he did not want to.

"But do you..."

She held his arm in her hands and placed her head against his shoulder.

116

"I know," she said. And that was enough.

Paul unzipped his smock and shook it off to place around their shoulders. In another hour the sun would throw the first morning rays into the valley. Though he wanted that moment to arrive so he could get back to camp, he also wanted time to stop so he could enjoy being next to Roza just a minute more.

Above the horizon, a satellite left a brief streaming trail across the brightening sky.

* * *

Once they were on the metalled roads, Seagood could drive again. With his head lolling on the seatbelt, Paul slept. He woke as the road noise changed and stretched as far as he was able, then twisted to check on the others.

Everyone was asleep, Roza leaning on Nick and Elire on Aden. He let them stay like that until they reached the traffic lights outside of camp.

"Rise and shine everyone! It's zero-nine-fifteen. Welcome to Slim Lines, Headquarters of British Forces Kosovo and Multinational Brigade Centre."

Roza sat up quickly and blushed. Nick rubbed his eyes and tried to stretch but was too squashed between the hastily packed tent and the rear door. The back window was filthy with the spatterings of mud. After they had parked outside the press office, Paul invited them all in for coffee. Telling Seagood to get everyone a brew, he checked in with Simon.

"The Serbs now have complete control of the buffer zone and the Presevo Valley," Simon said. "And except for those two poor sods on the reconnaissance team, no one else was injured,"

"No Serbs either?"

"No. Dragusha proved to be all bluster. Apart from the mine, there was no one there." He reached out a hand to shake Paul's. "Your message plan worked a treat. The Brigadier's delighted. Well done."

In the press office, Nick and Aden had made themselves comfortable on the sofa. Elire was perched on his desk. Roza squatted on the pile of rucksacks, yawning, while Seagood made coffee.

"You don't have the name yet, Paul, do you?" Nick said, scraping a hand over his unshaven chin.

Paul shook his head. "It will take twenty-four hours to tell the family, same as usual. I'll tell you as soon as I can."

Aden nodded. "It's a real pity about those guys. It was a good operation. And an excellent press facility."

"It doesn't matter, though," Nick observed, checking the messages on his phone. "Back home they're still obsessed with cows. Whatever we write will hardly get coverage."

"How are you going to present it?" Aden said, looking at Nick.

Paul turned his back on them as he helped Seagood take the teabags out of the mugs. It was as well they couldn't see his face as a sudden surge of anger flooded through him. He grated at their casual attitude to the soldier's death.

"You could always tell the truth," he said, more forcefully than he had intended. He turned round, a mug in either hand. "We shone a light into that valley for others to follow. It cost the life of one man. And because of his sacrifice, nothing else happened."

Leading Article, The Times, Saturday 5 May 2001
Return of Presevo Valley a Model for Balkans Peace

While the British Government has been managing the very public slaughter of thousands of cattle, the assistance of the British Army, under the leadership of Brigadier Alex Birtwhistle, has once again proved invaluable in the execution (no pun intended) of national policy.

The same is happening in the far-flung reaches of Europe where a gradually expanding NATO butts up against the former Yugoslavia. Here, British Forces are masterminding one of the most magnificent peacekeeping operations ever to take place. In 1999 they stepped in to prevent an epidemic of ethnic cleansing more horrific than anything seen on mainland Europe for fifty years. Since that war, Kosovo has slipped off the front pages of many newspapers, but the tireless and even-handed professionalism of our forces has continued.

On Tuesday night, British servicemen supervised the gradual return of Serbian security forces into the Presevo Valley, an area previously designated a no-go area due to the presence of Albanian terrorists. The event had been heralded as a flashpoint, an opportunity for some to advance the bloody cause of unifying the Balkan diaspora into a 'Greater Albania'.

But British forces prevented this without a single bullet being fired. By Wednesday morning, Serbian troops had occupied the entirety of the Presevo Valley and all Albanian terrorists had been pacified. Now the world can watch while President Kostunica of Serbia proves he has the moral authority to govern his whole populace – Albanian as well as Serbian – with the balance and accountability that we ourselves enjoy.

But it did not come without a price. On Tuesday night, Trooper Darren McCrae, 21, of the 9/12 Lancers, was killed by a landmine while conducting a reconnaissance of the Presevo Valley. He was shining a light, if you will, into the darkest recesses of the valley so that our former enemies would be safe. Once again we find British Forces at the centre of an international story. Once again we find British Forces putting right what politicians failed to envisage.

In 1998 Prime Minister Tony Blair persuaded the UN Security Council to legitimise the use of force against the vile and unelected regime of Slobodan Milosevic. For this he should be lauded. But few in Downing Street will have foreseen the long-term implications. As usual, it has fallen to our armed services to make it happen through their selfless dedication and focus on the task in hand. They are an inspiration. As we approach Mr Blair's second election we should remember Trooper McCrae and the many others like him. Mr Blair's reputation is partly founded on the shoulders – and the graves – of others.

PART THREE

Chapter 8

"Ecstatic, Paul!" said Brassy on the telephone. "The Chief was called by the top spin doctor from Number 10 last night..."

Paul smiled. He sat back in his chair, feet crossed on the desk, while Brassy spoke in a jubilant manner without a pause.

"...we got five 'agree stronglies' for Balkan policy at these study groups they run. Even more than the minimum wage!"

Paul glanced at the television. The orange globe spun and dissected on its axis.

"It's not just *The Times*. The Grauniad and the Torygraph are on message too."

Paul pulled his feet off the desk and shuffled his chair forward on its casters. "That's great. So what's next?" he said.

Brassy was silent for a moment. Paul imagined him glancing at the wall planner.

"Well, here's the thing," he said. "We still don't know the date of the general election."

Paul had a pen ready in his hand. "Don't follow."

"You haven't seen the process through, so you won't know," said Brassy. "When an election's announced, the public sphere is placed in purdah."

"In what?"

"Purdah. Hindi word. It means we cannot be seen to influence the outcome."

"I thought you wanted..."

"Yes I did. And that's the point." Brassy said. "We can only influence how people think up to the date when the election is announced. As soon as the date's set, we stay shtum."

Paul frowned. "I can't say nothing for a whole fucking month! We have a complex, medium-intensity operation here. There's a weapons amnesty, an election…"

"Relax, Paul," Brassy said, "you can talk to your locals all you like. What you can't do is talk to the internationals. No formal briefing of any kind."

Paul said nothing. If he couldn't talk to Aden, he couldn't talk to Reuters, and Reuters broadcast to everyone. As did the BBC. "It'll hamstring me," he said.

It was not just the operation Paul was thinking of. There was the question of his annual appraisal. He'd got Kosovo 'on message', but if he wasn't allowed to keep it there, he could be stitched up.

Brassy seemed to know what he was thinking. "Don't worry. You'll get the report you need. But the law's the law."

"So just to be clear, when the date for the election's set, I can't talk to either Nick or Aden."

"No."

"So when's this poodar thing?"

"Purdah. We don't yet know."

"How am I meant to plan?" said Paul.

Brassy explained. "It's the foot and mouth crisis, Paul. The government is never going to announce an election if it's on the back foot, so to speak."

"Is it?"

"Oh yes," said Brassy, laughing. "The Min of Ag is in utter meltdown. Everyone is running for cover. The Prime Minister's had to step in, and that means he's putting himself at risk."

"And they're using the TA to kill cows?" said Paul.

"Yes. The army's come through yet again! Good old Bertie Birtwhistle up at 142 Brigade. We're providing the wherewithal to destroy the cattle and the land on which to bury them."

"Where?"

"Catterick. Salisbury Plain. I tell you, if you've got a gun dog, don't let it run behind the ranges. It'll come back with a bone the size of a horse's dick!"

Paul chuckled. "So the government are only going to announce the election once the disease is on the wane."

"Bingo!" said Brassy.

* * *

If he couldn't talk to the internationals, Paul would need to invest more time with the locals to make sure they trusted him.

With Radio Black Eagle, this proved highly stimulating. He and Elire started having lively on-air debates in which she argued for Kosovan independence and he sucked his teeth, throwing up potential obstacles that the fledgling state would have to overcome. He was safe doing this even though he was way off script. Brassy never cared what he said to the locals, and neither Nick nor Aden would be listening to Radio Black Eagle.

On Thursday, Paul collected Stefan from Gracanica and took him to the UN press conference in Pristina. His body odour was repellent, and he stuck so close from the moment they got out of the Landrover that Paul could never get away from it.

"Relax, Stefan. No one knows."

"I not go out village since two years before. Of course I am afraid."

Paul felt sorry for him. He was just swept along in this tide of ethnic strife. He had few friends and hands like a woman. The radio station was the best way he could employ himself, though who paid him, Paul had no idea.

The conference provided little information. Breitman was nowhere to be seen, and Carla Alvarez spent twenty minutes explaining what was being done about the water supply to a town she called 'Pec stroke Peja,' combining both the Serbian and Albanian names. At the end, when the German captain banged his gavel and people rose to leave, Stefan became exited.

"I know that woman," he whispered. "She is from Mitrovica, Serb area."

He disappeared to talk to her. Paul hoped that the possibility of being with a woman might persuade him to wash his clothes.

Roza had come in case Stefan forgot that he spoke some English. She stretched her arms wide. In so doing, her breasts pressed into the front of her blouse.

Paul said, "Are you ok? I haven't managed to speak to you since…""

She smiled. "Yes. I am fine."

Everyone in the room was gathering their notebooks and waving at friends. Nick and Aden walked down the stairs. Paul nodded to them and they back.

Roza placed her feet on the back of the row of chairs in front and hugged her knees. The skin of her arms was tanned, the fine hairs bleached by the sun. Paul wanted to stroke her forearm with the back of his finger.

She nudged him with her elbow. "What?"

Paul shook his head slightly, then checked to see Stefan was safe.

"I enjoy it, being with you," Roza said. "I enjoy it very much."

She didn't need to say more. There had been a moment they had both shared, a moment of tranquillity in the centre of a war. Nothing could take that from them, and nothing could develop it. He'd felt like a teenager rather than an officer of the British Army. But with her sitting next to him, watching the auditorium empty, his cock started to swell. Susan had never made him feel like this.

Stefan appeared on the row below looking awkward at having to disturb them. "Ok, Major, we go?" He held a business card in his fingers.

"You have her number?" Paul asked.

"Yes. We go university, Belgrade."

"Is she a journalist?"

A broad grin broke out over Stefan's face. "She has newspaper in Mitrovica. I have radio station in Gracanica. Maybe we work together."

His joy was evident.

"She's pretty," Paul said. "Who brings her?"

"French officer," Stefan said. And sure enough, a captain with a blue kepi was following the woman down the stairs.

"Better get in quick, Stefan. French officers, you know?"

Stefan blushed. He shook his head. "She is not like that."

They weren't going to achieve anything else in the UN building so Paul agreed they should go. The drive to Gracanica provided an opportunity to find out more about Stefan's view of the world.

"Do you think President Kostunica should hand over Milosevic to the International Criminal Tribunal?"

Stefan didn't hear the question. Paul repeated it, shouting over the tyre noise.

Stefan nodded. "Milosevic bad man," he said. "He kill many people."

"He was an elected head of state," said Paul.

"No!" Stefan said, shaking his head. "He take power, but not democracy way..."

"Not by popular vote," Paul said.

"Like this," Stefan said. "But question for me: why is United States wanting Serbian people to go ICTY, criminal tribunal, but they are not sign it?"

"Not signing what?"

"America. It does not sign International Criminal Court – ICC. Is America above law?"

Paul could imagine Stefan sitting in a café, smoking and having loud political debate with his neighbours. "I don't know, my friend. I've never thought about it."

"Is good you think," Stefan said. "America very powerful. But power brings..."

"With great power comes great responsibility," said Paul, nodding.

"Like this."

Paul admired Stefan. But it was a simple truth that, in the Balkans, moral authority and military power were the same thing.

* * *

"I hear they are singing your praises back at the Bunker," said Simon. Paul saluted and sat facing his desk.

"I'm trying to press a number of buttons," Paul replied. "It's not about telling the press what we're doing. It's about using them to shape public perception."

"Yes it is," said the Brigadier. "And I want you to know that I'm very pleased. I wasn't certain about taking the press up to the Presevo Valley, but the coverage has shown you were right. They appreciate we are willing to give our lives for the sake of peace."

Paul didn't know what to say. "Thank you," he managed.

The Brigadier continued, "And now that you've shown what you can do, there are a few other things I'd like you to sink your teeth into."

This was good. He might be given free rein to say what he wanted to say and do what he wanted to do.

"I said from the beginning that I need you to build trust with the Albanian population, because one of my tasks is to reduce the number of weapons in circulation."

Paul nodded. The Brigadier had mentioned this on his first day in Kosovo, but he had done very little about it.

Montrose continued, "The whole of Kosovo is having a weapons amnesty this month. I want you to make sure we get more weapons handed in than any other Brigade area. Especially the Americans."

Paul grinned. He liked a clear target.

"And there are two other things I need you to think about too. The first of these, since you're so politically minded, is that the UN are setting up an assembly."

"A what?" said Paul.

"A regional assembly, to run Kosovo. Guided by the UN and protected by NATO."

Paul shook his head and frowned. "Kosovo isn't a sovereign state. How can it have a legislature if it's not a state?"

The Brigadier smiled at Simon, who nodded. Then he said, "We knew you'd get this, Paul. The answer to your question is that it's not a government, and not a parliament, it's a regional assembly."

Paul pondered. "Like Scotland. It will make decisions about some things but not others."

"Precisely!" said the Brigadier, poking a finger into his own thigh. "I expect the distinction will be difficult for people to understand. Or should I say, it will be easy to misunderstand."

Paul lifted the beret off his knee and turned it round so the capbadge faced him. He stroked it with his thumb. "The Serbs will be an important audience in this. I don't have access to the mainstream Serb media."

The Brigadier raised a palm towards him. "No, but the Belgrade media is outside your scope. You can, though, talk to the people in the enclaves. To make sure they vote."

"It's going to be a multi-ethnic thing?" he asked.

"It'll have proportionate representation from all over Kosovo, including the Roma and the Serbs. The UN Secretary General is convinced the minorities will not take part. But I want you, Paul, to prove him wrong. I want you to make sure voter turnout in the Serb enclaves is the same, if not more, than for the Albanians."

The Brigadier studied him.

"That's quite a big ask..." Paul said.

"I know, Paul, I know." The Brigadier slapped his hand against his leg. "But take it as a sign of the confidence we have in you. The infantry battalions won't be able to affect this outcome except by leafleting people. The training team are engaged with the Kosovo Security Corps, therefore the

Albanian population. And the reconstruction team are, well, doing tactical things. Only you, really, have the reach we need."

There were forty thousand NATO troops in Kosovo, and about the same number of UN personnel. Of these, about twelve thousand were under Brigadier Montrose's command. And of those, only Paul, his teenage driver, and a young interpreter were being tasked with this strategically important activity.

"This is just the sort of mobilisation activity I enjoy," Paul said.

"Excellent," said the Brigadier. "And that's just the sort of response I'd expect."

There was a lull while Paul looked at Blanche, who was watching him closely. Her gaze was unsettling.

Simon said, "What you'll do now, of course, is develop a plan then come back and brief us on it."

Paul pulled himself upright in the chair. "There'll be limitations to what resources you can give me?"

Simon sniggered. "There will, yes. If you think you'll get ten staff and a dedicated helicopter, think again."

"Who will approve my messages?"

"I will," said Simon. "And there's another thing you should know. Blanche?"

She spoke without moving the rest of her body at all. "Paul, that lead you gave us. It has borne fruit."

"What lead?" said Paul.

"The girl."

"Little Anja? She's led you to the bomber?"

Blanche shook her head. "She led us to a place, and at that place we found evidence. And that evidence provided us with a DNA profile. And that profile matches a file in the German criminal register. And as of this morning, we have a name."

Paul's eyes widened. "You're going to make an arrest?"

"We're going to make a number of arrests. At some stage in the future," said Simon.

"That's excellent!" said Paul, beaming.

"Of course this is, at the moment, classified," said the Brigadier. "We're telling you because your journalist friends might notice things happening."

Paul nodded to show he understood. "You want me to focus on the elections and the weapons amnesty. And at some stage you're going to tell me about arresting the bus bomber."

"That's pretty much it," said Simon.

"Not quite," said the Brigadier. "There's more to it. I want you to understand how I see things."

He held up the paddle of one large hand, fingers splayed, to count his points on each finger in turn, starting with the little one. "In ninety-nine we cleared out the Serbs. Last month we gave them back the Ground Safety Zone. Now we're doing three things: setting up an assembly, increasing the perception of stability by reducing the number of assault weapons in people's houses, and proving that the law is more powerful than nationalism."

He looked over the top of his fingers at Paul. "And you're going to make these three known."

As he spoke, Montrose held out his hand, palm towards Paul, with the thumb and two fingers extended.

Paul smiled. "If you ever say that to an Albanian, Sir, don't use your hand like that. It's a Serb salute."

The Brigadier frowned, then chuckled. "That's why we want you to do this, Paul. You've got the knack."

* * *

It was a huge honour the Brigadier had just paid him. Paul really was at the forefront of everything – making Kosovo peaceful, setting it up for independence, getting all sides of the population to build a new society. What was that phrase Elire kept saying? That Kosovo needed to be 'reborn'? Well, if that was the case, he was the doctor.

But would the Albanian television stations allow him to say that the Serbs needed to vote? Which party should he support? Or should he remain neutral?

He made a list of questions. Then he got another piece of paper and linked concepts. Then he got yet another piece of paper, but didn't know what to do with it.

It was late. Everyone else would be in the Officers' Mess, or in bed. Back home they would be watching telly.

The computer pinged. Paul wiggled the mouse to get rid of the screen saver, then brought up his email. The title said: '*For Major Paul.*'

"Dearest Major Paul," it read. "Just to say I enjoy working with you and thank you for all the opportunity you give me to improve my English. Yours sincerely, Roza Xhaferi (your Albanian and Serbian interpreter)"

As if he needed telling.

Paul stretched, then placed his hand on his chin to read the email again. At that very moment she was at home, thinking about him.

Chapter 9

Paul unrolled the flipchart onto the briefing room table. Using his pistol, a bottle of green ink from Simon's office, and his notebook, he kept three of the corners flat. The Brigadier placed a finger on the remaining one to keep it down.

"This is my proposed message plan," said Paul, talking from one side of the table while the Brigadier, Simon, and Blanche stared down at the document from the other.

Paul was proud of the work. Lying awake at night an idea had come to him about how to structure what he needed to say.

"As you can see, I want to hit the locals through the TV, radio, and print newspapers. I can use the internationals as well, but only to the point when the election is announced."

The Brigadier folded his arms and the corner of the flipchart curled up. Simon bent it back on itself.

Paul continued, "My behavioural goals are simple: hand in your weapons as you don't need them anymore; take part in the elections; and support the rule of law. It's an echo of that old Northern Ireland phrase: the ballot box is better than the bullet."

The Brigadier nodded as he toyed with his lower lip. "You don't seem to have very much evidence for the rule of law."

Paul stood upright and folded his arms. "I'm waiting for you to provide it," he said. "There's no point *telling* people that the law has long arms. You have to *show* them."

Paul checked that the door to the Operations Room was properly closed. He dropped his voice.

"Arresting the bus bomber would be the best way to do that. As soon as you tell me more, I'll plug it into the plan."

The Brigadier looked up. "How would you see that panning out?"

Paul smiled. "We could do it any number of ways. But the popular thing at the moment is real time cop shows – shoulder mounted cameras following a dawn raid. I'd like to do something like that, using Aden Short."

Simon pulled a face. "Not sure that'll work."

"Why not? It's graphic. It's dynamic. The Albanians are a culture that honours force."

"Yes, yes," said the Brigadier. "But you're missing the point. This will not be a police operation. We are keeping security tight."

Paul was silenced. "Ah, I see." He stared at his plan. "But that's fine. We can do the same with the infantry battalions."

Blanche shook her head. "We're not using the infantry battalions either. We've brought in external assets."

"Really? Who?" said Paul, but then the penny dropped. "The SAS?"

Simon nodded. "It's not the bomber that's the issue. It's his support network among the Kosovo Security Corps."

"The people we're training to be the future police force?"

"Exactly. There are some bad apples in the barrel."

Paul placed his hands behind his back, hooking them into his stable belt.

"Not sure what I can do. You'd need to tell me…"

"We will, Paul. But get rid of the idea that you can watch the arrests. The SAS won't allow that level of intrusion."

"But what about the Iranian embassy back in eighty-one? That was filmed. The two guys on the balcony? That's become an iconic image. Could we not do the same?"

Paul was chancing his arm because the Brigadier was an ideas man. But he seemed to be in two minds. "I think not,

Paul. Getting the specialist assets deployed was, well, a bit harder than I'd expected."

Paul frowned.

Montrose explained. "Let me say that the Bunker has a slightly different view of this operation than I do. They'll not support the idea of the SAS being used for publicity."

The Brigadier was trying not to criticise his masters. It was a mark of his integrity. Paul opened his mouth but Simon made a very slight shake of his head. Paul had pushed it as far as it would go.

"Very well," he said. "I'll do a post-operation press conference instead. It won't have the same power, but it'll do the job."

He'd been lying in bed when the idea of a live arrest came to him. The possibilities had kept him awake for hours. He knew he was right. Not only would it show what the rule of law meant, but it would imply that superior military skill only came from having a mature democracy. Therefore, involvement in the elections would be essential.

"But the rest of this is very good work, Paul," the Brigadier said, tapping the table. "We can't do everything. But keep Simon informed."

Paul braced as the Brigadier strode out of the room towards his office, then relaxed when he'd gone. With only Simon and Blanche left in the room, the conversation became easier. "What was that about?"

Simon shook his head. "Politics, Paul. The Chief of Joint Operations doesn't support us. He says the arrest operation is too risky."

"Why?"

"He says it's not a matter for NATO. Basically, he's afraid of people getting killed."

"Are they likely to? It's just an arrest; like being back in Northern Ireland."

Simon shook his head. "Not quite the same. The law's clear in Northern Ireland. Here it's as murky as Lochnagar."

Paul said nothing as he tugged the flipchart towards him and rolled it up. "I had no idea it could be so complex."

Simon shrugged. "Neither did we. The Commander's been told that his cock is on the block if the operation fails. So please don't let him down."

"Don't worry."

Simon picked up his bottle of ink and pushed Paul's pistol across the table.

"If it wasn't for that reason, I think your plan would have been brilliant."

Paul holstered the pistol. "Well, there you go. My experience is that Special Forces enjoy being filmed. It enhances their reputation."

Simon cast a glance at Blanche. "Yes, and I can imagine the commander in question would love being the centre of attention."

Blanche nodded.

"They're here on a recce?" Paul said.

Simon placed a finger to his lips. "They're out on the ground."

"I didn't see anyone..."

"They were briefed elsewhere." Simon folded his arms. "In fact, I wonder if you know the commander in question. He's from your regiment, and about the same age."

Paul straightened. "It's fucking Richard Rawlins, isn't it?"

* * *

The television screen showed apocalyptic pictures of cattle pyres somewhere in Dumfriesshire. Through drifting smoke, a stiff cow's leg poked out from the pile of carcasses.

It was late, but Paul needed to finish the script for his next radio interview before he went to bed. And he was annoyed. He didn't understand why they were stopping him. It was the best way to cover the arrest. Simon knew it, and so did the Brigadier.

With his chin resting on his hand, he doodled ideas on a blank piece of paper. He was so absorbed in his thoughts that he didn't notice Seagood make him a cup of tea until she placed it next to him.

"You look like you need that, Sir," she said.

She was eighteen, and the RAF equivalent of a private. He was fifteen years older, and a major, and yet she could read his mood as well as anyone.

"Thank you, Jane," he said, reaching for the mug. "That's very kind."

She looked as if she was about to touch his shoulder as a gesture of complicity, but drew back as if in deference to his rank. "I'll be going, Sir, if you don't need me."

"See you tomorrow," he said, then turned back to the computer.

Ideas were forming in his mind.

Was it Ariel Sharon or Moshe Dayan who ignored orders to stop advancing and as a result captured the whole of the Sinai Peninsula? How was this different?

If he asked permission to do what he wanted, they would say no. But none of them – Brassy, Simon, Blanche; not even Brigadier Montrose – really understood what Message Operations could do. Since when were soldiers praised for sitting still when attack was necessary?

Paul wiggled the mouse to make the computer come alive.

* * *

It was lunchtime. Seagood said she was going to get some scoff. "You coming, Roza? Sir?"

Roza tucked her shirt into her jeans. Paul saved the script he'd been working on and pushed the computer keyboard away. "Since you ask so nicely, I will."

The three of them sauntered over to the cookhouse and joined the back of the soldiers' queue. Roza and Seagood chatted while they waited. They seemed to enjoy the fact that Paul had chosen to be with them rather than taking the much shorter officers' line. At the counter, Paul collected a tray, a portion of lasagne, and a shovel of chips. Under the heat lamps, the plate was untouchable. He snatched cutlery and some brown sauce from the containers and looked round to see where Seagood and Roza had gone. The officers' section of the cookhouse was screened off by a wooden lattice and pots of plastic plants. Seagood and Roza had sat at one of the long tables adjacent to the main aisle. They had kept a place for him.

"You're in the cheap seats today," Seagood chirped, as she slid a large aluminium teapot with a misfitting lid along the table.

Roza met his eye. He winked at her, but then felt silly. It was stupid, flirting like that. Saying nothing, his mind still spinning ideas and arguments, he started to eat.

He looked up when a group of four strolled down the central aisle; the Brigadier, Blanche, Simon and a tall, broad-shouldered man wearing brown brogues, crisp jeans, and a double cuff shirt.

"You know him, Zotëri Major?" said Roza.

Paul nodded.

Seagood giggled. "Is he single?"

That made Paul smile. "He's an old buddy."

"What's he doing here?" said Seagood. "And who are they?"

Paul looked over this shoulder. On a table by the main door were ten or twelve men in dirty civilian clothes. They were unshaven. They saw Paul looking and fixed him with steady, unflinching glares.

"Ooh, they look hard," chuckled Seagood. "Are they here long?"

"I'll get you an intro," Paul said as he finished his meal.

Paul knew the man with the Brigadier only too well. Richard 'Rolly' Rawlins. They'd trained together at Sandhurst. Their trust in each other was unconditional, the result of the shared experience of pain, terror, and relief. They'd spent three days in a bothy in Scotland, snowed in by a blizzard. They'd shared women, once at the same time. They'd stood side by side when a gang of youths attacked them outside a chip shop. When Paul had gone down with a bottle to the head, Rolly had stood over him, fighting them off.

But since their lieutenancy, their paths had been divergent. Rolly made captain in three years while Paul took four. Rolly passed SAS selection and breezed through the promotion exams. Having badly broken his leg early in his career, Paul never attempted to join the SAS and only just scraped through the promotion exams. Whereas Paul was an Acting Major, Rolly had been given substantive promotion at the youngest age possible.

He watched Rolly follow Simon and the Brigadier through the lattice screen into the officers' eating area. It was funny watching Blanche trying to attract his attention.

Seagood leaned over the table to whisper. "Are those men, you know, SAS?"

"Possibly."

"Were you in the SAS, Sir? Is that how you know them?" said Seagood.

"If I was, I wouldn't tell you," he said, and smiled. He watched with amusement as her eyes widened, then grinned and shook his head. "No, I never was. Too many injuries." It was something he would never lie about.

After waiting for Roza to finish her fish, the three of them slid their trays into the stacker and Paul said he'd be along shortly. First, he wanted to catch up with his old mate.

Behind the lattice screen, Rolly was sitting at a circular table with Simon, Blanche, and the Brigadier. Rolly had his back to Paul and was talking when he appeared.

"We don't see a problem with the lift. We'll be ready for the order..."

Blanche placed a finger on her lips. Paul nodded at the Brigadier before intruding on the conversation. Placing a large hand on Rolly's shoulder, he imitated Al Pacino: "What d'you say I buy you a cup of coffee?"

Rolly looked up. "Matey! I thought you were here. Great to see you!"

They shook hands for a long time. Paul said, "How long you in camp?"

"Twenty four hours. Shit, shower, shave, and back out."

"You got time for a chat after you're done?"

"Sure!"

Rolly looked at the Brigadier, who gestured with his hand out in front of him. "Major Rawlins, I have no further need of you today. By all means…"

"Then let's go to my office," Paul said.

"Right," Rolly said as he got up from the table. "But I've had two hours kip in the past forty eight; you know what I'm saying?"

"Don't be such a homo," Paul responded with a bravado he could not really justify. "Come on."

He led Rolly across the central square, walking slowly to bask in the reflected kudos of being with the SAS commander.

"We do need to talk, matey," Rolly said. "There's something I want to tell you."

Inside the office, Roza and Seagood lay sprawled on the sofa reading the newspapers. Seagood's jaw dropped open when they entered. Paul said, "Ladies, would you mind giving us a bit of space?"

The two women left, beaming at him. Seagood threw Rolly a glance as she opened the door. Rolly smiled back at her, making her giggle. When they'd gone, he slumped onto the sofa and placed his feet on the coffee table. "That your team?"

Paul nodded. "My driver and interpreter."

"The interpreter's cute."

"Yes she is. Want tea?"

Rolly placed a hand on his stomach and pulled a face. "You won't have a decaf?"

"A what?" scoffed Paul, as he clicked the button on the kettle. "You gay?"

Rolly shook his head and snorted. "Matey, it's caffeine. It inhibits motor control and heightens anxiety. You think it keeps you on the edge, but actually it does the reverse."

Paul held a bag of sugar in one hand and a teaspoon in the other. "I'll have to pop out to the macrobiotic food store and get some in. And while I'm there I'll get a CD of whale music and a yoga video."

Rolly chuckled. "Just hot water. That'll do fine."

After making their brews, Paul pulled over his desk chair, the casters running unevenly over the linoleum tiles.

"So this is Message Operations?" asked Rolly, looking round. "Nice office."

Paul took a sip of his tea, ignoring the implied jibe. "This is me."

Rolly nodded towards the crown on the front of Paul's shirt. "It's got you promoted. Congratulations."

"I'm acting. Not substantive."

Rolly drummed his fingers on his leg as he continued to look round the room. His angular and powerful presence made Paul recognise that their relationship had changed. He was outmanned. Even though Rolly was allowing him to make a show of being mates, the fact remained that one of them was an SAS commander operating undercover, and the other was desperate to get promoted on a last ditch staff job.

"When are you going to Staff College?" Paul asked.

"Not this year. I'm going back to the Third Battalion as a company commander. Then Staff College after that."

Paul nodded, slurping his tea.

"Family well? Your sister doing ok at university?" Rolly asked.

Paul nodded. "Yes, thank you for asking. She's fine. And so are the folks. In rude health, to tell you the truth."

Rolly never talked about his family, so Paul kept to professional matters. He said, "The work's going well? You're... getting lots of experience?"

Rolly swept a hand through his hair. "I'm in an airport in some shitty country more often than in London. We're just so busy."

Being in the SAS was obviously everything people said it was. He was getting trigger time. "You're... having fun?"

"Loving it. I was in Iraq last week, and Pakistan the month before that. Never needed my passport in over a year."

Paul chuckled. He looked at the toe of his boot. "You know me and Susan split, right?"

"Yes, matey, I did." Rolly said. "One of the things I was going to talk to you about..."

Paul cut him off. "I think it was the constant deployment that came between us. What with Sierra Leone and Oman, I was only home for six weeks."

He studied Rolly, who had rested his head back against the wall to stare at the ceiling. One of his brogues had a worn patch in the centre of the sole.

"She binned me just after Christmas," Paul said, trying to keep the emotion from his voice. He took a sip of tea and stared at the emerging hole in Rolly's shoe. Silence descended between them like cigarette smoke.

Rolly spoke quietly and slowly without taking his eyes off the ceiling. "Matey, I started going out with her at Easter."

The blow was immediate; a slow, sinking feeling in Paul's stomach. The energy drained out of him as he tried to voice something. He felt utterly helpless.

"I thought... I hope... She's..."

He felt his face reddening and leaned forward to place his mug on the coffee table.

"Matey, she said you were one of the best..."

It had been meant as a compliment. Paul pushed his chair over to his desk and pretended to check his emails. He wasn't upset. He was angry. How dare she? After all those chats about authenticity and being grounded, she chose fucking Rolly Rawlins!

Rolly said, "You don't mind, do you? You'd split."

A sudden flash of rage ignited in Paul. "You gotta stop going after my sloppy seconds. It's becoming a habit. You did the same with Clare when we were subbies."

He leaned back in his chair. Two grown men, and he was the lesser of them. He interlaced his fingers on top of his head. "I hope you'll be very happy. She's a bit needy at times, but you'll like that."

Rolly spoke carefully. "You really don't mind?"

Paul thought of Susan's body beneath his. How she gave a little grunt when she came. On the night he'd got back from Sierra Leone, when the skinny man with the afro had eventually let him in the door, he'd followed her upstairs.

"Paul, it's so good to see you," she said when they were finally in the privacy of her flat.

"Is that it?" he laughed. "I've been away for six months saving Africa from post-colonial decline!"

He dropped his bergen by the fire place in the living room, then walked her backwards towards the bedroom.

"I've been thinking about this for weeks…"

He could tell she didn't want to: the tilt of her head, the line of her lips. But she didn't refuse him, and made little grunting noises as he powered into her. He wanted her to want him, wanted her to love him the way he loved her. After exploding inside her, he collapsed with fatigue.

"I love you, Susan."

He'd slept for three hours, then woke to find he was alone. Susan was sitting straight backed on the Edwardian settle in the living room. She was drinking a cup of peppermint tea, the saucer in one hand.

"Come back to bed," he said.

She followed him, and even gave herself to him again. But at four o'clock, as he dressed to catch his lift to Catterick, she watched him with an expression he could not read. He knew it was not going to last, and the more he tried, the quicker it would end.

Reaching for his watch on the bedside table, he knocked it off and had to search for it under the bed. There he found a pair of brown leather brogues, not his, neatly tucked out of sight.

"I'll see you, Susan," he said. "I know I'm away a lot right now, but we can go away for New Year if you like?"

He walked round the bed to sit on the thin ledge of mattress next to her hip. She rolled onto her back. He stroked the bare skin of her arm. "Where would you like to go?"

"I'll think of something," she said.

Had those shoes been Rolly's? The relationship with Susan was ending anyway. Did it matter if Rolly had accelerated it? Or stolen her from him? Truth be told, Rolly would be far more use to him than Susan ever was.

Paul looked at Rolly and shook his head. "No. I don't mind. But you can do me a favour."

"What's that? Anything, matey."

Paul shoved Susan from his mind with a short, stark shake of his head. "It's about work."

"Sure."

Paul explained in outline what he wanted to achieve, stressing that there would be no photos of his, or his men's faces.

"It'd be like watching a drugs bust on a film, following guys in with the door ram. It's important, to show the rule of law."

Rolly said nothing.

"There'll be no risk to you, but maximum benefit to the local population. They'd see that killing innocent Serbs gets them arrested."

"What does the Brigadier say?" said Rolly. "Or CJO back in the bunker?"

"I'm working on it," Paul replied. "They both know it's a good idea, but are nervous of what you'll be prepared to do. If you say yes, they'll let me arrange it."

Rolly may have taken his girl, but Paul was going to win this battle of wits.

"I think I can do that for you, matey." Rolly said after a long while. "We might need to tinker with the details, but we can get you something."

A surge of relief. Paul didn't want to thank him as that would acknowledge the hierarchy between them. Instead he said, "Message Operations, Rolly. It's the future. Does more than kinetic warfare ever can. It shapes the battle space to allow conventional forces to operate safely. It's an intellectual game. I love it."

"So, in a way, we doing the same thing," Rolly said.

"Yes, we are, in a way," Paul replied. "Cutting edge warfare, both of us."

* * *

The studio at Radio Gracanica was more spacious than Radio Black Eagle, but less well equipped. The plywood furniture was angular, home-made, and painted yellow. A single microphone slotted into a holder that looked like a shower fitting. The room wasn't soundproofed, and the chugging of tractors occasionally reverberated through the wall.

Stefan looked more nervous than usual, the sweat making his hair greasy. "Tell us please, Major Paul, why UN and NATO want election?"

"They want to create a regional assembly that will administer Kosovo."

Paul waited for Roza to translate, then, "This will be a good thing. It will give you accountable people speaking on your behalf."

"Why this necessary?" Stefan said, avoiding his eyes.

"It is necessary so that Kosovo has a democratic structure that makes decisions about where money can be spent."

"But Kosovo is not country. It not need assembly. There is already parliament, in Belgrade."

Paul answered sentence by sentence. "As you know, Stefan, UN security resolution 1244 paves the way for the UN to administer Kosovo under the protection of NATO.

It acts in place of the Yugoslav federal government. Because the government was no longer functioning..."

What could he say? That the Serbian parliament lost control of its army? That it actively administered genocide?

"...and lost the moral authority to govern..."

Stefan's face became pinched. "Will this government be cruel to Serbian people?"

Paul shook his head. "No, Stefan, let me correct you there. Firstly, this is not a government. It is an assembly, with limited powers of decision making. A government has responsibility for defence, foreign affairs, monetary policy. This assembly will not have such a role."

"What powers it have?"

Paul held his eyes. "I don't know what powers have been agreed, Stefan. But as soon as I know, I will come and tell you." He changed his tone. "But what I can say is that the assembly can only have moral authority if it represents the Serb people resident in Kosovo. There are still a hundred and sixty thousand of you."

"So, Major, if Serbian people do not vote, this assembly will be immoral?"

Paul had not thought of this. "Stefan, look at me. This assembly is going to happen. You need to tell your listeners to get involved. Pretending it isn't happening is not the answer."

After the interview, Stefan thanked him for coming. He turned to put a record on the turntable, holding it between his palms to inspect it for dust. When he wasn't looking, Paul shook his head at Roza. She shrugged.

Outside, in the kitchen, Paul refused coffee but accepted the offer of water. Sweat was running down the inside of his shirt.

"You've got to ease up on the rhetoric, Stefan. It doesn't help to make the interview into an angry exchange."

Stefan shook his head. "My friend in Mitrovica, she say different. She say conflict make good radio. Then more people listen and have debate."

Paul pulled a face. "If that's the way you want it, Stefan, but be careful…"

He was about to say more when the telephone rang. Stefan answered it just as there was a heavy banging on the front door. Paul's mobile rang in his pocket.

"Paul Illingworth."

"Sir, it's the Watchkeeper. We're getting a report from callsigns in the air that there's a vehicle on a side road in Gracanica, parked up but with very limited guard around it. The number on the roof suggests it's yours but you're not signed out in the book. Can you confirm…"

Shit, Paul thought. He would get a bollocking for this.

"Er, yes, it's mine. Are we under threat?"

"There's a large body of people moving towards you…"

With no windows looking to the front, Paul could not see outside. Someone banged on the door again and there was the faint sound of Seagood shouting his name.

Stefan had one hand over the receiver of the telephone. "You must go," he said.

Paul pointed at his face. "We'll talk later," he said.

Grasping Roza's hand, he unbolted the doors to get her into the Landrover as quickly as he could. Seagood was waiting by the door.

"Thank God, Sir. There's this gang up the road…"

"Shut up, I'm driving."

As Paul opened the driver's door, a brick landed on the road in front of the vehicle. Seagood winced as she slammed the passenger door. "Oh my God!"

A second brick reverberated on the side of the Landrover as Paul started the engine. Pulling out into the road, he had the option of turning left, towards the crowd, or right towards the fields along a route he didn't know. "Shut the windows. We're going through them."

He pushed at the stubborn gearstick several times. "Get in you fucker!"

The vehicle lurched as he lifted his foot off the pedal. Keeping one hand on the wheel, he pulled out his pistol and placed it under his left thigh, pulling down the safety catch with his thumb.

"Is that gonna go off?" cried Seagood.

"Shut up. Sit back, smile, look them in the eye."

The crowd was no more than thirty people, but they were young men armed with farm tools. They were too loosely scattered to be an effective road block, and didn't appear to have a plan.

Paul's telephone was still on, and the Watchkeeper's voice was talking at the far end. He changed hands on the steering wheel and lifted it back to his ear.

"Hello? Yes it's me. I'm in Gracanica with SAC Seagood and my interpreter, Roza Xhaferi. I forgot to sign out. There's a crowd of hostile males... wait out..."

He put the phone on his thigh as he came to the front edge of the crowd, but made no attempt to slow down.

"Jane," he hissed through gritted teeth. "Check your fucking door's locked.

Using her first name broke her fear. She checked the lock then stared, wide eyed, through the windscreen with a painted grin on her face.

Fists banged on the side of the vehicle. Something hard hit the roof. Paul looked in the rear view mirror. Roza yelped and picked up a wheel brace. Paul checked quickly over this shoulder.

"Where's your fucking rifle, Jane?"

Her whole body trembled. "It's in camp..."

Very slightly, Paul accelerated. The banging on the sides of the vehicle became less frequent. A stone hit the spare wheel on the back door, making a loud crack.

"We're through," Paul said, as the road cleared in front of him.

He picked up his phone. "Hello? Line check?"

The Watchkeeper's voice was steady. "Sir, we're watching you live from a callsign in the air. Be aware that was not the main crowd. There's another one as you turn left back to the main road."

"Bugger. Here, Jane, hold the phone."

Placing both hands on the wheel, he accelerated to normal driving speed. At the road junction, he stopped, ostentatiously looked right and left, then put his foot down.

"Where's this other crowd?"

Just as he said this, the second crowd appeared around the long left hand bend; about a hundred people walking very slowly towards him.

"Is Stefan fault," Roza said angrily from the back. "He does not understand what he is doing with radio."

Paul was not sure if Stefan was to blame, but if there was evidence of the power of radio, this was it. On the Message Operations course he often told the students how *Radio Milles Collines* had whipped up the genocide in Rwanda.

He slowed the vehicle, and carefully reached for his pistol. Taking his hands off the steering wheel, he cocked the weapon.

"Oh my God!" said Seagood, her breathing fast.

"Just smile," Paul said through clenched jaws.

The crowd moved as if in procession, melting round the front of the Landrover like water. As they passed, they fixed him with their eyes. He put the hazard lights on, but this made little difference.

"Hello, excuse me..." he said, without sliding the window open.

Someone banged the side of the wagon. As he looked over to Seagood, someone else slid his window forward and grabbed his arm, pinching it through the shirt. He lifted his elbow off the sill to make them release him.

He wanted to drive faster, but he couldn't. "Roza, stay low," he said in a voice as normal as possible, a false grin on his face.

She needed no telling, and sank out of sight. He was moving so slowly that faces could peer into the back window cupped between two hands. Thankfully the glass was caked in dust.

Paul couldn't help thinking of the two corporals who got lost in the one-way system in West Belfast when he was a young officer. They had accidentally driven into a funeral cortege. The crowd had recognised them as British soldiers, dragged them from the car, and killed them both before they could open fire.

If there was one thing Paul knew, it was that he wasn't going to be killed without firing all fourteen rounds in his magazine.

"Excuse us please..." he called.

The Watchkeeper's voice came over his phone and Seagood held it to her ear.

"Yes it's us, they're all around us... they're all around us..."

"Don't panic!" Paul hissed. "We're fine."

But just then, a hand made a grab for the car keys through his window. Paul elbowed the man hard in the face. Someone else rattled the handle on the outside of Seagood's door, making her scream and pull away.

Another hand snatched at Paul's shirt sleeve again. He pressed the brake quickly, catching the man's elbow joint against the window. The man cried out and withdrew his arm as Paul pressed the accelerator again.

Paul shut the window and snubbed the lock. As he did so a young man clambered on to the front fender and started shouting at the crowd. Again, Paul pressed the brake and the man fell off backwards. People raced to pull him out of the way as Paul put his foot back on the accelerator.

Seagood's door opened. Someone pulled the beret from her head. She screamed, hands protecting her face. A bearded face appeared in the doorway, but seeing it was a girl in the seat, looked gormlessly at Paul.

Paul snatched the pistol from under his leg and punched out with the muzzle towards his eyes. He hit true, and the face fell away. The door slammed shut.

"Lock the fucking thing," he shouted.

"How do I do that?" she cried.

Paul let go of the steering wheel to reach over and click the snib. As he did so, the Landrover rocked up and down as if crossing a speed bump.

Someone screamed, leaving Paul with the terrifying thought that he'd just driven over someone.

Hands started banging more aggressively on the outside. Something struck the rear window, cracking the glass. Roza picked up the wheel brace as a weapon. She smacked the inside of the door with it.

"You try, you die," she screamed in English.

Paul put his feet on the gas and the clutch and revved the engine without increasing speed. He pressed the horn.

Suddenly the way cleared around them. But it wasn't Paul's use of the horn.

An orthodox priest in long black robes and a square hat walked slowly towards them swinging a golden orb. Smoke wafted around his legs.

Paul braked.

The priest walked past without looking at him at all. Behind him there were as many people as there had been in front, but no one struck the Landrover. The crowd thinned, and disappeared.

Paul grabbed the telephone.

"They've past us, but they're on the way to the monastery. Is there a callsign there?"

Seagood's face drained of colour. "We're not going back in, are we?"

The Watchkeeper's voice remained implacable. "Negative. Our assessment is that their intent is merely to show presence."

There was a deeper, gravelly voice in the background, which the Watchkeeper acknowledged. "And you are to report to the Chief of Staff as soon as you're back, Major Illingworth," she said.

Paul checked the wing mirrors of the Landrover. The crowd had gone, so he put his foot down.

Fuck, was he going to get a bollocking! He deserved it too. He had gone out unprepared, undrilled, under-armed. He had not signed out. If he wasn't careful, Simon would ground him and he's be stuck in camp like all the other staff officers.

Clear of the village but before the main road, Paul glanced at Seagood. She was trying not to cry. She held one hand to her nose. Paul pulled over and undid his seatbelt. Her pupils had dilated and the lips looked very dark.

"Look at me. How many fingers."

She blinked, shook her head, and spluttered a cough.

"It's normal to be scared. A crowd is a dangerous thing."

Roza reached over the bulwark to wrap her arms around Seagood's shoulders. Seagood held her hands, and started to sob. "I didn't know what to do…"

Paul placed a hand on her arm, exaggerating his Yorkshire accent. "It's fine, luvvie. Eee, what bastards eh?"

She snorted a laugh. "Sorry, Sir. Are you ok yourself?"

She nodded at Paul's arm, and he noticed that the shirt had been torn. Blood was running over his hand.

"The bastards cut me. Here, you'd better drive. Let me staunch this." He kicked open the door to swap seats. Giving her something to do would make her concentrate. "Can you?"

She nodded. "Yes, Sir."

Once underway again, Paul pulled his seatbelt round his body with his good arm, the snib never quite connecting with the receiver. The blood started dripping off his fingers and onto the seat.

"Let me help," said Roza, reaching over the bulwark to press his bicep between both her hands. "You are my hero, Paul," she said.

* * *

"You're a fucking tit. That could have been bloody serious."

Paul hadn't been able to salute with his arm in a sling. To show remorse, he stood rigidly to attention.

"Sorry."

"You endangered that wee driver," Simon continued.

"Sorry."

"Not to mention," interjected Blanche, "putting an Albanian interpreter at serious risk in Serb territory."

Paul scowled at her. Who the fuck was she to be part of this? She was his peer, not his superior.

"Don't let it happen again," said Simon. "Or I'll have to court martial you for damage to the vehicle."

"That won't happen," said Paul.

Simon folded his arms. "I have not told the Commander. Ultimately you had to drive through a hostile crowd, that's all. But you should know, as an infantry officer seeking promotion, to plan for the worst case scenario."

He got it, and being told off repeatedly just made him angry. He clenched the fist of his uninjured arm. "I'm fucking sorry."

Shaking his head, Simon rested his elbows on his desk. "Now, let's put that incident aside. There's something I need you to do. It's not related to the other operations, just a bit of harmless PR for UK plc. I need you to cover the Kosovo Security Corps parade that the training team have organised for tomorrow afternoon."

Paul shrugged. "Sure. Why's that so important?"

"The training team have been complaining that the work they do is not getting attention. They feel undervalued." Simon sniggered as he said this.

Paul said, "I can't promise to get them into the papers just because they're training Kosovo's future police. It's not a story that would grab an editor."

Simon nodded. "I know, Paul. But they would value some support. They like to think that their work is crucial to establishing a stable and peaceful future. As indeed it is."

Paul sniggered. "By taking former fighters from the Kosovo Liberation Army and training them up as policemen?"

Simon nodded.

"Actually, I deliberately haven't covered them because it is quite easy to misinterpret what they are doing. To the casual observer, it might look like the British were training up the future army of an independent Kosovo, something that wouldn't go down well in Belgrade."

Simon leaned back in his chair and folded his arms. He glanced at Blanche. "I can see that. But it's not the truth. They're a security force, not an army."

"They're not being given weapons training," said Blanche, as if that answered all possible questions.

Paul shifted his weight. "They didn't really need weapon training after a two-year insurgency against the combined Serb army."

Then a thought came to mind. "But that being said, giving the Security Corps some local coverage would mitigate the impression that we're becoming too pro-Serbian."

"How do you mean?" said Simon.

"We handed back the Presevo Valley, in essence an anti-Albanian stance. We are trying to arrest the bus bombers, the same. By holding the Security Corps up as a paragon of virtue, we are showing the Albanians we are being even-handed."

"And that should build trust with them," Simon nodded. "I like that."

Blanche made a slight nod. "Build a trust that deceives them into thinking we have no concerns about them," she said.

* * *

With his arm in a sling, Paul had to reach over the keyboard with his left hand to grab the mouse. Using his middle finger to click the button required effort, and the cable, caught in the tangle of wires underneath his desk, didn't stretch far enough to be useful.

The television had the sound turned off. The tickertape headlines at the bottom of the screen announced that the leader of the opposition had agreed to delay the general election due to the foot and mouth crisis. It was after ten. Paul had finished sending out invites for the parade to all the local journalists he knew. He thought about inviting Nick and Aden, but thought better of it.

He still had to write a report about the damaged Landrover.

Describe the position of the vehicle at the time of the accident, the form said.

"Surrounded by angry mob armed with shovels and hoes," he muttered to himself, but then typed 'Driving down the middle of the road through a large crowd of pedestrians.' His arm in a sling, he used one finger to locate and press each key.

The door opened behind him. Paul looked over this shoulder wondering why he had never turned the desk to face the door.

"Good evening Zotëri Major," said Roza. "I see the light is on so I come to ask if you need me."

She stood a few inches from Paul's elbow in the sling. She had recently applied perfume and the scent penetrated his senses like a vivid dream. He pushed the chair back a little and looked up at her, following the line of buttons up her blouse to where the fabric creased between her breasts.

"You were very brave today," he said. "I saw you grab the wheel brace." She would be a lioness if she was cornered. And a tigress in bed.

Roza smiled. "It was you who were very brave. You saved us all." She reached out to touch his shoulder.

He looked at her hand, longing to touch the warm, olive skin. Her jeans fitted tightly round her hips and across the front of her stomach. At the top of one thigh, the denim had worn through the white fibres to reveal a patch of skin lighter than her arms.

She placed a hand over the hole. "I am sorry. I must repair this."

Paul stood to face her. Using his good arm, he took her hand and squeezed it. "Don't."

The two of them looked at each other for several moments. Paul traced the patterns in her iris, the display of hazels and ambers that bled into dark green. Her lips were very thin and bright pink. When she pressed the palm of her hand against his, he felt a yearning deep inside his groin. The sound of the sentries chatting outside the window reminded him that the main gate was only a few metres away. He leaned over the desk to tug the cord for the blind and closed it.

He shouldn't be seen with her like this, but his movement had broken the spell.

"I have to work, Roza, I'm sorry," he said.

She pushed the ends of her fingers into the pockets of her jeans, allowing her wrists to fall outwards.

"Okey-dokey," she said. "I understand." Very slowly, she walked to the door as if pulling against a rope that bound them together. "I go," she said. "I have night duty in interpreters' hut. Just me."

The clumsiness of it all, the sordidness, made Paul shudder. "I'll see you in the morning, Roza," he said.

Though after the door had shut, and he was once again alone with her perfume dancing in his nostrils, he stared at the computer screen for half an hour without typing a thing.

* * *

"Is this it?" said Paul, crouching over the map and glancing through the windscreen of the Landrover.

"Yes," said Roza from behind the bulwark.

"This very famous place, Major Pol," said Elire. "We all know it."

"I'll relax then," Paul said, pointing Seagood towards an obvious parking area. "Stick us in there and we'll walk."

Once parked, Paul opened the back door to let out Elire and three other local journalists who had responded to his emails. "Welcome to the Kosovo Security Corps capability parade, ladies. If you'd all follow me..."

The journalists were excited, like children on a school trip. As soon as they'd stretched and decided it was too warm to wear a coat, they skipped through a green metal gate guarded by a British soldier. Beyond it was a sizeable crowd cheering the events on a sports field beyond. Leaving Paul behind, they squeezed through the crowd.

"I'll be leaving at two," Paul called after them.

Only Roza stayed close. "So this is a famous place?" he said. "I have never been here before."

Beyond the gate, the area was dominated by a square stone tower about a hundred feet high. To the front, on a dais made from scaffolding, a small collection of worthies – some civilian, some military – watched two teams of men compete in an assault course competition. The crowd, held back by security fencing, cheered and applauded. Occasionally, someone shouted a word Paul recognised.

"*Oochaka, Ooochaka*!"

"What does that word mean?" Paul asked. "I remember it from the very first interview we did at Black Eagle. The woman who rang in, she kept saying it."

"It is not a word," Roza said. "It is the letters, U-C-K."

"It's an acronym?"

"Yes, like this. *Ushtria Çlirimtare e Kosovës.*"

"That's easy for you to say," chuckled Paul. "What's that?"

"It is Albanian letters for what you call the KLA, the Kosovo Liberation Army."

Paul snapped his fingers. "Sorry, I was being thick; UCK, of course."

"They are heroes," Roza added. "They drove the Serbian army out of Kosovo."

She held her hands in front of herself like a small girl.

"I think it's more accurate to say NATO drove the Serb army out of Kosovo," Paul said. "But I don't deny that the KLA put up fierce resistance."

Roza indicated the men on the field. "After the war, NATO take KLA fighters and make them into Kosovo Security Corps; KSC. They will defend us after NATO has gone."

She gave a slight shrug. The way she looked up at him made him wonder if she was being reproachful.

He said, "The Serbs will not attack again."

"We are safe when you are here," she said quietly.

Did she mean NATO, or him? Or both? Paul touched her arm, nodding towards the tower. "Tell me what that monstrosity is," he said.

Roza smiled, her teeth broad and white. "We call it *Gazimestan*. It means the place of heroes."

"Why so?"

"Here is site of battle between Serbian army and Albanians in 1389."

"Did the Albanians win?"

"Yes, of course. Many peoples killed on both sides, but Albanians win. This field is called *Kosovo Polje*, the field of the black birds."

Paul imagined a battlefield with the dead and dying being picked over by crows. "So that tower is a monument to the Albanian victory?"

"Actually no. It was made during communist time. On the front, you see when parade is finished, there is a poem about Serb people who did not fight and so the battle was lost."

Paul sniggered. "So this is a monument to a battle at which the Serbs got their arses kicked?"

Roza nodded. "Yes indeed." She looked suddenly angry and Paul thought he should save this conversation for after the parade. "Excuse me. I need to take photos."

He wished he had done more research before coming. It was as well he'd brought Roza. Climbing onto the stone platform on which the tower stood, he took a few shots over the heads of the crowd. A British soldier patrolling the perimeter looked up at him, but left him to his work when he waved his NATO identification card.

He then took photos of the parade from behind the dignitaries. The Royal Artillery colonel commanding the training team saw him and nodded when Paul held up the camera to indicate what he was doing. To the side of the dais was a row of wide concrete funnels. What an ugly design, Paul thought, as he propped his back against the lowest one to take shots of the dignitaries. The sling round his injured arm was an embuggerance, so he slipped it off and stuffed it into his pocket.

He then crept underneath the crowd barrier to get a series of shots of the race. He concentrated on the point where the teams had to cross a six foot wall and then crawl through a low wire entanglement. The event made him smile. He always enjoyed a good assault course.

"Keep going!" he shouted.

At the far end, the teams had to run round a bollard before racing back to the start in a straight sprint. The crowd cheered, shouting the names of those they knew. Paul got a very good shot of a man skidding in the dust.

Both teams wore olive overalls and boots. On their right arm was a red badge on which the black eagle of Albania spread its wings above the Albanian name for their organisation.

Paul was refitting the lens cover on the camera when a hand tapped his injured arm. He winced as he looked up. It was Nick, standing behind the fencing with both hands resting gently on the top rail.

"Paul, are you honestly going to tell me this is not a military organisation?" he said.

They shook hands with Paul crouching so as not to get in the way of people watching. "They're for civil order duties, Nick, you know that."

Nick waggled his head from side to side making a slight scoffing sound. "That badge on the arm of their coveralls? It's identical to the one the Liberation Army used during the war."

Paul could not deny the scene looked very similar to what infantry recruits did in Catterick. He said, "A police force also needs teamwork, leadership, physical fitness…"

Nick looked at him with a sad expression. "You know this is the site where…"

Paul cut across him. "Yes, I know. A battle in thirteen something…"

Nick was silent for a moment. "Actually, I was going to say it was where President Milosevic came to give a big speech in 1998. He read that poem on the wall by the entrance to the tower. Basically, he made a great show of Serbian triumphalism. He told the Albanians they were worse than dogs."

Paul studied him trying to work out what his political allegiances were. "I bet he regrets that now," he said. "Nothing like a bit of political hubris to entertain the media."

Nick nodded. "Like the sort you're making?"

"How do you mean?"

Nick said, "All these men are former KLA fighters. You gave them uniforms and badges. You are giving them military training. To the Serbians you're creating a de facto army. And right now you're parading them in front of the Albanian media – I noticed you didn't give me a call about this event – on the site of a historic battle at which the Ottomans defeated the Serbs."

Nick's manner was never aggressive, but his words always hit home. Who was being triumphalist now?

Paul said, "We don't teach weapon handling. And the coveralls are just…"

"I'm not criticising, Paul," Nick said, raising his hands. "I don't know what you do with a rebel force like the KLA after a war has ended. I recognise that you need to find work for them or they become a threat to stability."

"You train them to be a force for good," Paul replied. "If Kosovo does become independent – and I'm not saying it will or it should – it will need a police force."

Nick smiled. "That is true. But it's also true that the Democratic Party is just the political wing of the Kosovo Liberation Army, and still depends on the same bribery, smuggling, and coercion that funded the war against the Serbians in the first place. Did you know that?"

"No, I'm afraid I didn't," Paul said. He turned to watch the men on their second circuit of the assault course. The crowd cheered louder as they approached. He dusted off his knees. "No, I did not know," he repeated. "But what else would you have us do?"

"I don't know," Nick said, nodding with his head towards the dais. "But that man there, the one in the suit talking to the artillery colonel? His name is Florim Agani. He was the political leader of the Democratic Party during the war and is as corrupt as they come. Most of the heroin that gets into France has come through his channels. And NATO has made him head of this quasi-military organisation."

* * *

The bunches of green grapes hung in compact, tight knots along the supporting wires. Because she was small, Anja's job was to work the lowest vines, picking out individual fruit that had turned brown or been attacked by wasps. She had to nip them out with a pair of scissors that had a sprung handle and a blade like the beak of a parrot.

She squatted, feet wide apart, to reach up underneath the heart shaped leaves. On the opposite side of the row, Tata laboured along the higher branches. The pair moved steadily and evenly from one plant to the next, each dragging a red plastic crate along the ground into which the cuttings were thrown.

Tata grunted from time to time, or stood and stretched his back. After an hour, Anja found she was getting further ahead than her father, so spent time doing the upper branches as well.

"That one is next, Tata," she said, pointing with the scissors.

"Thank you," he said, exhaling heavily down his nose and into his beard as he lowered himself down by pulling on a wooden stake. Then, kneeling on one knee, he bowed his head and mumbled to himself, his hands grasped together.

Anja studied him. A red blister had formed in the web between his thumb and forefinger. His arm was the colour of a beetroot.

"You want me to do this row?" she whispered.

Breathing heavily, his eyes downcast, he shook his head. "The saints have told me I must do this," he said, but after picking out two more bunches, he once again had to stand and lean backwards, his hands on the back of his hips. He pushed the crate with his foot and sat on the edge of it. Then he stretched out his legs, and grunted as he did so.

"Tata?" said Anja. "When will we know if they have arrested the hunter?"

Tata shook his head, drawing in a knee to his chest and hugging it. "I do not know, my love. I have asked the British major, the one with the red hat, but he did not know. I think there were things he did not wish to say. Or say to me."

Anja studied the soil. It was grey and dry. Tiny pebbles reflected the sunlight. A small patch of grass grew where the irrigation pipe had a hole in it. She pulled it up to find the roots were longer than the green blades. It came out easily, without tearing.

"If they find him, will others come looking for me?" she whispered.

Tata sobbed, then smothered the sound with a choked cough. "I don't know, Anja," he said. "I just don't know."

Chapter 10

The lobby of the Grand Hotel was empty, save for Nick and Aden in a nest of sofas at the back. Aden waved when Paul came in.

"Where are the suits?" Paul asked as he took a seat.

"It's the election," said Nick.

"The one here?"

"Of course the one here. They'll be lobbying for contracts in exchange for cash."

Paul nodded, watching the tall waiter strut to the window and stare out through the chiffon curtains with his hands behind his back. His shadow fell long and slim along the marble floor.

"Is that how it works? I have no idea."

Aden snorted. "Haven't you noticed all that building work along the Mitrovica road?" He cast a glance at Nick, giving Paul a sense that they thought him wonderfully, beautifully naïve. He let them do so. It would serve his purpose.

Nick reached into his trouser pocket for his fags. He offered one, but Paul shook his head.

"It kills me in the heat," he said, watching closely as Nick cupped a flaring match in his hands and inhaled the first drag.

Again Nick held out the packet, his eyebrows raised. Paul shook his head more firmly, but Aden took one and tapped the tobacco end on his leg before lighting it.

"Who do you think will win the election," said Paul, placing his arm along the top of the sofa.

Nick exhaled smoke through his nose as he thought how to respond. Aden answered first. "Usual form after a secessionist war is for the nationalists to get it."

"Would that mean the guy you pointed out, Nick?"

Aden nodded. "Agani. The guy you put in charge of the Security Corps. Nasty fucker. He'll win the Albanian vote by playing the independence card alone. And since that means ninety-eight per cent of the population…"

Nick raised a finger. "I'm not so sure. The liberal, Rugova, is a very special man. He's like a Mandela, or a Ghandi, in his way. Of course they all want independence, but Kosova people know Rugova would make the better statesman."

Aden's frowned. "He wasn't at the peace conference. Nor was he here during the war…"

To Paul, the outcome of the election did not matter. He didn't worry who was in power; only that someone was. "All I really care about is that people vote. Even the Serbs."

Both Nick and Aden made immediate, disparaging grunts. "A death sentence," Aden said.

"What is?"

"Representing the Serbian minority. You're bound to get killed."

Paul sucked his teeth. "Not sure. I can think of several countries where minority parties hold disproportionate power."

"Such as?" said Nick.

"Northern Ireland, for a start. The minority parties hold the balance between the protestant and catholic blocs. They are king makers."

Again, Nick and Aden exchanged glances, but Paul noticed a difference in their expressions. He was playing his cards well. He felt superbly in control.

"That's a first world country, Paul. Democracy is long established, as is the rule of law." Aden swept his hair out of his face with one hand.

"I'm sure you're right," Paul said, shrugging. "I don't have anything like your experience. But Kosovo is not as backward as some people make out. The law is established."

Nick and Aden both sniggered. Nick rocked back in his chair, one hand on his belly, laughing loudly and exhaling vast puffs of smoke before being reduced to coughing.

Paul's shoulders shook at the shared humour. "You don't agree?"

Nick waggled a finger as he coughed into one hand, his body still in spasm. Eventually, he hawked up phlegm and reached with one hand into the pocket of his trousers to produce a large, ironed handkerchief, which he used to wipe his lip. "No, Paul, I don't agree. I've seen corruption. And Kosovo ranks right up there with Nigeria and Indonesia."

The debate was in balance and Paul felt it time to play his queen. He couldn't *tell* them Kosovo was stable. He had to *show* them.

"Maybe, maybe not," he said. "But in the few months that I've been here, I've seen a major change in attitude."

He waited for the journalists to ask the next question. It was Aden who took the bait.

"How?"

"Two things. They're not much, I suppose, in the grand scheme of things. But I think they're significant."

"What?"

"Well, firstly, as you know, I've been campaigning for a weapons amnesty on the local radio and television stations. I've been asking people to hand in their weapons from the war."

"And?"

"Up at camp I've got a forty-foot freight container rammed to the gunnels; everything from a World War Two carbine to an M16, and enough AKs to equip an African revolution." He pulled a carefree shrug. "Come and have a look."

Nick and Aden looked at one another. Paul knew he should play his king while he had their attention. "And this week I watched something I've never seen before."

This time, it was Nick who bit. "What was that?"

"A Kosovo Albanian in a Series 5 BMW stopping at a red traffic light on an empty road."

He let the implications sink in. It was a simple metaphor, but layered with complexity.

"Seriously," he said, "on an empty road, with no traffic crossing, he waited for the green light."

Nick nodded thoughtfully. Aden studied Paul with a guarded expression, his hair casting his face in shadow. It was time for Paul to play the ace.

"But anyway, to business, since we're talking about the rule of law. I need to tell you something that's top secret and if you spill the beans I'll have to kill you."

It was a joke, but he knew them well enough to make it.

"In the not very distant future we're going to make a series of arrests."

"For what?" Nick said.

"For involvement in a hideous and unnecessary crime," Paul said. "Involving a bus."

He had their attention.

"I'd like you watch the arrests taking place. So you see how the rule of law is being applied, even in Kosovo, one of the most corrupt countries in the world."

* * *

Back in the Press Office, Paul found he'd left the television on overnight. The headlines on the red tickertape along the bottom of the screen said that the foot and mouth crisis was now under control. The phone rang just as he was pulling the pistol from its holster. It was Brassy.

"The Prime Minister can't delay the election any longer, so the announcement's coming. After that, you're in purdah."

Paul sucked his teeth. "I need more time," he said. "I need the internationals."

"What for?"

He had never told Brassy what he wanted to do with the arrest operation, knowing the idea would be shot down. "I can't tell you."

"Has this got something to do with the arrest operation?"

"Possibly."

Brassy was annoyed. "Listen, Paul. The Chief of Joint Operations had a two-hour phone call with your Brigadier last night. If this operation goes wrong he'll be Corporal Montrose, sweeper of the royal parks in Outer Stornaway. So don't be fucking coy. What are you planning?"

Paul evaded the question. "Taking the bus bomber down is a good thing, surely? It's all about promoting the rule of law, proving we're a force for good. It plays straight into the Five Themes."

Brassy's voice changed. "You don't see the bigger picture, Paul. There's a much wider view."

Arrogant twat, Paul thought. "Go on then. Tell me this *wider view*."

"It's not the bomber, it's his support network. Your Brigadier wants to arrest them as well."

"I know. So what?"

There was a silence. Paul heard a door being closed in the background.

"This is between you and me," Brassy said. "The support network is drawn from the Kosovo Security Corps. The police force you've been training."

Paul shrugged. "I know. So what?" he repeated. "The international press are deeply suspicious of them."

"Precisely!" said Brassy. "And what's happening later in the year? I'll give you a clue. The same thing's happening here as well."

"An election?"

"Yes, a fucking election. And which side do you think will win? The peacenik Rugova, or the leader of the KSC…"

"Florim Agani, the nationalist."

"Precisely."

Brassy said nothing more, as if that had been enough.

"I still don't get it," said Paul, more angrily than he meant to. "What are you not telling me?"

Brassy sucked in air and exhaled slowly.

"There's an aspiration in Downing Street, Paul, to make Kosovo independent. There's a view at the very top that Rugova will not deliver. Therefore we are tacitly supporting Agani and the nationalists."

"Don't talk bollocks," Paul said without thinking.

"I beg your pardon!"

"I'm sorry, Colonel, it just came out. But how can we support Agani if his supporters committed such a heinous crime?"

The blood strained behind his ears. His voice had risen in pitch and he made a conscious decision to talk slower.

"It's a bloody business, Paul," Brassy said. "But that's the game. *Realpolitik*, as they say in Deutschland. War is an extension of politics after all."

Cobblers, thought Paul, anyone can quote Clausewitz. "Still don't buy it. If Agani's involved in that sort of political intimidation, we shouldn't be touching him with a barge pole."

"It's the game, Paul."

"No it's not. And I bet very few people support such a ridiculous idea."

Brassy's voice was sing-song. "It comes from the top."

Paul mimicked him. "I don't believe you. Ethical foreign policy." Then, more soberly, "I really don't believe we would support someone linked to terrorism."

"Oh grow up!" said Brassy. "How do you think we got peace in Northern Ireland, if not by talking to Gerry Adams and Martin McGuiness? The man who is now, I remind you, Minister for Education."

Paul bit on his lip. "You're blocking the arrest operation because you don't want to damage Agani's election campaign?"

"We're not *blocking* the operation. Just making sure there's no fall out. Your Brigadier's been told that if he fucks up, he'll be out of there by Friday."

"Bugger me."

Paul did not know what to say. A whole spectrum of intrigue was opening up before him.

Brassy said, "Did you think this was just about making Kosovo safe and stable? Come on, Paul!"

Paul felt his energy drain. To have to face such conniving on a daily basis, the Brigadier must have balls of steel. "I thought you wanted them brought on message."

Brassy snorted. "This is the message, Paul! This is the message. And your job is to make sure the press don't get wind of the fact that the bomber's mates are linked to a political party."

"But I've already..."

"You've what?"

Paul realised his mistake. If he stayed shtum, he might be able to cover his tracks. "Nothing."

"Get this right, Paul. You've only got a few days left to keep the press quiet. Purdah starts as soon as the election is announced. And don't for God's sake let Short or Oakeshot know about the arrests."

Chapter 11

Lying in bed, his hands interlaced behind his head, Paul realised that he had hardly thought of Susan at all in the past two weeks. The conversation with Rolly had only served to emphasize the point that he was getting over her. The exquisite bitterness had gone. What remained was a dull rage that she had left him for Rolly of all people.

Keeping busy made all the difference. He was working eighteen hours at a stretch and the remaining six hours were spent either in the gym, asleep, or lying on his back, staring at the struts supporting the roof tiles.

He didn't buy it. He didn't believe there was a policy of supporting Albanian extremism so that Kosovo became independent. That was the sort of muddle-headed thinking that took place during colonial times.

But why did he question the policy? It was very clear that Radio Black Eagle favoured Agani's party, as did most of their listeners. The alternative, Ibrahim Rugova, was an academic. During the war he had appeared on television alongside Slobodan Milosevic to demand an end to the NATO bombing of Belgrade.

Why did Paul favour him?

A couple of days before, driving to Gracanica to collect Stefan for the UN press conference, Paul had asked Roza who she would vote for.

"Rugova," she said, touching her throat as she spoke. "He is the best man."

That was why.

***

"Simon, I need advice," said Paul, after saluting and removing his beret. "May I sit down?"

Simon scowled. "You normally saunter in here and sit down without saluting even when the Commander's in the room. You never tell me what you're planning, so you obviously think a line infantry officer, and a proponent of conventional warfare, wouldn't understand what mighty deeds Message Operations are capable of. And you've even put polish on your boots. Out with it, laddie. What have you done?"

Paul chuckled, sat down, and placed his beret over one knee. "I don't bother you with minutiae, Simon. But this time I need top cover. I'm getting something from the Bunker I don't believe."

"What's that?"

Paul told him what Brassy had said, during which Simon sat back in his chair looking at the ceiling with his fingers steepled in the same way the Brigadier did.

"Fuck me," he growled. "You're saying the Bunker actively want the former freedom fighter to win an election? That'll mean utter annihilation for any Serbs left in the enclaves."

Paul nodded, playing his cards one by one. "Doesn't it remind you of, say, Zimbabwe?"

"Well I'm not sure about that parallel," Simon said. "But it doesn't sound right."

Paul said, "Agani would never be able to form a relationship with President Kostunica in Belgrade. It'd be like turning the clock back to ninety-nine."

"Exactly." Simon drummed his fingers on the desk. "So what are you thinking?"

"I go back to my original suggestion, Simon. This arrest operation. I want to film the capture of the support network. We should not be picking sides. That's for the Kosovo people to do. We should be neutral." He paused and adjusted his beret on his knee. "But if a candidate is a bad apple..."

171

Simon folded his arms. Paul had learned that on such occasions he had to hold Simon's gaze. "This is the right thing to do. We must show everyone that the law is the law."

"And I presume you've spoken to your mate, the SAS commander."

"I've known him since Sandhurst; he's vain, as all pretty people are. He'll do it, providing it's off the record."

Simon's face darkened. "The thing is, Paul, the Commander liked your idea so much he mentioned it to the Chief of Joint Operations, in a call the other night."

Paul nodded.

"He told CJO that we were considering using the SAS as part of a Message Operations programme, not just to lift some *bad apples*, as you say."

"And…?"

Simon shook his head. "I was in here. But I could hear CJO shouting through the wall. He lost his fucking nut."

"Why?" The suggestion that his ideas had got Brigadier Montrose into trouble embarrassed him.

"Have you met CJO?"

"No."

"He's Royal Navy. He wouldn't know a rifle from a hand grenade. He's a career staff officer who's spent most of his time at some NATO headquarters drinking wine with the Germans."

It was not like Simon to be so disloyal, so he obviously meant it. "He threatened to pull the Commander out of theatre if this operation goes badly."

So Brassy had been right. "But why would they pull him? Don't they want the bombers arrested?"

"They want the bomber arrested, sure. But there are others involved who…"

"Are members of the Kosovo Security Corps."

Simon looked at him. "And since we're training said organisation, it would look bad if that were made public."

So that was it. A far more likely story than some conspiracy about political manoeuvring; this was simply about face saving. The British had trained the people who supported the man who blew up the bus. Hardly the actions of the global masters of counter insurgency warfare.

"What this means, Paul, is that nobody wants to see the operation in the papers. You'll have to find other evidence for your 'rule of law' activity."

"I don't have time," said Paul. "As soon as the UK election is announced I'll not be able to brief Aden and Nick about anything."

Simon shrugged. "Perhaps that's a good thing? If the Brigadier got a bollocking just for mentioning the idea, remember that shit rolls downhill."

Paul was downcast. "I still think it's the right thing to do."

"That may well be, Paul," said Simon. "But that does not mean we are going to do it. Have you told your press friends anything?"

Paul coloured, but shook his head. "Of course not..."

"Because if you had, you could kiss your annual appraisal goodbye."

"I haven't said anything."

"Good. Because it's tomorrow night. And I don't want to get caught in the flak either."

* * *

Thirty six hours. That's all he had. Paul fingered through his notebook looking for Rolly's new number. He found it and dialled, but it went straight through the voicemail.

He rang Nick, but after the dial tone had rung a couple of times, he pressed the red button and killed the call. He sat at his desk, staring at the words bouncing round on the computer screen.

He was close, very close. But something was getting in his way. Did he have the balls to go through with it? Or would he let someone else take the game?

Under the keyboard he noticed a small pink envelope. He pushed the keyboard back and slid the envelope towards him. The words *Zotëri Major* were written in neat, small handwriting. Inside was a card with a cheesy cartoon of a teddy bear being lifted off the ground by a heart-shaped balloon.

Paul's heart thumped. His hands shook. How utterly stupid. How girly. And yet, how…

Opening the card, it simply said, in English, *Thinking of you, my hero. Your interpreter, Rozafa.*

As if he needed to be told.

And then the phone rang.

***

The air conditioning in the Grand Hotel had gone into overdrive. It was freezing.

Aden appeared from the lifts. "Cheer up, Paul, it can't be that bad!" He was jittery and red faced, his shirt open to the third button and the sleeves rolled up above the elbow.

"You just got up?" asked Paul, a smirk dancing along his lips.

Aden unrolled his sleeves and did up the cuff buttons. He held one nostril and sniffed. "Just a bit of business upstairs. You know."

Paul shrugged. "Whatever floats your boat, mate."

"You don't?"

"God no! I haven't touched drugs since I was a freshman."

Aden's face clouded for a moment as Nick appeared through the main door and walked towards them, raising a hand in greeting. "Jasper did, once or twice," he whispered. "If you want to, I won't say anything."

What more had that man done? How did people like that go to Staff College and get promoted? It was a sham, the whole thing.

When he joined them, Nick slid his old leather briefcase down the back of a chair and slumped down next to Paul on the sofa. The tall waiter appeared in Paul's peripheral vision so he held up three fingers. The man raised his nose, nodded curtly, then spun on his heel to disappear into the kitchens.

"You're becoming a man of influence" smiled Nick, patting Paul's thigh. "You're getting known."

A sudden shiver ran through Paul's body. It was true. If he could pull this scam off, he could do anything. He said, "You working on anything, Nick?"

Nick shrugged, reaching into his pocket to poke around for his fags. "Just an idea I'm researching. More for a book, actually."

"How's that coming?" said Aden, pinching his nostrils as he talked. "Will your agent cover it?"

"The Observer have said they'll serialise it."

"Fantastic!" said Aden, clapping has hands.

Nick winked at Paul as he lit a cigarette. "The man who really captured the public imagination at the start of the war was a farmer. His resistance to Serbian oppression became legend."

"What about him?" asked Paul.

"His name was Adem Hoxha." said Nick. "He founded the Kosovo Liberation Army. It took an entire battlegroup to kill him. I'm writing his biography."

Paul nodded. "Are you speaking to his family?"

Nick chuckled. "There aren't many left, after the war," he said. "One of his great quotes was 'Family come first, but Nation before that'."

"He sounds like the sort of pleasant, even-handed liberal we'd like to have running Kosovo in the future," Paul said.

Nick lowered his voice. "Don't joke. The man's photo is in every house you visit."

"Sorry."

The coffee arrived and Paul panicked that the waiter may have overheard him. He placed a five deutschmark note on the tray hoping to secure some loyalty.

"So what have you got? When is this thing you mentioned happening?" asked Aden.

Paul placed a palm down on either thigh.

"I've got a problem," he said. "I told my masters that I wanted to bring you along. At first they said yes, what a great idea. And that's when I told you it could happen. Now they're saying I can't do it."

"Why?"

Paul shrugged. "Because of some of the units involved."

Aden's face lit up. "You've called in the SAS!"

Paul nodded slowly, then, "I regret that I cannot confirm or deny rumours about the presence of D Squadron in Pristina. And I can't take you out to watch the operation."

He said nothing more. Nick and Aden looked at each other.

Aden said, "Who's going to be arrested, Paul?"

Paul shook his head. "I don't know yet."

"But it's more than just a guy who pressed the switch on the bomb?"

Paul shook his head. "I couldn't possibly comment."

"What time and where?"

"Tomorrow morning, I don't know."

"Can you brief us afterwards?"

"Definitely. A full brief. In my office. Before the UN press conference on Thursday."

"Can you do that?"

"Sure," said Paul. "It's a British operation; I can say what I like." And then his masterstroke. "And if you can promise me that you won't dob me in, I might bring a friend here for a drink, tomorrow night, who could tell you more than I ever could. Off the record. No photos. No names. No one gets hurt."

"You bet," said Aden.

"We can do that," said Nick.

* * *

Rolly was in camp seeing the Brigadier. Through the window of the Press Office Paul watched him enter the headquarters building, then watched him leave half an hour later. He was in combats but without a beret or badges on his uniform. The signallers at the gate looked like they were going to salute, but didn't.

Seeing him stroll towards the cookhouse, Paul opened the door to the Press Office. "Rolly!"

Rolly turned, waved, and walked over. Once inside, he slumped onto the sofa. "Matey, London are saying you're trying to put me on the front pages. You trying to do for me or what?"

"Just a bit of psychological warfare, that's all."

Rolly lifted a boot to rest on the coffee table. "And I also hear CJO wants to have your Brigadier's head on a plate."

Paul shook his head. "Mate, I've had good leaders and bad leaders in the regiment. You know who I mean. But that Brigadier is a fucking star."

Rolly said nothing, looking round the room.

"I can believe that. And CJO is a cock."

Paul put his hands in his pockets and rolled his shoulders backwards. "Rolly, I've a favour to ask," he said.

* * *

The alarm went off at four. Paul woke immediately, eyes wide. He'd slept all night and was ready for what he had to do.

In the Operations Room, the Watchkeeper had drawn a grid on a whiteboard. Down the left hand column were listed four targets for arrest, each identified by a code name: Pear, Apple, Banana, and Tomato. The staff officers took their usual seats in silence, fitted headphones and typed passwords.

Blanche was sitting on the Watchkeeper's desk, drinking a cup of coffee, legs dangling over the side.

"You been up all night?" asked Paul.

She nodded, blowing across the top of the mug. Paul touched her elbow.

"Is the Commander ok?"

She made a see-saw nod of her head.

"It'll be good," Paul said. "We'll get them."

She almost smiled. "Where are you going?" she asked.

Paul swallowed. This was his big test. "I'm going out on the ground to be at the radio stations if they ring me. In case anyone sees anything and calls in." He held her eyes, but she looked too tired to care and didn't challenge him further.

In the central square, Seagood had the Landrover prepared. She was bouncy, far too much for that time of the morning. She grinned, and turned the steering from side to side as Paul got in beside her.

"This is so cool..."

In the back, her rifle was locked into the weapon mount. Paul patted the heavy holster under his left armpit and then the camera bag in the foot well. These were his weapons of choice for the day: a telephoto lens, a quick mind, a sharp tongue.

"Where to, Sir? Are we picking up Roza?"

"If anyone asks, that is exactly what we are doing. But first of all we're going to a place by the airport. I'll direct you. Let's go."

Seagood pulled out, the engine coughing. It was cold without a jacket, but as soon as the sun rose it would become one of those dusty, baking, Kosovo days. The tyres made a high pitched hum on the tarmac as they sped along the empty ring road. The city seemed to know something was happening.

His phone rang. It was Nick.

"Paul, I didn't think you'd be up. I was going to leave a message."

"Always awake for you, Nick. What's happened?"

"The Serbian government have arrested Slobodan Milosevic. There was a shootout at his villa in Belgrade, but a SWAT team took him into custody."

"Fucking excellent," said Paul.

Nick laughed. "Is that your official response?"

Paul chuckled. "No, a personal one. Are you wanting a statement?"

"Yes, I do. On the record."

With the phone held to his ear by his shoulder, Paul pulled out a notebook and pen. "How about this: 'All NATO Forces are committed to building peace and stability in Kosovo and throughout the Balkans. We applaud the decision by President Kostunica to arrest former President Slobodan Milosevic and hope he will now send him for trial at the International Criminal Tribunal on Yugoslavia'. Will that do?"

The Landrover slowed as it approached the traffic lights on the Mitrovica Road. There was no other vehicle at the junction and Seagood stopped, looked left and right, then drove through the red lights. Paul frowned at her. His look made her giggle.

"Sorry Sir," she whispered.

Nick spoke in his ear. "They've not sent him to the Criminal Court. They've just arrested him. His supporters are rioting outside his house. There's a rumour his daughter's been killed."

"I'm not in the office, Nick, so I'm speaking blind. If you remove the clause you don't like, will that do as a quote?"

"It's good. Can you be that assertive, really? Are you driving?"

"You'll get more information later, Nick," said Paul, then closed the phone down.

His mind was ablaze. This was excellent news. Why had Kostunica chosen this moment to arrest Milosevic? Paul didn't know, but he could use it. This was more than the law being done. This was morality in action. He shouldn't really make statements about international events without consulting Brassy and Major Breitman, but he didn't care. This was going to be his day.

"Next left, then slow down. Stop by those trees."

Seagood parked the Landrover behind a thin bank of silver birches along the side of a cornfield. The airport was about half a mile away. The tail fin of a Hercules was silhouetted against the lightening sky. Along the lane was a small warehouse with a carpark in front of it and a residential property to one side.

"Lights out!" hissed Paul. To get to the locations he'd agreed with Rolly, close enough to use the camera but not so close as to fuck the operation up, he'd have to approach on foot.

He gave Seagood a sharp order. "Engine off. No light, no sound. You understand?"

He had never given her orders in such a manner before. She pulled a face but sat very still, both hands on the wheel, shoulders braced backwards.

Easing the door open, Paul slid out and pulled the camera strap free of the seatbelt. He then pressed rather than shoved the door to close it. He had his beret on with a silver badge, and no camouflage cream. He'd better be careful or he'd look a fool.

Using trees for cover, he walked on the outside edges of his feet to silence the tread. At the edge of the factory carpark, he stopped.

Along the wall, two cars were parked nose in. To the right of these, and recessed into the wall, was a wooden doorway. Paul wanted to get closer, but a movement off to the right told him to stay still. He knelt, listening.

Sliding the power switch for the camera, he became conscious of the light emitted by the screen. He pulled it against his chest to smother it.

A muffled explosion came from inside the residential compound. He looked round, but couldn't see anything. A dog barked aggressively, then yelped.

An engine roared somewhere off to his right. Lights came on. A van drove at speed into the carpark and skidded to a halt. The side door opened and two men got out, taking fire positions either side of the recessed doorway. Both were masked and had short barrelled weapons held at shoulder height.

Peeking through the fluttering leaves of a birch, Paul raised the camera to his eye and pressed the shutter switch.

Shouts from within. The doorway opened from inside. There were lights inside the compound making for a perfect silhouette. A man, bound and hooded, was pushed out of the doorway to fall onto his face. The two men outside the door picked him up by the arms and bundled him into the van.

"Gotcha," Paul said, shooting off as many shots as he could before the van sped off. "That's Pear. Now let's get Banana."

* * *

At nine o'clock, the mood in the Operations Room was tense. The Brigadier was trying to look calm, but he kept stroking his fingers with his thumb, an action Paul had not seen him do before.

The Watchkeeper was updating the whiteboard. She had drawn a line through the words 'Pear' and 'Banana' and stood with her hands resting on the back of a chair, a red marker sticking out between her fingers.

Blanche opened the door that lead to the briefing room. "Apple," she said, smiling at the Brigadier, and the room erupted into applause. She then whispered in Simon's ear. She had showered and changed since Paul saw her earlier. He may not like her, but he could not help respecting her cold determination.

They had got three of the support network, but *Tomato* was still to be found.

Paul stood half way down the room leaning against the wall. Simon saw him and flicked his head towards the door. Paul went outside and waited.

"Where've you been?" said Simon.

Paul shrugged. "Out on the ground in case the radio stations called me about Milosevic's arrest."

Simon looked suspicious.

"Nick Oakeshot rang me at five looking for a statement. How's the Commander? Has the Bunker been on the phone yet?"

Simon shook his head. "No, they've not. But it's early. They will."

"So do I go public now, or wait till we get Tomato?"

"We wait, Paul. We wait."

* * *

It was ten o'clock. Paul sat in the Press Office with Seagood on the sofa. They didn't talk.

Roza knocked on the door and entered. Her face was radiant. "They have arrested him!" she said. "They have arrested Milosevic!"

Paul nodded. "Yes. And we will be talking to all the radio stations today, Roza. It's going to be busy."

There was something in his voice that told her he was hiding something.

"What is it?" she said. "What you not tell me?"

Paul stood up and shoved his hands deep into the pockets of his smock.

"There's a big operation today, Roza. We're going to arrest some bad people."

Roza frowned. Her eyes flitted between his. She looked hurt.

"Why you not tell me? I could have been here? I could have had time to prepare…"

Paul placed a hand on her shoulder. "This is absolutely no reflection on you. But the people we are looking for…"

Roza placed her hands over her nose. "It is the bus. Anja…"

Paul nodded. She was very quick.

"There are four of them. We have got three so far, but the last one is the one we want most."

"The one she calls 'the hunter'."

Paul nodded. Roza looked angry.

"I couldn't tell you. It was secret," he said.

"But you can trust me."

"I know I can, Roza. It's just…"

"Just what?" A splurge of blood pumped into her neck, colouring the skin.

"I'm sorry, Roza..." There was nothing he could say really. She was an Albanian civilian. No matter how much they liked each other, there was no way he could let her in on Brigade plans.

The phone rang.

"Paul, it's Aden. Any news?"

"Not yet. Are you in Pristina or have you been asked to go to Belgrade."

"I'm going up tomorrow. I've told my desk I should stay here to see your mate tonight. Otherwise I'd be up there now. So is it happening?"

"It'll happen, Aden. I promise. I'll be at the Grand later."

The tension knotted inside him. He paced around the office. When the main news came on, he watched the scenes of Milosevic's arrest: men in black jackets and jeans firing shots by a metal gate, then the sudden rush and shout of capture. In another clip, a large crowd threw stones at government buildings. The police, in riot gear, withdrew under their assault.

"He still has many supporters," Paul said. "I thought he was unpopular."

Roza shook her head. "Very bad man," she said.

* * *

The Brigadier was no longer in the Operations Room. In fact, there was a cold, depressed air among the staff. The phones were not ringing, and everyone was sombre.

Paul pointed at the door to the Briefing Room. The Watchkeeper shook her head. "Don't disturb the Commander, Sir. But the Chief of Staff's in his office."

Paul went through, and found the Brigadier and Blanche in Simon's office. His face was long.

"I think I should go out anyway," Paul said, "to Radio Black Eagle at least. I can use Milosevic's arrest as my evidence for the rule of law. Even if we don't find Tomato, we got three others. We should say *something*."

Blanche immediately shook her head. "If you say we've made arrests, Tomato will run to ground."

Paul shrugged. "Maybe. It depends how it's done. We could also flush him out. Spread misinformation. How close to him are you? Do you have eyes on?"

It had been a question too far. Simon looked at him and shook his head. "We can't say. And everyone's a bit highly strung. But you should go and talk to people. At the very least, make an assessment of what they are saying about events in Belgrade."

"But if you find him, you'll tell me? I really need to know."

"I'll call you," Simon said.

That was enough. Paul thanked them and left.

***

At Radio Black Eagle, Paul reached out to shake Elire's hand. Her fierce eyes held him firm.

"So, Major Pol. What is it I hear about some loyal members of the Kosovo Security Corps being arrested in the night time?"

Paul shook his head and smiled. "I know nothing about that, Elire. I'll check back at camp and ask, if you like?"

He hadn't warned Roza how to handle Elire, but hoped she'd take his lead.

"So it is true?" Elire said, folding her arms and cocking one foot on the stiletto heel of her shoe.

"Is what true? I was expecting to talk about Milosevic. I'd like to have a chat about the rule of law; how even former presidents must answer to it."

Elire scoffed. "Come on, Pol! The reason Kostunica make him arrest is because Mister Clinton say he cut aid for Serbia people. It is bribe."

Paul had not seen it that way.

"You do not understand," Elire said. "This is business. America wants Milosevic to go to ICTY. Kostunica wants money."

"I think there's more to it than that. It's about proving..."

Elire made a dismissive wave of her hand. "Yes, sure. Big ideas. But mainly money. In Balkans, money is most important thing behind ethnic city."

Paul smiled. "I thought it was family."

Elire looked surprised that he'd know so much after only a few months. She was about to say something else when Paul's phone rang.

Simon's voice: "Tomato. Now knock 'em out."

Paul clicked the phone.

"Actually, Elire, there was something else I wanted to talk about. I have a statement I'd like to read when you next do a news broadcast. Will that be on the hour, or would you like to do it now?"

They were playing *Rio* by Duran Duran.

"We do it now," said Elire.

* * *

It was dusk before Paul and Roza got back to camp after all the interviews. The sinking sun threw orange and pink splashes across the horizon.

Radio Black Eagle had been the most aggressive after he'd read the statement. Elire demanded to know why the arrests had taken place. Did NATO not trust the Kosovo Security Corps? Did Paul know that these men were all heroes who fought against Serb oppression?

At Radio Rilindja the interviewer was a woman with thick glasses and a floating, sensuous way of walking. Paul watched with amusement as Roza bristled. The interview was a joy. Paul must have mentioned the phrases 'rule of law,' 'multi-ethnic,' and 'peace and stability' a dozen times.

Radio Gracanica had not started as easily as he had expected. He thought Stefan would revel in the news of the operation but found he was nervous. He asked if the

Albanians would make reprisal attacks? Were Serbian people safe?

Paul explained calmly that the arrest of the bombers, and of Milosevic, was a good thing.

"It's the law reaching out its long hand, Stefan. Kosovo must be safe for all its people. Serbia must show it can behave as a modern state."

Despite his fears, Stefan agreed. "Oh yes," he said. "This is wonderful, really wonderful." Then, live on air, he said something in English he had written down on a piece of paper. "We the Serbian people of Gracanica wish to thank the Major for helping to bring justice to our land."

At the end of the interview, as they scraped their chairs on the tiles, he was almost in tears. Bowing, he took Paul's hand and kissed it.

The gesture silenced Paul completely. These villages were so totally dependent on what he represented.

In camp, Seagood spun the Landrover round to halt next to the Operations Room. "There you go, Sir."

"Thanks, Seagood. But I'll be going out into town again in a bit. You'll drop me off and then collect me later."

"Ok. Shall I take Roza home, Sir?"

Standing by the door, Paul peered round into the back of the vehicle.

Roza shook her head. "It's ok. I wait for you."

"You sure?"

"I am sure. I wait."

Paul met her eyes. "Roza, we've delivered some very difficult messages today. There are people who don't think NATO are neutral. And who think we will…"

"I know it, Zotëri Major. It was good today. You were very strong."

The empty longing kicked at his insides. If only they could be having this conversation without Seagood present.

Roza said, "I am very happy to be doing this. For you."

Such an addendum. It made his stomach contract.

"You can take me home later. When you go out," she said.

And at that moment, Paul realised what she was saying. He hoped Seagood could not tell, from listening to their voices, of the spark between them.

"Be ready in an hour," he said.

In the Brigadier's office Paul found him sharing a bottle of local red wine with Simon and Blanche.

"Drinking on duty?" Paul laughed. He saluted and then stepped over Blanche's legs to shake the Brigadier by the hand. "I just thought you should know, Sir, that I had a Serbian journalist crying when I told him the news about the bombers' arrest. I can't describe how powerful it's been. The roads are empty throughout the city. The shops are closed. And the female population of Gracanica want to have your babies."

The Brigadier's face broadened into a grin as he extended his long arms sideways in an expansive gesture. "And there's validation," he said. "Who needs a word of thanks from CJO? These are the people that matter."

Paul winked at Simon, who nodded back. "Thanks for everything you've done, Paul. It's been down to you that this whole enterprise can be called a success. They now know that we stand for law and order and that we're neutral. We couldn't have got that message out without your contacts."

"It was good, even if I say so myself." Paul nodded. "I'm still buzzing from the interviews…"

"What is the public mood?" asked the Brigadier.

Paul rolled his beret up in one hand. "I think we hit them in just the right way. The liberal people will know it's right. The Serbs are overjoyed, although nervous of reprisals. And the nationalists? Well, let's just say they've been taught a lesson."

Simon's smile broadened. "What a great day!"

Paul looked from one to the other, but since the bottle of wine was almost finished, he decided he'd said what he needed.

"If you don't mind, I've been up since three."

Blanche cast him an evil look. Her eyes were sunken. She'd probably had three hours sleep in the past forty-eight, and the Brigadier even less.

"You get yourself to bed, Paul. And thank you for an excellent day," said Simon. He had a rucksack at his feet, with another bottle poking out the top.

"Where are you going?" asked Paul.

Simon shrugged. "The SAS have invited us to a celebratory barbecue at their compound. It seems there's a bit of rivalry between the teams who did the arrests.

"How so?"

Simon chuckled, and made a sly glance at the Brigadier. "I'll tell you later," he said.

Paul nodded. If he wasn't in the circle for this one, it didn't matter. Rolly would tell him.

The Brigadier got to his feet and extended a hand. "It has been a good day, Paul. I want you to know that I greatly appreciate the way you do things. It has been noted."

* * *

In the press office, Rolly was ready on the red sofa, knees apart, reading a magazine. He'd washed and shaved and his hair was brushed back in a casual manner that made it look perfectly unkempt. Seagood was sitting beside him. Paul had to smile at the sly glances she was casting in his direction.

A man Paul didn't know was standing in the middle of the floor, arms folded, noisily chewing gum and watching the television. He was short, square shouldered, and bald. He wore a tight tee-shirt, belted jeans, and desert boots. In the back of his jeans was a pistol. When Paul entered, he twisted round on his heels, summed Paul up in a second, and turned back to the television.

"Paul, this is Manny. He's coming with me."

"Good. Ready now?"

Seagood leaped up and grabbed the vehicle wallet from the coffee table. She smiled at Paul like a child smiles at their parent when they don't know anyone else at a party. "Roza's in her hut. Shall I meet you outside, Sir?"

After she'd gone, Paul shook Rolly's hand. "Well done. A good lift?"

Rolly was being ostentatiously casual about it all. "Yeah, you know."

Paul said, "It was a bit tense here until you got the last one."

Manny snorted a laugh and shook his head. "Utter fuckup," he said, exuding the sort of energy that told Paul he'd never understand.

"Got your story straight?" said Paul.

"Matey," said Rolly, "there's no way we're going to tell the truth; that's one thing for certain."

* * *

Mother Teresa Street was empty. In fact the whole city was unusually quiet for a Friday night. There were some bars open, but not many people in them.

Rolly had taken the front passenger seat of the Landrover, leaving Paul, Manny, and Roza to sit in the back. Paul felt the pressure of Roza's hip against his, and how she used the turns to amplify the contact. He didn't stop her, and Manny was too focused on the road to notice.

At the Grand Hotel, they all got out. Manny pulled his tee-shirt out of his jeans to hide his weapon. Rolly was wearing a collared shirt, and did the same for the same reason.

Seagood shouted out from inside the vehicle. "What time, Sir?" She was blocking the entrance to the hotel and wanted to get out of the way.

"Be here at ten," Paul said, raising his eyebrows at Rolly. That would give them two hours.

"Ought to be enough," said Rolly. "Once we're done here we should get back to the compound."

Manny sniggered, but did not meet anyone's eyes.

Seagood left and Paul indicated the doorway. "Shall we?"

Roza touched his arm, her face a question. He winked at her, placing a hand in the small of her back. "Come have a drink."

The lobby was empty save for a woman in a red waistcoat behind the reception desk and a man who looked very drunk indeed, standing by himself, almost asleep on his feet. Rolly and Manny spread out, eyeing spaces on the right and left.

Following a short, dark corridor, they found the bar, a plush affair of mood lighting, cocktails, and spotlights. The circular tables were enclosed within booths and occupied by the same barrel-chested businessmen that usually occupied the lobby. This time they had company.

From the far corner, Aden waved. Sitting next to him, Nick looked like an awkward uncle in white socks and comfortable shoes. Manny and Rolly did a visual sweep of the room, then slid out of the lit area as Paul went to shake the two journalists' hands.

"This is Rolly and Manny. They'll tell you what they can, but please don't press it. If you do, they'll just leave. And it goes without saying that I expect good coverage out of this."

Nick was shaking Rolly's hand. "You don't have to worry there, Paul. The election back home will be announced soon. With Milosevic being arrested in Belgrade, there would be no point writing a critical article. No editor would publish it."

The idea that they had to write what was popular was news to Paul, especially from someone as principled as Nick.

Nick shrugged. "We all have to be mindful of what the public wants."

The four men settled down, Manny insisting on sitting where he could face the door. Nick and Aden shuffled round to the back of the booth.

"Shall I get drinks?" Paul suggested. "Or leave you to it? I need to walk Roza home, but then I'll come back."

"I've got this," said Aden. "The beers are on *The Sunday Times*." He turned to Rolly, his face like a child's. "So did you find the bombers?"

"We did," said Paul, quickly. And I've also got some photos for you, which I'll give you when I come back.

He threw a glance at Rolly, who nodded. He left them all to it.

"Why are you laughing?" whispered Roza as they walked out of the bar.

"I can't wait to read what they tell them," he chuckled, then once again placed a hand in the small of her back, letting it slip down to the top of her jeans once they were in the dark corridor. He removed it as they walked through the lobby, then replaced it again once they were outside.

"Where do you live?"

"This way. You come with me?"

She tugged at a strand of hair that had got caught in her lips. She was as nervous as he was.

"Is it a good idea?"

She looked down.

"I want to show you my home."

"You father is there? Your brother?"

"No," she said. "I am alone."

She smiled then, and Paul felt strangled. His desire and his duty were pulling in opposite directions. His hands shook. How stupid was this?

"Take me," he said, and walked beside her in silence round the block and down a narrow street. Roza kept her eyes on the pavement, neither looking up nor at him.

Paul's wiser self told him to see her to the door and then turn back. His lusting self knew he had an undisturbed hour.

"This is it," she said, indicating a block of flats.

A white concrete wall was daubed in political graffiti. The letters 'UCK' were everywhere. The external concrete steps were a dull grey. Roza took each one slowly, scraping her feet as she did so. He followed close behind, her bottom just in front of his face. He could reach out and touch it.

As they turned the corner of the stairs, Paul took her hand. The skin was warm. On the landing, she turned.

"We must be quiet," she whispered. She unlocked the external door and pulled it slowly, making sure it did not squeak. Paul slid in behind her, finding himself in a narrow corridor with blinking strip lights.

Roza walked smartly away, twirling a set of keys in her hand. He watched her. She stopped and turned. "Come," she said, and selected a key to unlock the door to her flat.

He followed her inside. The room was lit by a desk lamp. The smell of spices hung in the air. A deep sofa was covered by a sheepskin throw. Roza sat down to pull off her shoes, but he did not copy her.

"This is lovely, Roza," he said. "It's very cosy."

Above the archway into the kitchenette, a photo of a large bearded man carrying a machine gun over his shoulder was set within a thin frame. Below it was a quotation Paul could not read.

"My uncle," she said. "My mother's uncle."

"He is famous, Roza, this man?" Paul asked.

"Yes. The Serbian army kill him at the start of the war. He was in *oochaka*, Liberation Army."

She went to the fridge and poured herself a glass of water from a plastic container. She looked nervous.

Paul's heart was racing. "I have heard of him," he said. "Very brave man."

Roza looked at him.

"I didn't know you were related." Paul said. "You never mentioned it."

Roza brought him a glass of water and stood very close to him. He took the glass. To the right of the archway was a low cabinet made of veneered wood. Paul picked up a framed family photograph, Roza surrounded by older men and women.

"Look at you!" Paul said. She was perhaps sixteen years old, and camera shy. She slouched with her arms folded.

"So where is your cousin? Mimi, the one who…"

Roza took the photo from him. "She is not in this one," she said, then took hold of his hands and led him to the sofa.

He sat down to unlace his boots and placed the glass on the floor. She stood in front of him, her hands on his shoulders.

He took hold of one wrist. She stroked his head with her other hand, feeling round his skull. Then she placed her palm against his cheek.

She sat astride him, pulled herself towards him, and placed her mouth over his. After a long and expert kiss, she said, "I am giving you myself, Zotëri Major."

The hollowness inside him made Paul desperate. His mind ached. He wanted her in a way he had wanted no other woman. She was so lovely, so trustworthy.

But he forced her backwards off his knees.

"I can't! Don't you understand? I want to. But I can't!"

The Sunday Times, 15 July 2001
SAS Capture Balkans Bus Bombers
Aden Short in Pristina and the Staff Editor in London

Soldiers from D Squadron, 22 SAS based in Hereford were responsible for the dramatic arrest of four men responsible for the brutal killing of twelve ethnic Serbians in February this year.

The night time assault, nicknamed Operation Fruit Salad, brings to a close the tragedy of many Serbian families bereaved by the terrible events when Albanian terrorists planted a road side bomb that destroyed a bus of Serbians in Northern Kosovo...

PART FOUR

Chapter 12

Brassy was incandescent. "Did I not explicitly tell you not to use the SAS?"

"You did, Colonel."

"We neither confirm nor deny the presence of Special Forces. Ever. You do know that, don't you?"

"Yes, Colonel."

"Then why did you? It's of strategic importance to keep the mystique."

"It wasn't me."

Brassy was astounded. "Who else could it have been?"

"No idea. But it wasn't me. These journalists have their own networks, you know. Inside the SAS."

"So you're denying it?" His breathing was angry down the phone.

"Completely!" Paul said in a high voice. He wanted to sound put out. Brassy was insulting his integrity.

On the red sofa, Seagood was reading the Daily Express. On the front page was a picture of Lady Diana. She wasn't listening to his conversation and even if she was, Brassy would never ask her what she knew.

"I don't believe you, Paul."

"I'm very sorry to hear it. But it still wasn't me. Are you getting your ear chewed by the Chief?"

"No, I'm not," Brassy snorted. He said nothing for a while, and Paul waited for him to soften. "Fortunately, the coverage was favourably received by Number 10. It makes the country look strong, projecting force in this way."

"Really?" said Paul, drawing out the word. "Just before an election, and purdah starts, there's a headline that announces we are a powerful force for good in one of the shittiest corners of the world?"

"That's all very well, but..."

"It's almost as if someone planned it," said Paul in a wistful manner.

Brassy exhaled angrily. "You were lucky. But if they'd failed, or if the journalists had gone to press too early..."

"Like I said, Colonel, where that story came from, I have no idea. Try asking the SAS."

Brassy made a grumpy noise in the back of his throat.

Paul said, "Is the coverage good? Are there graphics?"

Despite himself, Brassy smothered a chuckle. "Yes, there's a fantastical diagram of how the operation was conducted."

Paul laughed. "Is there a guy abseiling out of a helicopter?"

"Off the side of a building."

"Is there a little explosion against the wall?"

"Yes."

"And is there, like, six stages or something described in detail down the side."

The paper must be open on his desk. "Seven."

Paul laughed, full throated, then controlled his mirth. "Fax it through? That's how you know it wasn't me. In truth, the last guy, Tomato, was only captured because one of the infantry patrols turned up by accident."

"What on earth do you mean?"

"A little bird told me. The SAS fucked it right up. They got the right car, and shot out the tyres, but it was armour plated and they couldn't open the doors. Tomato was inside but didn't surrender."

Paul chuckled, finding Rolly's humiliation a cause for personal amusement.

"But the SAS only had shotguns. Nothing could shatter the windows. Tomato kept driving on his rims and they couldn't stop him. They only flipped the car when an infantry unit arrived with a Landrover."

Brassy said nothing. It sounded like he was alternating between laughing and being angry. "That's not what they told CJO. And I still think you're lying about the publicity."

"Come on, Colonel! Why let the truth get in the way of a good story?"

"I'd ask you not to take me for a fool, Paul."

He'd gone too far. "I'm not, Colonel," he stammered. "I genuinely did not have anything to do with that story. But the fact that it got global publicity is something I can use."

"Not with the internationals you won't."

"So the election's been announced?"

"Yes. One month's time."

"But I can still speak to the locals?"

"Yes. But you may not brief Short or Oakeshot on anything."

"Very good," said Paul, and clicked the red button.

Lying was becoming easier by the day. But it didn't matter when it was for the greater good.

* * *

After his weekly interview with Radio Rilindja, Paul rang Aden to ask if he was free to meet at the hotel.

"Sure, my friend," the journalist said, "I need to show you something anyway."

Seagood dropped him off at the entrance and said she'd park up nearby.

"Thirty minutes," Paul said.

"Are you going to get Roza, Sir?" she said, a smile on her face.

"No. Why would I?"

Her smile disappeared. "No reason, sorry," she said, and Paul slammed the door. If Roza had been blabbing, he'd look a complete tit. He wasn't going to have the equivalent of a private knowing his business. He was way too important to have that hanging over him.

Inside, the lobby was as busy as Paul had ever seen it. He had to walk round a party of Russians, and another of Chinese, before he found Aden. Sitting at the back, the correspondent had his hair tied up in a ponytail.

"It's the assembly election," Aden said. "All sorts of wheeler-dealing."

He smoked with quick, jerky movements. He rolled the end of his cigarette against the side of the ashtray to keep the ash short.

"Great article," Paul said. "The Prime Minister loved it."

Aden chuckled. "Cool! But so you know, I had nothing to do with the graphics. That's all done in London."

"It was great, Aden. Really good reporting. And you enjoyed the chat with my mate?"

Aden nodded. "Yeah! They were really cool guys. It was a good facility you laid on there, Paul. Just the sort of access we should be getting."

Praise indeed, from such a seasoned reporter. Paul really was the best. In fact, he was only just hitting his stride. If a small white lie could produce such an outcome, what could he do if he tried to be really devious?

"But please. Not a word to anyone," Paul said. "I'd be in the shit."

Aden winked and tapped the side of his nose. "I never reveal a source," he said.

Paul nodded. He trusted him. "So what did you want to show me?"

Aden stubbed out the cigarette and cast a sly glance round the room. He slid a hand into his rucksack and pulled out two rolled-up newspapers.

"That's Albanian," said Paul, unrolling one onto the table. "But this isn't a Pristina paper. Where's it from?"

On the front page was a picture of a man who had been shot dead. He lay on his back next to a white car. One arm was extended to the left, the fingers curling slightly. In the background, armed police in helmets and body armour adopted fire positions round his body.

"Where is it?"

Aden shook his head. "It's Tetovo. Northern Macedonia. There's a growing Albanian insurgency, the next place it has spread to. That's what I wanted to show you."

He unrolled the other newspaper and placed it on top of the first. This one had a more broadsheet look to it. The photo was the same, but smaller. The text was Cyrillic.

"This is in Serbian." said Paul.

"Macedonian. The Albanians you kicked out of Presevo, they've moved south, to Macedonia. They attacked a police station on Saturday and killed a man. Now the Macedonian government are sending in the military."

"Is that the policeman?"

"No, he's a guy trying to throw grenades at the police. Have a look at the photos again."

Paul did, and then he saw it. In the Serbian broadsheet photo, something small and cylindrical lay next to the outstretched hand. In the tabloid photo, the object had been airbrushed out.

"Cheeky fuckers."

"This paper, with the grenade removed, is for the Albanians around Tetovo." He pulled out the second paper and slapped it down over the first. "This one is from Skopje."

"It's for the Macedonians."

Aden nodded. "The war's not finished, Paul. The Albanians didn't get NATO to help them win Presevo, so they're now after Tetovo. But the Macedonian government has deployed a mechanised brigade to crush them."

Paul looked at him. "I can't comment on the actions of the FYROM government, Aden. It's outside my scope. We're not involved there."

Aden rolled up the two newspapers and handed them to Paul. "You are involved. Your supply convoys come up from Skopje and the Greek coast. You need Macedonia."

Paul saw what he was saying. "We'll have to support them, even if that means operating against the Albanians?"

Aden nodded. "Which may cost you some loyalty here in Kosovo."

The two men looked at each other. Paul leaned on his knees. "Clever doctoring of that photo. It makes it look like he was killed for no reason."

Aden nodded. "That's the sort of war this is becoming. And for a journalist, that makes it all the more important that you tell the truth. We trust you, Paul. We know you're honest."

* * *

There was no time to waste. Balkan people only respected force. He had to make the point that the function of the press was to report the truth. To distort events was not just incorrect, it was immoral. His next interviews with the radio stations would focus on the doctored photos and he would drag up case studies from Sierra Leone and Rwanda to make his point.

Sitting at the computer late on Wednesday night, words flew from his fingertips. He knocked out page after page of argument and indignation. When he eventually dried up, he sat back and interlaced his fingers behind his head to look at the two pictures he had got from Aden, which he had cut out and tacked to the wall by his desk.

If he could get the press to report accurately, then how the population behaved would surely follow. Or to put it another way, if he wanted to influence how the population behaved, he had to be certain that the press was accurate in its reporting.

He was about to watch the news when the door opened. It was Roza, peeking round to see if he was alone. She entered uncertainly.

"Roza, I'm working on something."

She swallowed, but still approached to stand close enough for her hip to touch his elbow. "I have not seen you," she said. "After you come to my house, you have not been talking to me."

Paul took the ends of her fingers, then remembered to pull down the blind on the window.

"I couldn't. I've been very busy, that's all. Are you ok?"

She nodded, but her lip quivered.

"Look, I'm sorry. But I couldn't... You know there are rules."

She nodded, licking her lips with the tip of her tongue. She leaned forward and kissed him. Her hand was cold on his cheek.

"I had to do that," she said, lifting a knee to rest on the triangle of chair between his legs. Paul placed his hands on her hips.

"And I want it," Paul said. "But not here. You'll lose your job. As will I."

She must know he was right, but for a moment he was afraid she was too immature to recognise it. He interlaced his fingers into hers, studying how the tendons ran over the knuckles.

Her mouth wavered, but then she smiled. Her blouse was tight across her chest.

He said, "I rely on you totally. You do know that, don't you?"

"I know," she said, then extricated her fingers from his to walk across the office floor and sit on the red sofa. She put her feet on the edge of the coffee table, knees pressed together, hands on thighs. "I sit here and watch you," she said.

She really was quite lovely.

Paul smiled as he reached for the mouse. "I'm writing about press integrity," he said, sending the document for printing. "Tell me if this will work in Albanian."

"Okey-dokey," she replied, rising to get the document from the printer before he did.

As she set about reading it, he cleared his way through a few emails then decided that was enough. It was nine o'clock. In his bottom drawer was a half-finished bottle of wine. He dug it out, pulled out the cork, and waved it to offer some to Roza. She shook her head.

He watched how she hooked her hair round her ears and followed the text with one finger. He rose from the desk and joined her on the sofa.

"Shift up," he said, sitting close enough to fill his nostrils with her perfume. Roza giggled as he used his hips to edge her along. "So what do you think?"

"I like it, Zotëri Major," she said. "I like it very much."

"What do you like?"

"I like how you say the press have duty."

"You agree with that?"

"Oh yes, very much." She was silent for a while, then, "during the war there were many rumours. People saying many things, some are true, some are not. It makes people afraid."

Paul nodded to encourage her. He was too close for her to face him. He placed a hand on her shoulder. She did not shake him off, so he extended one finger to stroke the skin behind her ear.

"What are you thinking about?" she said.

He did not know how to answer. Would he tell her the truth?

"Nothing," he said at last.

Even if they managed to get over the security issues, it would never work. Susan had left him because he was away all the time. His tour of Kosovo would end in a couple of months. She would soon have to face the fact that he was leaving. He couldn't even speak a word of her language.

"You seem sad," she said, placing a hand on his thigh.

"Not sad," he replied. "Just thinking, that's all. Missed opportunities."

The skin of her face had tanned into a rich oak colour. She shuffled a little away from him so she could turn more. She took his hand. "First time, I learn English with a cartoon," she said.

Paul smiled. "A cartoon?"

"I want you to learn Albanian." she said. "I buy one for you. Then we read it and you translate."

Paul frowned. Had she known what he was thinking? Was that not a sign? His heart thumped in his chest. "In here, every evening?"

"Yes," she said.

* * *

That was the thing about war, its central paradox. For most of the time it was more peaceful than peace itself. People made friends quickly, ate quickly, fell in love quickly. They talked only of issues that mattered: food, fresh water, who could be trusted and who could not. The domestic concerns of peacetime – soap operas, shopping, celebrities – were meaningless.

Walking across the central square of the camp, Paul looked at the distant building that had once housed the Serbian army. Targeted by precision munitions during the war, it slumped down at one end as if drunk, all five storeys collapsed on the one below. The explosion must have been a sight to behold.

Paul entered the Chief of Staff's office and saluted. Simon and the Brigadier were studying a map on the wall. They had placed pins along the boundary between Kosovo and the Former Yugoslav Republic of Macedonia.

Blanche was sitting on the other side of the room, reading a file and chewing the side of her forefinger. She looked up briefly, then went back to her reading.

"The journalists tell me there's a mechanised brigade moving north from Skopje to reinforce the police around Tetovo," Paul said. "The Albanian extremists are the same ones that were in the Presevo Valley. The Macedonians are going in hard."

The Brigadier and Simon looked over their shoulders to listen.

Paul continued, "They think NATO will have to join them in fighting the Albanians around Tetovo because we need the main supply routes up from Thessaloniki and Tirana."

The Brigadier and Simon looked at each other.

"That's certainly the risk," the Brigadier said. "But you have more pressing things to worry about at the moment. How are you getting on with the weapons amnesty?"

Paul said, "We've got three-hundred rifles of varying ages. I'd like to hit a thousand before the assembly elections. I've spoken to my equivalent in the American brigade. He works at their headquarters in Bondsteel."

Paul pointed at the American flag in the south-eastern side of Kosovo.

"He's had about six weapons handed in since June."

"Six!" said Simon.

Paul nodded. "They're nowhere near us. In fact, I was going to go down there, with your permission, Sir. I want to touch base with him about the assembly election."

The Brigadier frowned. "Isn't that the job of the NATO press office, to co-ordinate between the brigades?"

"It is, Sir," Paul replied. "But the NATO spokesman's another American. He's called Breitman. The press call him *Eighty-five*." He paused and smiled. "That's their estimation of his IQ."

Simon and the Brigadier spluttered into laughter.

Simon said, "Actually, Sir, it'd not be a bad idea if Paul was to make friends down there." He tapped the map with a finger. "Given the reinforcement request we've received."

The Brigadier nodded. "Paul, the Americans have asked us to help plug the gaps in the border. The terrain is so hilly they're not having much luck. It would do no harm if you dovetailed your plans with their Message guy."

"He's called Randy," said Paul. "Randy Snookis."

"Of course he is," said the Brigadier. "And yes, you've my blessing to go. They'd value a bit of advice, I'm sure."

* * *

Later that night, as Paul worked, the door opened and he immediately checked to see the blind was drawn. Throwing his pen down, he spun round on his chair with a smile on his face.

"Who were you expecting?"

Blanche stood in front of him with her green beret rolled up in one hand. Her face sagged like a balloon half filled with water.

"Not you," Paul said, then spun back to face his computer. If she could ignore him, he would ignore her.

"I've come to ask you a question," she said.

Paul spoke over his shoulder.

"About...?"

"About your interpreter, Rozafa Xhaferi."

He sat back in the chair and interlaced his fingers on his belly. He spun his chair round. "Why?"

"Because that's my job," she responded curtly. "What is the nature of your dealings with her?" She folded her arms underneath her breasts. *Bleach Henderson*, the signallers called her. Kills all known morale. She seemed to revel in the nickname.

"I talk, she translates. She helps paint the walls of this office. She protects British military property when it is under attack by a mob of angry Serbs. And she enables you to talk to mixed-race children who led us to the identities of the men who bombed the bus. Apart from that, not very much. Why?"

Blanche studied him. He placed his hands on top of his head and studied her. "Was there anything else?"

She turned and left without saying anything. No apology, no explanation.

A surge of anger swept through him as he wondered why she had the right to enter his office and assess his integrity and his professionalism. The fucking cow.

Shaking his head, he wiggled the mouse and returned to the script he was working on, but the irritation nettled through his concentration.

It was late anyway. He would just check his emails, then go to bed.

But when he brought up his hotmail account, the first email was from Roza. It said, simply, *Zot□ri Major* in the title section, the English letters unable to cope with the Albanian umlaut.

He clicked the title and found a tightly spaced email that said how wonderful she thought he was. And how much she'd enjoyed Saturday.

How different she was from Susan, how unpretentious and unadorned.

Paul clicked the reply button and started typing. His email account was secure. It had a password no one would be able to crack, not even the acerbic Blanche Henderson. But he stopped.

He should not encourage her.

* * *

Hiding in her new favourite place, Anja squatted on the roof beams in the hayloft over the radio station. Looking down through the holes in the plaster, she watched Stefan talking gaily to his girlfriend on the telephone, then walk to the music room to change the record when it finished.

She could also see people out on the street through a brick that had lots of little holes in it. There were spiders' webs and other creepy things in them, but she poked them out with a cooking skewer. That was how she knew Roza had come to see her. A green car stopped outside and three people got out: the man with the red hat, the fat woman she didn't like, and Roza. The fat woman was carrying a big book. They knocked on the door and told Stefan they wanted to speak to her.

Anja wasn't sure she wanted to be spoken to. With her feet on the roof beams, she looked down through the holes while first Stefan, then Stefan and Mama, then Stefan, her Mama, and Tata all looked for her. She giggled.

Roza looked up. "Hello Anja," she said in Albanian. "Are you ok up there?"

Mama and Tata came into view. They were not happy. Tata said something to Mama and strode back to the cottage. Stefan went back to the music room.

"Come down. Come down right now!" said Mama. But Anja didn't want to move. It took more threats and an angry expletive before she shuffled along to the rusty ladder and descended into the long grass and the nettles at the back of the building.

"Don't do that again. We were worried!" her mother said in Albanian. She put a hand on Anja's shoulder and pinched through to the bone.

"Ow."

The fat woman in the green hat spoke to Roza. Roza said that the woman needed to check something. She was going to see some photographs and if she recognised any of the people, she was to say. Would that be ok?

Anja nodded. "Ok," she said.

The fat woman opened the book. On the right hand side were two photos of men, neither of whom she recognised. Their faces were round, well fed, and clean shaven. They looked ordinary.

But when she turned the page, there was only one photo to look at. The face was thin, dirty, and the eyes very, very dark.

Anja ran to her mother. Memories haunted her: the horrible teeth, the popping fire, the soldier being sick.

"No..." she whined.

With her arms around her mother's hips, she buried her face into the folds of her body so she wouldn't have to see those eyes again.

Chapter 13

Paul could feel her looking at him. She kept smiling to herself, then turning back to the newspaper on the coffee table.

"Seagood, what's on your mind?"

She giggled, but shook her head. "Nothing, Sir. Just thinking."

He returned to his script. He was waxing lyrical about the fact that a peace dividend meant increased trust between families, and increased trade between villages, and by extension collaboration and integration between counties. The need for trade prevented the need for war. Trade brought deeper levels of trust because markets could deliver economic success to both sides. Guns could only deliver victory to one. He wanted to say something like 'markets over magazines', but wasn't sure the alliteration would work in Albanian.

Seagood got up and adjusted her jacket and beret. She had an impish smile on her face. It made Paul scowl. The girls had been talking.

She walked towards his desk and placed a small folded letter on the mouse mat. Then she burst into giggles like a schoolgirl and fled out of the door.

The folded paper was pink and smelled of Roza's perfume. *Zotëri Major*, it read, *why you never write to me? I think of you nearly all the time. You are very special man. R.*

A feeling of intense embarrassment fell over him. Did Seagood know everything?

He had to grip this situation, grip it before it got out of hand.

* * *

It was like being on holiday. The hard-top Landrover was being serviced again, so Seagood had been given a soft-top for the day. Paul helped her pull the canvas back over the roll cage. He fitted his sunglasses, a pair of fakeleys he'd bought at one of the stalls outside the main gate. He pushed the window forward. Once they were on the main road, he pressed play on a portable CD player by his feet and turned up the volume. The baseline kicked in and Paul tapped out the beat, nodding his head in time.

It took an hour and a half to drive to Bondsteel, the American base outside Gjilane. When they got closer, it was easy to identify.

"Jesus Christ," said Paul.

It was vast. The entire British headquarters took up an area the size of three football fields. Bondsteel had an American football field at the far end, the posts poking above a solid concrete wall that must have been ten feet high.

"How the fuck did they build that?"

A sign told them they were entering an area protected by the United States military and they should do as instructed by the guards. Paul took off his glasses and pulled out the NATO identity badge he kept on a cord round his neck.

"Major Illingworth. I have a meeting with Major Snookis."

The soldier was thick set, and padded out further by body armour, helmet, weaponry, and thick leather gloves. He must have been boiling.

"Thank you, Sir. Have a nice day."

Seagood drove through the chicane and followed the one-way system. A squad of men dressed in identical shorts and tee-shirts jogged slowly along the road ahead of them, then wheeled off towards a helicopter landing site.

On the chopper park, three Blackhawks and a Chinook were being serviced. Their rotors sagged down on all sides. Further along the road, Paul was amazed to find brick built buildings, a bowling alley, a store the size of a supermarket, a pizza joint, an ice cream parlour.

"Wow," said Seagood. "This is amazing!"

The place made Paul depressed. "All the gear and no idea," he muttered. "Turn left. It's that building there."

Randy Snookis was about the same age as Paul. Thin shouldered, he wore issued glasses which, though robust looking, were still cool. "Welcome Major," he said, saluting in the American style.

Paul hastily returned the compliment. "Hello, mate. Paul Illingworth. We've chatted on the phone."

"Yes, Sir," said Snookis. "You want to discuss media handling in the context of interdicting hostiles crossing the south-eastern border?"

"I do," said Paul, a smile tickling his lips, then, "Seagood, why don't you got back to the pizza shop and get yourself a coffee. I'll see you there in half an hour."

Following Randy through the building, Paul found his opposite number had a planning office larger than the briefing room at the British base. One wall was covered in white boards on which information was collated in rows and columns. Three soldiers, all slim, tall, female, and black, worked at computers. Against the far wall stood a podium with an American eagle on the front and a huge flag behind.

"You give press conferences here?"

Randy shrugged. "Yeah, I guess. But Major Breitman up at NATO headquarters, he's said he'll do all the major statements. He doesn't like the brigades having their own press operations. Says it makes the press confused."

He was quite right. Paul was often making statements in the name of NATO rather than just the British brigade purely by virtue of the fact he was located in Pristina. And the press liked him more. Randy was looking at him. It was obviously Paul, rather than anyone else, that Breitman wanted to constrain.

"I'd happily comply with any NATO policy," Paul said, "providing I have faith in the person delivering it."

Randy checked over Paul's shoulder to see whether his staff had overheard.

"Let's go in here," he said, indicating a small room containing only two chairs and a table. "We can talk freely."

Paul thanked him for making time, and laid out his thinking.

"I can't talk to the two internationals in my area. There's an election in Britain and the rules prevent it happening."

Randy nodded. "We have the same, sort of."

"Ok, good. But there's no rule against me passing a message to them through you. And since they'll soon be down here watching how you cope with preventing Albanians crossing the border into Macedonia, I thought we might like to see if we could work together."

Of course they were working together. They were both part of NATO. They had the same mission statement. But that was where the alignment ended. Each Brigade operated in its own way. The British wanted Pristina to get domestic media exposure. The Italians wanted the western sector to control the flow of weapons to the mafia. The Germans wanted any area that would allow them to demonstrate their military maturity. Kosovo was the first place they had served since 1945. The French wanted Mitrovica because it had the largest Serb population and the French had a historic affiliation with the Slavs. The Americans, by contrast, wanted the south-east sector because it was a low threat area and the risk of casualties would be minimal.

"I couldn't say what you want me to say, Major," Randy said. "My statements have to be signed off by a one star general."

"All of them?"

"Yeah. We have a process. I draft them, then forward them up through the chain of command. If there are amendments to be made, I make them and resubmit. When they get approved, I can say them. Some of them require political approval, if it concerns a matter that is about more than just the military goals."

Paul suppressed a snigger. He couldn't remember the last time he'd had a conversation with a journalist that was purely about military matters. The day before, he had spent an hour with the editor of the Koha Ditore newspaper talking about the benefits of a three party system.

He said, "So how do you... I mean, can the process keep up with a fast moving story?"

Randy obviously knew what he was trying to ask. He didn't have the look nor the manner of an infantry officer. He had joined up as a Public Affairs Officer because he had once written an article for his college paper.

"Major, it's different for us. Our reporters don't criticize like yours do..."

They were both dancing round the issue. Paul realised that Randy was refusing his request.

"But heck, if there's a text you want me to feed up through the approval process, I'd be only too happy to help."

Paul smiled. "It's been good of you to make time, Randy. At the very least I hope I'll be able to give you a call if something happens."

"Be my guest," Randy replied.

Walking through the expansive office, Paul was again amazed by the reach and power of the American military. But how bureaucratic!

Randy saluted him again at the door, then shook his hand.

"Been a pleasure, Major. I respect what you've done in Pristina. But we just can't work like that. There's a process."

"I know, Randy. I know. And it's there for a reason. I guess you are just more stable down here than we are. You've made that so."

It was a good way to finish. Despite his rigid thinking, Paul liked the man. As the door shut behind him he retraced his steps along the road back towards the helicopters, then turned right towards the shops. Seagood looked tiny sitting at a table by herself in the empty café, a huge ice cream sundae in front of her face.

"Sir, look! They didn't take deutschmarks and I didn't have a dollar, so the lady gave me it for free!"

Paul patted his pocket. He couldn't fail to pay for something. Behind the polished aluminium counter was an Albanian waitress. She pointed at him and smiled, recognising his face from the television.

"You want? I give you."

Paul shook his head. "Thanks, no, it's fine."

He sat opposite Seagood and she pushed the glass towards him, offering the spoon.

"Have some of this, Sir. It's really nice, but it's massive. And I don't have herpes, honest!"

Paul burst into laughter. He'd never have thought her capable.

She said, "Always careful, me."

The ice cream was rich and not too cold. It was delicious. He studied her face, then pushed the glass back across the table. "Have you got a boyfriend back home?"

She shook her head. "No. We split just before I came out here. He was a corporal, at Lyneham, but he was shagging about, so I dumped him."

There was a cold precision about her that Paul had never seen before. She seemed to have life experience beyond her years.

"What about you, Sir?" she said. "How are you getting on?"

There was a thin smile on her face. It wasn't fitting for him to be having a relationship with an interpreter and even less fitting for him to be having a conversation about it with his driver. She was smiling at him.

"Seagood, whatever you think you know, please don't mention it."

He clenched his jaw. If she blabbed, the whole camp could know.

"I haven't said…"

"Never. Do you understand?" He glared at her.

"All right," she said, pushing herself back from him and holding up her hands.

"I'm serious," he said, chopping his arm to point with his hand extended. "I don't want to hear that chatter."

She blinked as she turned away. She mouthed the word *sorry* as she got up to find the loo.

Had that been too heavy-handed? Maybe, but it needed to be said.

* * *

Roza was subdued as she sat next to him on the bench at Radio Black Eagle. She didn't meet his eye or respond to the soft touch of his elbow against hers. Elire, by comparison, was as warm as she'd ever been. Since Roza was being so incommunicative, Paul was inclined to ignore her.

"So, Major Pol, you want to talk about guns, why we no longer need?"

"Well yes, Elire, since you ask, I would like to talk about that."

"And what have you to say?"

"I have a question for your listeners, Elire. I want to understand what is the situation, in a stable and peaceful Kosovo – possibly one that is becoming independent at some stage in the future, hypothetically speaking – where a gun would be necessary? Describe to me the circumstance in which someone would use a gun. Or tell me how it benefits a man to have a gun he cannot use."

Elire liked these debates. "There could be animals. There could be dogs or wolves."

"Ok. But the best thing for vermin would be a shot gun, or perhaps a small bore rifle. But surely not a seven-six-two semi-automatic?"

Elire laughed. "But what about the bad people, Major Pol? What happen if they come?"

Paul paused. He had learned to deflect such questions. "In America they can own guns, yes? It's part of the constitution. And yet a few facts for you. Did you know that having a gun in the home increases the likelihood of the home owner being killed by a gun by seventy per cent? Did you know that?"

"No, I didn't know that."

"Well it's true. And did you know that having guns at home increases the chance of your children being killed by *that* gun. Your own gun. They take it out and play with it but they don't have the training..."

Elire made a noise while shaking her head. She winked at him.

"And suicide. After wars, people get hurt by the things they have seen. Having a gun increases the chance of suicide by something like five times. Just imagine what it would be like for you to come home and find your son, your husband... someone who bravely fought against oppression..."

"No..." said Elire.

"So that's why I want to applaud the people of Pristina." Paul said. "I want you to know that you have handed in far more weapons than any other region. In fact, more than all the other regions put together."

The interview ended well. "Well thank you Major Pol, spokesman for British Multinational Brigade Centre, we thank you for coming to talk to us and we like what you say about handing in our weapons and hope you'll come again next week and talk to us again.

"I will, Elire, thank you very much."

Paul pulled off the headphones after the lights changed. Elire balanced the stylus above the side of a Spice Girls album. When they walked out into the corridor, she stood very close to him.

"Today very good, Major Pol. Very exciting radio. We get many people calling in later. I tell you."

"Thank you Elire. I really do mean what I say. A mature democracy does not need guns at home."

He didn't mention independence, but he didn't have to. It was always on the tip of Elire's tongue. Her name, he'd learned from Roza, meant *Freedom*.

She winked at him and disappeared into the kitchen, swaying her hips as she did so. Next to him, Roza felt small and shrunken.

"Shall we wait outside, Roza?" he said.

He went ahead of her and pushed the screen door open. At the bottom of the steps, the grey collie was waiting. He descended with one hand out, fingers curved.

"Hey, girl."

The dog withdrew, dropping its head. It pressed its ears back and wagged its tail. The hair on its flank was patchy. Scabs had formed on the joints. It was limping, the left foreleg unable to bear weight.

"Come here, girl. Let me see."

He squatted on the bottom step. The dog licked its lips and took a jump forward on its right paw. It blinked.

A door slammed inside the radio station. The dog looked up at the screen door, then limped quickly back under the concrete piling.

"What a way to treat a dog," said Paul, pulling himself up to standing.

Then, looking at the sky for signs of rain, he led Roza to the bench they had sat on before. "We need to talk," Paul said.

She sat next to him, head slightly bowed and hands between her knees. "Please don't talk about us with Seagood," Paul said. "She works for me. I have a responsibility."

Roza nodded. Paul looked across the parking area at the houses on the other side. They had the same chain-link fences and low oak trees in their gardens.

"I think the world of you, Roza. You've been instrumental to what I've done here."

There was a 'but' coming. He didn't know how to voice it. She was the only person who understood what he was doing. And yet the hard fact remained that he was going home soon, and long-distance relationships never worked.

"I make a letter to go to London University, to study English," Roza whispered. "I have passport now, thanks to my brother. I come next year."

Paul turned, his mouth open. "That's... that's..."

She lifted a strand of hair behind her ear. "Does that make you happy, Zotëri Major?"

"It would make me happier than anything," he said.

She placed a hand on his thigh. It was small and square. Paul held her eyes, those lovely, loving eyes.

"I do this to be with you," she said.

The sound of a Landrover approaching down the lane made Paul look up. He removed her hand from his leg, but squeezed the fingers as he did so.

Chapter 14

It was raining, and the orange mud in the central square splashed his trousers as he ran to the Press Office.

Instinct told him to check the news before he went into the morning brief. All the phones were ringing. Seagood was sitting at his desk making a list of those who'd called.

"Excellent work," Paul said, patting her on the shoulder as he would a man. He felt the need to apologise for being so hard on her. "That's really brilliant…"

"You left your phone in here overnight, Sir. I put it on charge."

She'd forgiven him.

"What's happened?" he said, turning the television on.

"I don't know, but it's like when that helicopter crashed. That guy Nick rang, and Colonel Brazel."

"Anybody else?"

"Major Breitman. Major Snookis…" she giggled. "I like him. He's funny. Also Elire Ruci from Radio Black Eagle…"

She'd made a list.

"First class, er, Jane. Now, may I have my seat?"

On the screen, the picture showed a forested hillside topped with a mosque and a few houses along the ridgeline. It looked a lovely scene except for the plume of smoke hanging in the air next to a minaret. *Former Yugoslav Republic of Macedonia Fires at Kosovo village of Krivenic*, ran the tickertape headline.

Paul turned up the volume just in time to hear the anchorman say that a number of people, including a journalist, were reported injured.

"Oh fuck," said Paul.

Less than five minutes later the ticker tape had changed: *Journalist killed*, it read. Paul crossed his fingers. Please don't let it be Aden.

His phone rang. It was Nick, sounding strained and angry. "Paul, what can you tell me?"

"Who was it, Nick?"

There was silence, then, "I'm not certain. I got a garbled message from Aden's fixer. I've tried his phone but it's ringing out. Do you know anything?"

"No. Krivenic is in the American sector. I couldn't even tell you where it is."

"It's on the border, in one of the little lugs that stick out into Macedonia. The rebels were using it as a launch pad for their supply runs."

"How do you know that?"

"Aden told me. He'd been across to spend time with that rebel group of his. Look, Paul, what is NATO going to do about this?"

As Nick was talking, Paul watched the image change on the screen. It was now a picture of Aden taken a few years before, when his hair was shorter. He was wearing a red and white Palestinian shemagh on top of green fatigues. Above his face was the header: *Aden Short, 1971 to 2001*.

"Paul, are you listening?"

"I'm watching the television, Nick, and I think you should as well. Aden's been reported killed. I don't know what happened, but I'll find out and get back to you."

Nick said nothing. On the line Paul heard an Albanian radio station and other phones going off. It sounded like Nick was driving.

"If he's dead Paul, I will expect NATO to respond. If Macedonia is firing shells at a NATO protectorate, and a British national has been killed, you'll not be able to gloss over this..."

"Who said I was glossing over anything? Hold on and let me get an official line."

Paul hung up before Nick could say anything else. He could see why Nick was angry. The Macedonian troops would be for the high jump.

The soldier in him took over. He called the Chief of Staff on the landline, but on hearing that it had happened in the American sector, Simon was unmoved.

"What do you expect me to do, exactly?"

"Simon, we're being fired on. I expect you to call your oppo in the US sector and get fire down."

Simon laughed. "What good would that do? Are they still firing?"

Paul had to admit that it looked like the shelling had stopped. The plume of smoke above the village was thinning out. But he was still surprised that Simon should be so unbothered. His mobile rang.

"That's Brassy. Sorry Simon, I'll pop over in a minute." He grabbed the mobile and clicked the green button.

Before Paul could speak, Brassy said, "On no account are you to confirm that the shellfire came from the Former Yugoslav Republic of Macedonia. Do you understand?"

Paul said nothing. Brassy repeated himself, "Paul, listen. On no account, whatsoever, are you to either confirm or deny that FYROM was responsible for the shellfire that landed on the village of Krevinca fifteen minutes ago."

Paul still did not respond.

"Can you hear me? Line check, over?"

Paul coughed. "I'm here. But I don't get what you're saying."

Brassy didn't wait. "There's been an incident. Person or persons unknown have fired onto a Kosovan village called Krevinca..."

"Krivenic. It's called Krivenic..."

"So you know..."

"Of course I know; I'm watching the same news you are. And they're already ringing me for comment. It looks like Aden Short's been killed. He's *Reuters* and *The Times*."

"Fuck, is he *Reuters* as well?"

"I need a line, Colonel. I can't go round saying this has not happened."

"You say we are investigating, nothing more. You say an inquiry will be announced soon."

Paul coughed. "That would completely destroy my credibility. It's on the TV. There's a big plume of smoke. I can't tell grown-up journalists that someone has not been killed…"

Brassy's voice changed. "What can you see, Paul, really? What is actually on the screen right now?"

"Smoke," said Paul. "A plume of smoke above a village. It's live footage."

"Exactly. A plume of smoke. A village that, by the looks of things, has no power and no sanitation. It could be any manner of things. It never pays to get flustered, Paul."

Cunt.

"I'm not flapping. Don't ever say that I am, please. I'm just pointing out that we cannot say white is black and black is white. It doesn't work. We tried it before, in Sierra Leone, if you recall. It didn't work then and it won't work now."

Brassy went quiet for a moment. When he spoke, he used a quieter tone. "That was different."

"No it wasn't. If you have the International Affairs Editor of the London Evening Standard standing next to a four-foot tall soldier carrying a five-foot long rifle, you can't say that the Sierra Leone Army does not employ child soldiers. And you can't tell Nick Oakeshot, the Balkan editor of the BBC, that his eyes deceive him."

"I don't care. All our supply routes come through FYROM. You know that. NATO depends on their goodwill and it will not be to our advantage if we start escalating this incident."

"But…"

"I'm not debating this, Paul. This is the line: NATO is aware of reports of firing along the border in the American sector of Southern Kosovo. It is believed this was an isolated incident. An investigation is expected to be announced soon."

Paul had the phone in his hand, his mouth working. How could Brassy possibly think that would work?

"That's nowhere near sharp enough…"

"Get on with it and stop bleating."

The line went dead. Paul was shocked, then excruciatingly angry. How fucking dare he! The phone rang again. It was Nick.

"Well?"

Paul sucked in air. He repeated the line he had scribbled down on his pad.

"Oh come on, Paul! That's bullshit and you know it."

"We're going to announce an investigation," Paul replied, the energy gone from his voice.

"You're serious aren't you? You're saying that Macedonia did not fire on Kosovo?"

"I said we don't know who…"

"Yes we do, Paul. The villagers watched the shells land. You can't stick to that line."

"Nick, I'm sorry, but this is what we're saying at the moment. Asking me to say something else is never going to make this incident clearer. Are you driving?"

"I'm on my way there. I'm nearly at Bondsteel."

"Why don't you go speak to my US counterpart? His name's Snookis, Major Randy Snookis."

"I will, Paul, but you need to speak to your people. I'll not accept that line if Aden's really been killed."

Fuck.

"I've got to go," Paul said, inventing another call to get him off the line. He then turned the mobile off. The landline rang after a few minutes so he reached under the table to pull out the wall socket. The silence felt hollow, echoing with lies.

On the eight o'clock news, the shelling was the first story and got a full three minutes. Paul turned up the volume as the anchor-man trotted out all the cliché's: troubled Balkan region, notoriously porous borders, Albanian rebels wanting more than NATO could deliver. It surprised him that they did not mention Aden, but then he realised that they were saving themselves. Once Nick had confirmed he was dead, the story would lead in the evening.

The report closed with a bombshell Paul had not expected: "...despite all the evidence, NATO spokesman Major Paul Illingworth has denied that the firing came from the Former Yugoslav Republic of Macedonia. He said that an inquiry into the incident is expected to be announced soon..."

Brassy, you fucking cunt.

* * *

The following day, villagers from around Krivenic marched to the American base at Bondsteel carrying a banner that read *Who will protect us against the Macedonians?* Once outside the base, they were whipped into a frenzy by an angry orator keen to be elected to the assembly.

Paul had to dispel the fear. He had to get on the radio and television stations to stop the nationalists stoking the fires of Albanian victimhood.

The public mood in Pristina became unsettled. There was no rioting, but there was also no doubt that they felt the attack as keenly as the villagers of Krivenic. Simon ordered an increase in patrol activity for thirty-six hours while tensions ran high. The infantry battalion was told to reinstate the fixed guard at the monastery in Gracanica.

Paul could not talk to the internationals, but he could to the locals. With Roza at his side, he went on a back to back tour of the radio and TV stations telling everyone the official line he had been given from London.

At Radio Black Eagle, Elire looked like she'd been awake all night. When they arrived, she was sitting in the kitchen with a sad Albanian folk song playing in the background. Paul wondered if Aden's death was a personal loss as much as a professional one. She had been drinking.

"What you say, Pol? What can you say to these Macedonians who have blood on their hands? They kill famous English reporter. What is it NATO can do?"

Calmly, quietly, Paul said, "We must be careful at moments like these not to make too hasty a decision. An investigation is underway…"

But she was no more fooled than anybody else. Who else could have fired the shells?

The following morning he went to see Major Breitman at the UN headquarters, finding him by a water cooler in a corridor.

Paul skipped the pleasantries. "This line about the incident being under investigation is not working. Nobody buys it."

Breitman was a good deal older than Paul, his hair greying above his ears. "That depends on who says it," he said. "We're giving a press conference in an hour in response to public alarm. I'm sure I'll handle it."

Paul laughed. The man had never been outside the UN headquarters. He had no idea of the anger on the streets.

"Suit yourself," Paul warned, "but you're making a mistake."

How much of a mistake, Breitman shortly found out.

Nearly every seat of the auditorium was filled. The German captain with the gavel barked instructions to keep order. The translators and overhead projectionist stood nervously to the side. Breitman read a short statement that no one paid any attention to, then opened up the floor for questions.

"Here," Nick snapped, beckoning the sound boom towards him.

Breitman acknowledged him, "Nick."

"Major Breitman. Perhaps you could explain why NATO, the American Brigade in particular, has air defence artillery stationed in the villages along the border but is unable to say whether the artillery fire that killed nine people in Krivenic originated from Macedonia."

Breitman leaned forward, "The question of the incident in Krivenic is covered in the statement by the Special Representative of the Secretary General I have just read. There is nothing more I can add..."

"That did not answer my question. Are you telling me that NATO does not have artillery locating radar?"

With his mouth close to the microphone, Breitman's fumbling responses created an impression of stupidity.

"We cannot comment on the specifics of military capabilities..."

"Look, Breitman," Nick said. "There is, in Bondsteel, the headquarters of the American Brigade, a detachment of the 164th Air Defence Artillery, a National Guard unit. They are equipped with *Firefinder*, an artillery radar system. Please tell me if this system was deployed or not?"

The audience cheered.

Breitman blinked. "As I said before, I cannot comment on specific military deployments, Nick. You will know why that is..."

Nick did not let go. "If you cannot say whether the firing came from Macedonia or not, how can you reassure the people of Kosovo that it will not happen again?"

Breitman blinked again. "As the SRSG has said, we are investigating the reports of shelling in Southern Kosovo. Concurrently, there is a diplomatic mission to ensure that..."

"Is this mission going to Macedonia?"

The look on Breitman's face showed that he'd realised his mistake, but he continued to answer with his voice raised above the hubbub, "...there is a diplomatic mission to ensure that all states in the region, including Serbia and FRY Macedonia, agree how to prevent ethnic extremism spreading further..."

A stringy, curly-haired man in the front row snapped out a question in Albanian. The sound boom was directed to him. He repeated his question for it to be translated into English by the woman standing below the stage. Roza, sitting next to Paul, translated as he spoke. "He wants to know if NATO believe that Albanian people protecting their way of life and values and children are now being called terrorists by NATO and he wants to know who said this first and he wants to know if NATO will protect Albanian people in Kosovo because there are enemies on many sides. There are Serbs to the north and Macedonians to the south and everybody knows that Macedonians cannot be trusted...."

Laughter spread round the room as Major Breitman raised his hand. "Let me answer one question at once. The role of NATO in Kosovo is to provide peace and stability for all people..."

The room erupted into shouts and calls for attention. The German captain by the door banged his gavel. Breitman covered his microphone to speak to him. A handful of men at the back of the hall unravelled a huge red and black Albanian flag, flicking it open over the seats below them.

"Macedon is killing us..." a woman shouted.

Elire was sitting patiently a few rows down from Paul. She had her hand raised to ask a question. She turned to look at him and winked. At least she had not deserted him. Her anger was aimed at Breitman.

"As clear as mud," Paul whispered to Roza, then touched her on the thigh to indicate he'd had enough.

"Let's go, I'm on Radio Rilindja in an hour."

They walked down the steps to the main door, Paul winking at the German captain as they left. Outside, in the lobby, the air was much cooler.

The huge doors were open to allow a stream of people through the metal detectors. The café in the corner was empty, and Paul checked his watch to see if he had time for some caffeine.

Roza placed her hand on his arm, stopping him.

Coming through the metal detectors was a man of medium height and slim build. He was dressed in an avuncular manner, a silk scarf around his neck. Even as he walked through the detectors, he smoked.

"That's…" Roza whispered, her voice choking.

The man had a stick, which had to be fed back through the scanner after an alarm sounded. He seemed unconcerned, his face retaining an unwavering smile. His aides were being held up by the security staff, but he left them and walked straight towards Paul.

As he got closer Paul realised he was not that old, perhaps fifty or so, but smoker's skin made him seem much more.

The man fixed Paul with a look that penetrated his soul. He stretched out a hand and by habit Paul took it, then touched his heart with his fingers.

"You do great work for us, in very difficult times," the man said in English. "I wish to thank you from the bottom of my heart."

He patted Paul on his arm, then looked at Roza, giving her a slight but formal nod. She gaped back without moving. One of the aides touched the man's elbow. He was guided away.

"Who was that?" said Paul after a time.

"Doctor Ibrahim Rugova," whispered Roza. "You shake the hand of great man."

"He will be the first president of an independent Kosovo," Paul said, more certain of his words than of anything else.

But his reverie was broken by Nick coming out of the auditorium behind him. "Paul. A word."

The sense of peace and calmness that flowed around Rugova evaporated. Paul was splashed back into the cold swell of a media frenzy.

"I've got a radio interview in an hour. Is it quick?"

Nick indicated the cafeteria in the corner of the lobby. "It's not quick, Paul. But it is important. Give me a moment, please."

Behind him, there was an eruption of shouting from inside the press conference and the banging of a gavel. Paul allowed himself to be led to a brushed-steel table. He pulled out a chair and sat down. Nick did the same.

"I'm going back in when we're done," Nick said.

"This sounds ominous," said Paul. "What is it?"

He knew of course. Nick was behaving like a teacher about to scold an errant pupil.

Nick said, "I want to talk to you about Krivenic." Paul raised a finger but Nick silenced him. "Listen to me, would you? You have been among the best press spokesmen I have known in fifty years of reporting. You're straight, you work hard, and you understand the line between bullshit and influence. I respect a professional, because I meet a lot of amateurs."

Paul laughed nervously. Nick's manner became even more serious.

"Paul, you're young. You have integrity. And I can see you care very much for the people here."

He made a nod towards Roza sitting on another table. He was using her as an example, but Paul's cheeks still coloured.

"But you need to think about what you're doing. Morons like Breitman will spew the party line for ever. That's no bother." He placed a hand on Paul's forearm and gripped tightly. "But you, Paul. You are different."

* * *

The British elections would be in two weeks, and the Kosovan one six days later. A memo from the UN, sent by email, indicated that eligible voter registration for the Albanian population was 94% while the figure for the Serbs was only 7%.

Paul was struck by a terrible panic. He'd been so focused on the Krivenic shelling that he'd forgotten about the assembly elections all together.

He went to see Simon, finding him for once alone. "I may have dropped the ball. I don't think I'll get the Serbs to vote like the Commander asked."

Simon continued tidying the papers on his desk. "You can't live their lives for them, Paul." he said. "It's after eleven. Is this not best left for the morning?"

"I'm fine," Paul insisted, then rubbed his eyes.

"Don't burn yourself out. This can wait."

But Paul could not stop working, not with so stark a target. "The registration process only takes a day. All they need is a passport and a right of residency…"

"Paul…"

"Simon, this is important. The Serbs need numbers to get people into the assembly to represent them. Otherwise they'll have to depend on the Albanians." He walked over to the map, talking as if to himself. "Twenty thousand people left the enclaves after the war. Imagine if they were all voting!"

Simon placed his mug on the corner of his desk. "It's late. Come on. Let me buy you a beer in the Mess."

Paul ignored him. "Do they have to be resident? If they have property rights, could they vote by post?"

Simon raised his voice. "That's enough."

The order got through. Paul sighed. Fatigue pulled at his shoulders. He was suffering from adrenalin withdrawal.

He said, "You're right. I'll just tidy up. I'll be in the bar for lasties."

"Good man," said Simon. "I'll get you one in."

Paul slouched back to his office, finding it stale and musty in comparison to the jasmine scent in the cool night air. He propped open the door, then tidied the papers from his desk. He checked he had no emails, either personal or for work, then closed down his computer. He would mull on the issue. That usually threw up ideas.

Straightening the coffee table, he found the remote under a magazine and placed it on the corner of his desk. He checked the kettle was full, and washed the mugs. Last of all, he pulled up the blind ready for the morning.

He was about to go when Roza appeared at the doorway holding something tight against her chest. She grinned, bouncy with excitement. "Good evening, Zotëri Major."

"I was just leaving; it's been a long day."

Her face clouded. "Okey-dokey. But I bring you something. To learn Albanian."

It was the item in her arms. She bobbed up and down on her toes.

"Would you like me to sit?" he said.

She nodded, her smile broadening further. She seemed so desperate for his company. Her secret was exploding inside her.

Paul lowered the blind on the window, then shoved the fire extinguisher out of the way to allow the door to close. He sat in the centre of the sofa, while Roza stepped over his knees to sit facing him on the coffee table. Her hair had been cut.

She extended her arms to place the present on his lap. Her smile faded as he looked at it.

"You said you like it," she said.

The present, a flat oblong, was wrapped in yellow crepe and tied with sisal. He tugged a loose end of the string to unwind the bow. One loop shrank and the knot popped open. Paul brushed away the string to unwrap the paper.

"*Asteriks*!"

He slid the book out, turning it over in his hands. "*Gali Asteriks…*"

"You know this?"

"Oh, Roza, that's wonderful! I love these books. I always have done." He smiled at her, then leaned forward to kiss her cheek. "Thank you. That's very kind."

Roza swept hair from her face. "My English teacher said if you understand the names, then you are most way to speaking good English."

Paul laughed. "That's true. The Chief is called *Vitalstatistix* in English. Do you know what that is?"

She nodded. "Yes, it is the centimetres here and here. It is so funny. We do not measure women like this."

Paul looked at the cover then thumbed through the pages.

She touched his knee. "Every night we can do a page."

"That would be fantastic, Roza, thank you so much."

She clenched a fist as if she'd scored a goal. "Yes!" she said.

Her skin glowed. He couldn't help being drawn by the delicate grace of her smile. Her lips closed lightly over her teeth. She swallowed. Paul sat back on the sofa, resting his head against the wall. Their knees touched.

"I am a little bit in love with you, Zotëri Major," she said.

Paul's mouth went dry. Her heart was innocent.

"I love you too, Roza."

She giggled then, wriggling towards him, looking like she wanted to kiss. She slid off the coffee table to kneel before him, her hands on his thighs. If she came any further up his leg, she would be touching his cock as it stiffened inside his trousers. She knew this. Gently, she stroked her hands over his thighs.

He placed a palm against her cheek. "Please stop."

"But we are not doing anything."

She was showing her age. It might have sounded convincing to a teenager.

"Yes we are. We are breaking the code by which I belong here."

"What is this code?"

"I cannot be with you Roza. Maybe in London, but not here…"

He became exasperated. He grabbed her wrists, holding them tightly but not so much as to hurt her. "Look, I love Asterix. I'd really like you to teach me. But doing this… It's wrong!" He cupped her face in his hands. "Please sit on the table. I… I want to tell you about next week."

He thought she'd be angry with him, disappointed by his lack of commitment. But she pushed herself back to sit on the coffee table and leaned forward with her elbows on her knees to stare at him, smiling.

"What you want to tell me?"

"We need to do many Serb interviews next week. We need to go round all the enclaves and ask them to register and vote."

Her cheek twitched.

"You may not realise why this is important, but it is. I promise you. It will be better for Kosovo as a whole."

She wiped her nose with the back of one finger. "Why you want to speak to Serbian people? Why you interested in them?"

He shrugged. "It's the British way. We look after the little people. We tell the truth."

She studied his face, and he hers.

"You are telling me the truth? You love me?"

He could not pretend any more. "Yes, Roza. I do."

* * *

At the morning brief, the Chief of Staff was even more curt than usual.

"As of this morning, all patrols will be on hard routine. Helmets, not berets. In the rural areas, vehicle patrols will be accompanied by armour. Pristina may be relatively quiet, but in the enclaves there are improvised militias controlling the streets. The incident in Krivenic might provide fuel for further tension."

He looked round the room. "Who is going out on the ground today?"

Paul raised his hand: "Radio interviews; some in town, some in the enclaves."

"Make sure you sign out and back in again. Make sure you're armed and that your drivers have fuelled the vehicles. We've become tardy about these disciplines of late and I don't want to have to speak to anyone who gets caught out. Any questions?"

Nobody else raised their hand. Simon nodded. People darted for the door. But as Paul rose, he couldn't help noticing that Blanche was studying him, and making notes.

* * *

The tall British officer was in the radio station. Squatting on the rafters, Anja watched him and Roza enter through the metal door and walk below her to speak to Stefan in the kitchen.

Today Stefan smelled extremely bad because Anja had hidden the clothes Mama had washed for him. He'd had to wear his old ones for another day.

Roza made her excuses and left the two men to talk. That was ok as Stefan spoke English better than the English officer spoke either Albanian or Serbian.

Did they only speak one language in England?

But since she did not speak English herself, Anja shuffled along the rafters to the hatchway where the ladder was joined to the wall. She pulled the hatch a little bit so she could hear Roza talking on a mobile phone.

"I can't do that," Roza said in Albanian, one hand shielding her mouth.

Her voice was shaky. She sounded like she might start crying.

"No, I won't do that," she said, her voice rising in pitch. "I can't."

Anja didn't want Roza to start crying. She was afraid enough as it was and Roza was always kind.

Mama was walking down the path from the cottage. Roza quickly put her phone away. She greeted Mama nervously in Albanian.

Mama held Roza's hand.

"When will they tell me us about the trial, Rozafa?" she said. "They tell us nothing. The police say that everything is in the hands of the Americans. But they tell us nothing."

Roza looked like she was embarrassed to have Mama pleading with her.

"I don't know, Mrs Cokic. I have heard that the Americans have put the bombers in the prison in Bondsteel. But I do not know for sure. You want me to ask the British Major?"

Mama's face was flat in the sunlight. There were tears in her eyes.

"Yes. And will you ask him something else for me? He promised me a passport for my family."

Roza nodded and went inside, appearing below Anja's feet.

Mama stepped carefully round a clump of nettles and peered in through one of the windows. Anja slid silently along the rafters to be over the hallway.

The Englishman and Roza spoke in English and it sounded funny, a bit like Albanian and a bit like Serbian. They spoke very formally, like people who did not really know each other. They stood apart, not touching, their bodies turned partly to the side.

Anja's attention was disturbed by a bee. It buzzed past her towards the nest at the far end of the attic space. When she next looked down, Roza had gone outside and the English officer was talking again to Stefan.

Everything was cloudy. Nothing was simple.

BBC Online 1 August 2001 23.45 CET
Balkans civil war spreading throughout region as journalist killed

British journalist Aden Short was killed by artillery fire in Southern Kosovo this morning.

Short, 30, a veteran war correspondent, was investigating rumours of the mass murder of Albanians in the mountain village of Krivenic.

Eye witnesses reported the shellfire commencing at dawn, lasting up to half an hour and originating from across the border with the Former Yugoslav Republic of Macedonia (FYROM). Although the shellfire had ceased when Short entered the village, it restarted after his arrival. The vehicle he was traveling in received a direct hit and he died instantly.

It is believed that Macedonian security forces, including tanks, heavy artillery and special-forces, had recently been deployed into the area around the town of Tetovo, to quell unrest among the ethnic Albanian population. This has resulted in an exodus of Albanians who were fearful of the sort of reprisals meted out by the Serbian army during the Kosovo war of 1999. Hundreds are said to have fled north into the American sector of Kosovo believing NATO would protect them. In addition to Short, eight residents of Krivenic are reported dead.

The shellfire highlights the inability of NATO troops to control Kosovo's notoriously porous borders and prevent ethnic Albanian terrorism spreading across the region.

The Albanian rebels operating in Northern FYROM have responded to the incident by vowing to fight to the last man and bullet in defence of their freedom. In Macedonia, local tensions have resulted in at least sixteen deaths.

Meanwhile British Army spokesman Major Paul Illingworth denied knowing that the firing came from within the Former Yugoslav Republic of Macedonia, saying there was no evidence to suggest that it did. When asked who else could have fired on the village of Krivenic or whether NATO had specialist artillery-locating technology deployed in the area, he declined to comment.

Short leaves no family but is remembered for his courageous coverage of the first Chechen war in 1995, and the fall of Kabul to the Taliban in 1996. He had been based in Pristina since 1999.

Reuters News Agency: 1 August 23.59 CET
Balkans in turmoil as journalist killed

Reuters Kosovo correspondent Aden Short and eight unarmed civilians were killed by shellfire from NATO allies today.

At 07.00 this morning, villagers in Krivenic, a tiny agricultural hamlet overlooking the border between Kosovo and the Former Yugoslav Republic of Macedonia, were shocked by shellfire coming from their NATO-aligned neighbour. Nine people were killed in the firing, which lasted up to an hour, and was timed to catch the morning drive of milking cows.

NATO spokesman Paul Illingworth denies that the firing originated from the Former Yugoslav republic, insisting that no one knows where it came from.

The Sunday Times 5 August 2001
Times Journalist Killed by Macedonian Shells

Offices of *The Times* in Wapping came to a halt at four o'clock yesterday afternoon to remember the life of a journalist who had won awards for his fearless and uncompromising reporting from some of the world's worst hotspots.

Aden Short, 30, an ardent Greenpeace campaigner, was killed by shellfire from the Former Yugoslav Republic of Macedonia at around seven o'clock on Thursday morning. It is believed that the former Yugoslav Republic had deployed its vast military apparatus to quell an uprising by Albanian separatists. His death marks a sharp rise in journalists killed in the line of duty.

Short, who had gained unparalleled access to the rebels living along the border with the UN protectorate of Kosovo, was investigating war crimes in the area when the firing started.

His final submission, Life with the National Liberation Army, is published in the *Sunday Times Magazine* this weekend.

Chapter 15

The shower was wonderfully cool, washing away the grit and dust of the day. Paul leaned his head back so the water could pour over his face. He snorted into his hand and flicked the scabby mucus off his fingers, then rolled his shoulders to let the sharp pinpricks massage his neck and upper back. He watched the water swirl round his feet, thinking about what he had to do.

Nick had never called him after the chat they'd had in the wings of the UN press conference. His reporting on Aden's death had been fair, even though Paul was upset at being misrepresented. It wasn't *him* saying that it wasn't Macedonia firing the shells, it was *London*. Although he knew he had to toe the party line, he didn't like being made to look an idiot.

No one had been sent out by *The Times* to cover Aden's position and perhaps Nick would soften after a while. In actual fact, this was just like that time in his first few weeks when Nick and Aden had teased him and he'd held his nerve. The thought made him brighten. Yes, he would hold his nerve and Nick would eventually come running back.

Turning off the tap, Paul whipped back the plastic curtain and grabbed his towel from the hook outside the cubicle. He placed it over his face as he stepped out naked towards the row of sinks. The red matting was harsh under foot.

A woman spoke, "Do you mind?"

Paul quickly dropped the towel over his groin and wrapped it round his waist. "Sorry, I never heard the door open. I thought I was alone."

Blanche was wearing green tartan pyjamas and a pair of fluffy slippers. She was bending over one of the sinks, cleaning her teeth. Her belly rested over the front edge of the sink unit.

You're quite safe, thought Paul, turning away to towel himself down. Baring his arse felt like a small insult.

Blanche spat toothpaste into the sink and ran the tap to clear it. Paul wrapped the towel round his waist again, briefly admired the clean musculature of his torso in the mirror, then aligned himself with a sink to shave.

"Don't you do have to do that in the morning?"

Paul shook his head. "Queen's Regulations don't extend to personnel working in Message Operations." He dabbed shaving foam round his chin. "And to be honest, in this weather it's better to shave at night."

Blanche had wound floss round her fingers to insert into the gap between her front teeth. If he'd been quicker, Paul would have asked what time of day she liked to shave. After he'd rinsed the razor, he patted his face with cold water, brushed his teeth, and wiped down the sink with a snatch of blue towelling from the dispenser. Looking under the sink for his flip-flops, he thought he'd hurry out. Blanche was checking inside all the shower cubicles and he didn't want to be there when the pyjamas came off.

But she was checking to see they were alone. "Paul, a moment if you don't mind."

He turned to face her, shoulders low and square, pectorals tight.

She sneered at his machismo. "I want you to know that we monitor all the computers on camp. We do this to ensure that the signallers aren't stupid enough to give away operational plans. And we catch the locally employed civilians if they're spies."

Paul swallowed. Blanche studied his face. She revelled in her ability to destabilise. That was why, he guessed, she was good at her job.

"Are you having an affair with your interpreter?"

Paul could feel the colour rising in his neck just as the towel started to slip from around his waist. He made a joke of grabbing it before it fell away completely. "No."

"Are you having sexual relations with Roza Xhaferi?"

"No."

"Are you having an inappropriate relationship with Roza Xhaferi?"

"Just hang on a minute, Blanche. Who the fuck are you to start interrogating me?"

"It's my job."

Of course it was her job. But she was wrong. He had never crossed the line. His integrity was intact.

"I have nothing to say to you."

"So why is she sending flirtatious emails to your hotmail account?"

This was astounding. How fucking dare she? Had she read them? Had she seen his reply? When he went to see the Chief of Staff, or the Brigadier, were they laughing at how he'd bared his heart about Susan leaving him? Or how much he wanted her?

"Just a bit of friendly advice," Blanche said as she pushed past him and out into the corridor.

It was as if the shower had done nothing. He was again as dirty and exhausted as he had been before he got in.

* * *

At the following morning's brief, Paul arrived both angry and nervous. Was he going to get publicly shamed? Would people laugh at his emails to Roza or to his family? Perhaps Blanche would have them printed out and stuck on a wall for people to ridicule? Was it even legal that they should read his personal correspondence?

But as soon as he entered the room he knew something else had happened. Simon was in his normal place on the opposite side of the table. He mouthed, *see you after*, and Paul nodded. The exchange was noticed by others and a general air of tension developed until the Brigadier walked in. He was shaking his head.

Usual form at the morning brief was for Blanche to launch straight into her security assessment. This morning Brigadier Montrose didn't let her. Standing in the place where he normally sat, he leaned forward slightly to place his hands on the back of his chair.

"Ladies, Gentlemen, a great misfortune has befallen us. I've just been on the blower to the NATO Commander."

The room was totally silent.

"For reasons I do not quite understand, the man responsible for the bus bombing back in February has escaped from the detention facility inside the US Brigade Headquarters of Bondsteel. He is at large and considered dangerous."

Nearly every officer in the room had had a role to play in the arrest operation. A chorus of groans and astonishment rose.

"I know many of you will be rather disappointed by this news. I also recognise that a lot of people put an enormous amount of personal energy into the arrest operation."

His gaze fell on Paul, but Paul's reaction was to wonder how he must be feeling. No one in the room had invested more than Brigadier Montrose himself.

"We do not know how he escaped. We only know that the support network – Pear, Banana, and Apple – are still detained. Tomato is free. It goes without saying that I will be offering a personal reward of gratitude for anyone who locates him again."

The Brigadier pulled out his chair and sat down. There were so many questions unanswered that no one in the room knew what to say. How did he escape? How did he get out of the most secure complex in Eastern Europe? Why did the others remain?

Simon said, "Blanche, perhaps you could give us the security assessment as you've prepared it?"

Blanche rose and took hold of the snooker cue propped in the corner and used it to indicate Pristina city on the map. She coughed.

"The security situation for today, as at zero-six-hundred this morning. There was another attack by a gang of youths on the Gracanica monastery last night..."

* * *

"Randy, I want the fucking truth," said Paul on the phone, one foot resting on the bottom drawer of his desk. Roza and Seagood were sitting on the red sofa watching him, their mouths open. "How does a category A prisoner escape from inside a metal cage that's inside another metal cage that's inside Bondsteel?"

There was an edge to his voice. Fucking Yanks. How could they master counter insurgency warfare if they could not enforce the rule of law?

"If we're not careful this guy will become some sort of Albanian Robin Hood. We need a line that explains how he got out of jail, can't you see that?"

Randy answered with slow, mid-western precision. "In response to your question, Major, we regret to announce that one of our detainees is no longer under observation. We can say no more about the issue at this stage."

Paul snapped. "Come on, Randy! He's a fucking murderer. You saw what the press did to Breitman!"

"I'm sorry, Major, but that's all we can say at the moment. You have a nice day now."

Paul looked at the phone in his hand. "The fucking cunt hung up!"

* * *

Two full minutes after Paul knocked for the second time, the chains rattled behind the radio station door.

"It's just us, me and Roza," Paul shouted.

Stefan snapped the bolts back. He pulled the door inwards, checked up and down the street, then beckoned them inside.

"I'm sorry to hear about the monastery," Paul said.

Roza translated, but Stefan was already shaking his head. "Is very bad," he said. "Very bad for us, but also for you. Nobody vote if like this."

In the kitchen, Paul took a chair at the square table and pulled one out for Roza. Stefan made coffee. He seemed less sprightly than usual. Classical music emanated from inside the studio.

"Handel?"

Stefan nodded. He had a spoon in his fingers, waggling it up and down as he waited for the percolator to boil. Given his nervousness, Paul decided not to mention the incident with the crowd even though his arm was still bandaged.

"You need to get more people to come back, Stefan," Paul said. "The more you have, the safer you and your church will be."

Stefan did not respond. He made the coffee, and placed their glasses on the table in front of them. He drank his standing.

Paul's eyes followed the line of cables from the hole in the brickwork where they emerged through the studio wall. They were pinned neatly across the ceiling and down the far corner to disappear outside through a window.

Looking at the window, he became aware of a girl's face beyond it, small eyes set above thick cheekbones. She was using her hands to shade the glass. Little Anja; the bravest person in Kosovo.

When Stefan noticed her, he shouted, but the girl had already vanished. He turned back to them, nervously punctilious. "We go inside?"

Paul placed his coffee down then walked through to the studio. He and Roza sat in their usual seats on the bench against the wall. Paul felt good, waiting for the red light to come on. Roza was close beside him and by extending his elbow slightly, he could touch hers. She responded this time, and the warmth was quickening.

Stefan asked the normal set of questions about what was happening in the wider world and in Belgrade. Had

Mr Kostunica handed former president Milosevic to the International Tribunal? What was happening in Pristina? It was notable that he chose not to ask about the bomber, making Paul wonder if he should mention it first. He didn't want to appear like he was hiding something.

To the simple questions, he trotted out answers that now came easily: the Serb people must take part in the elections if they wanted a political voice. To fail to vote was to waste a vote. There was little point in denying the assembly's legitimacy afterwards.

Stefan nodded, his hair shining. "But tell us, Major Paul. Tell us if a person votes, he is a citizen, yes?"

Paul became suddenly excited. This was exactly the way he wanted the conversation to go.

"Absolutely. A voter is an active citizen. He is still a citizen if he does not vote, of course. But he isn't taking an active interest." He paused to let Roza translate, then added, "I've always voted, always."

"You vote in England elections?"

"I vote by post."

Stefan nodded again, slowly this time, "Good, good," he said. "And citizen. He has right to protect himself in England? Against robber? Against bad people?"

"Yes. You have the right to defend your house. Your health, wealth, and property, I think is the phrase. But it has to be using minimum force."

"But robber? Robber will not attack if he think you defend yourself?"

Instinctively, Paul muddied his wording. "A robber is a bully. And a bully picks on the weak. What I suggest people do about scaring robbers away is portray themselves as strong."

"But what of old woman? What of old woman who has no husband and no family? How she does tell to robber?"

Roza translated very fast. Paul felt powerful next to her.

"I think it is the responsibility of a society to protect the weaker members," Paul said. "That is what happens in my town, a small town in Yorkshire, in England."

"So the strong protect the weak. This is allowed."

"Yes, of course it's allowed. It's to be encouraged. The problems in society occur when people do not look out for their neighbours."

"So it is good to look after the weak, the old, the young…"

"Yes, of course."

"And to protect the weak, to make robber stay away, it is good to make it look like you are strong, yes?"

"Absolutely."

"Thank you, Major," Stefan said. "Thank you."

After the interview, Stefan followed Paul and Roza into the kitchen. He rolled a cigarette and offered his pouch of tobacco to Paul, who accepted, then noticed the front door was ajar. He strolled over to look outside.

Seagood was sitting cross legged on the grass with her back against one wheel of the Landrover, her rifle propped against the fender. She was playing cards with Anja, placing them down on the grass one by one.

"Snap!" Anja said, joyfully grabbing a pair and making Seagood laugh.

"That's it! You're too good you are."

Paul stepped away from the door so as not to break the spell. Stefan glanced out in his place. Seeing Anja, he dropped his cigarette and shouted her inside. The girl, terrified, disappeared past Paul's legs into the rear of the building.

Seagood looked crestfallen, the cards scattered around her feet: "I'm sorry, I just…"

Stefan shook his head. "She must be inside," he said. "We protect her, all of us. After bombing man escape Bondsteel, she say NATO help only Albanian people."

Paul started to respond, but Stefan talked over him.

"Major, after election, she thinks Albanian people kill us all."

***

248

That night Paul couldn't sleep. After an hour of tossing and twisting, he lay on his back with his hands behind his head, staring up at the roof tiles. A deep fatigue was dulling his mind. The same thoughts went round and round.

Was it true that NATO favoured the Albanians? It had, once, but had that not changed? Had he been caught writing to Roza? How did Blanche get away with doing such things?

There was snoring along the corridor. It made him smile. How strange to be thrown together into blocks like this, doing what they were doing. It wasn't natural.

Rising silently, he pulled on his flip-flops and walked slowly along the corridor to the toilet, naked except for the boxers he slept in. The automatic closer made the door slam behind him and he was angry with himself. He tensed, listening for grunts of wakefulness. After pissing, he washed his hands and was more careful with the door on his return.

But what was the point of lying in bed for another four hours?

He grabbed a regimental sweatshirt from the chest of drawers. Pulling it on felt exciting, almost surreptitious. He dug a packet of fags and a lighter out of his smock pocket and slid silently along the corridor towards the fire escape. At the fire door, he depressed the bar slowly so that it clacked free with the minimum of noise. Outside, in the warm night air, insects buzzed round the perimeter lights. He couldn't see the Guardroom, but could make out the nearest end of the interpreters' hut. Standing on the wooden staircase outside the fire door, he took out a cigarette and lit it, then waited as his eyes became used to the darkness.

It was serene. A crescent moon, balanced at an unfamiliar angle, cast a pure light into the spaces between the portacabins. Stars stretched across the sky as if flung like silver grain. Paul was unashamedly calm.

A light came on in the interpreter's hut, a yellow glow through frosted glass. He knew Roza was in there. Was she alone?

Thoughts of her filled his belly, a wanting like no other. He flicked the end of the cigarette towards the gabion perimeter, watching it spark and fall away into darkness.

Why shouldn't he?

He descended the staircase carefully to stop it creaking. On the gravel, he walked predator-like along the rows of accommodation blocks. Passing fire door after fire door, he continued until he could hear the sentries chatting at the main gate. In his flip-flops, he clenched his toes to stop the sole clacking against his heel. He stopped against the wall of the interpreter's hut and listened. A vague light shone through the square main window. Stretching up, he peeped inside. Roza was climbing into a sleeping bag. The top bunk was empty.

Would she cry out? Could he get in without alerting the guard? One foot at a time, he mounted the wooden steps that led up to the front door. The door opened outwards. From inside he would be silhouetted, a threatening figure.

"Who is that?"

He closed the door behind him. Torchlight shone in his face.

"Paul!"

He knelt, a finger to his lips. The torch went off and then Roza was on him, arms around his neck.

"Are you alone?" he whispered, his voice tremulous.

"Yes," she said.

The moonlight caught on her eyeballs, her teeth. She was shaking. They were both shaking. He pulled himself up to standing. She was wearing knickers and a tee-shirt. Her legs were smooth to touch.

"You've come!" she said, joy leaping in her voice. She pressed herself against his chest, pressed her lips to his. She tasted stale, stale but beautiful. She tugged him backwards towards the bed and ducked into the bottom bunk, pulling him with her. He followed, nervously but unable to stop. They couldn't both get inside the sleeping bag, but their feet could.

Her arms were hot. Her hips were round. Her waist was slim. Her hair was in his face, then swept away. He rolled onto his back to have her on top of him. They kissed. He placed a hand on her cheek and studied the light reflected in her eyes. He saw the answer to his desires. She kissed him again, tugging at his lip with her teeth. His heart pounded. She wriggled under him, knees wide apart. Slowly, he lowered his body down onto hers, his cock hardening with every passing second.

She was just lovely, so wonderful. He slid one hand under her tee-shirt and she responded by pressing a round breast into his palm. The nipple was large and stiff between his fingers. He pushed the cloth upwards so he could get his lips around it. She arched, thumping the wall with a fist. And then they were twisting round each other, pulling off their clothes, positioning themselves.

Paul looked into her eyes. Her answer was immediate. She tilted her hips and took him, gasping. She clawed at his skin as he entered her; entered the point where things could never be the same again.

Chapter 16

Part of him felt shame. He had used his position to bed her. Part of him was afraid. This would end in ignominy. Part of him felt unmoved. He had emptied himself into her and now he felt nothing. But part of him, the part he held closest, felt elation. He was alive, a master of his game and gloriously, wonderfully adored by a woman he found magical.

He was also tired. Afterwards, they had slept in the wrap of each other's arms for an hour. When the first glimmers of daylight had woken them, he'd sucked himself free of her embrace, terrified of being seen. Outside the hut he'd quickly lit a cigarette to make it look like this was his normal morning routine. He strolled as nonchalantly as possible back to his block. The fire door had closed. He banged on it until someone opened it from inside. Blanche. He thanked her, flicked his cigarette away in explanation, then strode off for a shower. It was unusual for him to be up so early, and she looked at him askance.

"I had work to do," he grumbled.

The lies came out easily now. She didn't push him further.

Later, in the afternoon, the lack of sleep weighed down on him. Nothing was in full focus. A sharp staccato knock made him look round. He called out for the person to enter but the door did not open.

He got up and pulled the door wide. At the bottom of the step was the Chief of Staff. "You got a minute?"

Paul trembled, but if the game was up, he would go with dignity. "How can I help you, Simon?"

Simon always wore his tammy at an angle, the peak pulled forward as far as it would go. The hackle looked a bit tired.

"There have been some security developments," he said. "We have an issue to do with loyalty and integrity."

Paul swallowed. The blood was rising in his neck but he felt strangely calm. If this was going to be his execution, he was not going to grovel. He'd worked his tits off, he hadn't had any leave, and there was only a few weeks left anyway.

His love life was his own. Being away all of last year had cost him his relationship. Who were they to say who he could shag and who he could not? She was loyal. She was true. And if she came to England, they could be together.

He said, "That sounds a little high minded."

Simon laughed. "Yes, I suppose it does. But I wanted to be clear in my mind before I took any action."

Paul said nothing. It occurred to him that Simon did not actually know what he'd done. "What have you got in mind? Firing squad?"

Simon seemed disturbed by his bluntness. "I fancy there's something more subtle we can do. But there's a question I need answered."

"What's that?"

"I need to know if you've had any dealings with Roza Xhaferi, if you're involved with her…"

So he really didn't know.

"She's my interpreter. She's very good, in both languages…"

The answer seemed to satisfy. Simon nodded, "But there's nothing between you…"

"Is somebody saying there is?"

"Not at all. It's just I didn't want there to be any collateral damage."

What did that mean?

"There's nothing going on. Other than a professional relationship."

Paul placed his hands in his pockets and spoke deeply, chin low, as they'd taught him to do on the Message Operations course. It conveyed gravitas. After leaving a silence, he looked up to meet Simon's eyes and saw the line had sunk home. "Is there anything else I can help you with?"

Simon shifted his weight. A slight breeze caught the hackle in his tammy and made it flutter. "No, that's it."

"Well if you don't mind, I've got two interviews today..."

"Yes of course. Thank you, Paul. But please, not a word to anyone."

* * *

Things were starting to unravel. It was as if the game was drawing to a close. In the Grand Hotel, even the waiter seemed to know. He could smell the fact that Paul's life expectancy was shortening and resolutely failed to notice him, darting from one group of barrel-chested, grey-suited men to another, his back erect and nose high in the air.

He could go fuck himself.

Alone, Paul sat in one of the single chairs facing out into the lobby, one leg crooked so the ankle of his boot rested on the other knee and the thigh fell out to the side. He had taken his smock off, leaving his shoulder holster exposed for all to see. The strapping that supported it was tight across his shoulders and underneath the armpit. He placed a hand on each armrest and waited for Nick to arrive.

Al Pacino, in *Scarface*.

He was in control of the message, he kept telling himself. He who controls the message controls perception. And he who controls perception, controls behaviour.

Nick arrived at one minute past the hour and Paul rose to shake his hand. The last time they had met, Nick had paid him both a wonderful compliment and a stark warning.

"I think we ought to talk about Krivenic, Nick. Straight."

Nick placed his leather suitcase to the side of his legs as he sat on a facing chair, a little too far away. He tilted onto one hip to delve for his fags, lit one, and with a single gesture ordered himself a coffee from the waiter on the far side of the room.

Paul said nothing.

"You're no good to me if you lie, Paul," he said, exhaling smoke.

Paul kept his voice calm.

"Grow up, Nick. What do you expect me to say on the record? FYROM is host to the entire NATO supply chain. Every boot, bullet, and beef burger comes across that border. We need access to a deep water port and a heavy-lift runway."

Nick shook his head. "That does not excuse them firing on innocent people."

"I'm not saying it does."

By keeping his answer short, it was Nick who had to come up with a better line of investigation.

"So what *are* you saying? That it's acceptable for Macedonia to fire on Kosovo because NATO can ill afford to criticise its actions? Are you saying this is just *realpolitik*?"

Paul held his eyes. He could feel the heat inside him, the heat of someone who acted on conviction. It was easy to sit on the side and criticise.

"What other line can I take?" he said. "You know as well as I do who fired the shells. You know as well as I do that it was an error of judgement. But it was an informed error. The Albanian insurgents have been streaming into Macedonia for months, using little towns like Krivenic as a launch pad. You said so yourself."

Nick looked away, then leaned forward to tap ash into an ashtray. The waiter appeared and swept Nick's coffee down in front of him.

"*Faleminderit.*"

Paul did not attempt to make eye contact with the waiter. He kept focused on Nick. "I don't like the line any more than you do, but I can't say anything other than what I'm told to say."

Nick sneered. "You're just following orders? Like in Nuremburg?"

Paul shook his head. "Of course I'm following orders, Nick. I'm a soldier. But comparing me to a Nazi is neither fair nor accurate."

He wasn't used to talking like this. He was usually deferential to the point of being obsequious. Talking like this made him feel powerful.

Nick said, "I think it's very fair. All it takes is honest men to accept the little lies. Then they buy the large ones. And bit by bit society falls apart."

Paul listened. There was truth in what he said, sure. But such apocalyptic doom mongering was flawed.

"NATO is not here to eradicate a whole race of people. It's here to provide peace and stability for all. Of course there will be eruptions of violence. But we'll deal with them in turn. It serves no purpose to stir it all up."

Nick scowled, his voice taking an angry edge. "Who's stirring up violence?"

"You are," said Paul. "Your reporting makes Kosovo out to be utter chaos. It's not. Just look around you." He waved in the general direction of the besuited men.

He continued. "I saw this in Sierra Leone. A reporter and a photographer were ambushed somewhere up country, just after we arrived."

Nick nodded. "I knew them."

"Exactly. Two journalists got killed and the whole place is described as Armageddon. *The rebels are rampaging through Freetown. There'll be rape, and cutting off little children's limbs.*"

Nick looked saddened. But Paul wasn't going to pull his punches. He said, "And it wasn't like that. Freetown was stable. Up country was pretty lawless, but they'd been told that. They chose to go anyway."

Nick said, "I know what you're saying…"

A flash of anger made Paul interrupt him. "Do you know what really grips my shit? When a soldier dies, when one of us gets killed, all he's worth is a few column inches in the local tabloid. Maybe a mention on the regional news. But it's nothing to what happens if a journalist gets killed."

He was snarling now. "And let's be honest. Which one of us is nearer the action?"

Silence sank between them. Nick picked up his fags and pushed them into the pocket of his trousers. He avoided eye contact as he reached for the handle of his briefcase. He was leaving.

But then he said, "Paul, you're no good to me unless you have integrity."

* * *

The humidity was insufferable. Walking any distance brought Paul out in a sodden sweat. The air was laden with a heavy dust that infected his lungs like fungal spores. Roza had gone inside the radio station to get some water, but he needed air before being locked in the studio. Sitting on the concrete steps of Radio Black Eagle, he hawked and spat. The phlegm was glutinous and discoloured.

As he waited, the decrepit collie appeared from across the street, slithering through a hole in a chain-link fence. It limped badly, head dipped low, body turned part sideways, tail wagging.

Paul held out his hand. "There, there, girl. Come on."

The dog was soothed by his voice. A metre away, the closest it had ever come, it tilted its body almost horizontal and licked its lips.

"There you go. You're ok, come on."

The scarring down the flank had got worse. Someone had shot it in the hip with an air rifle. The wound was small and the blood had dried into flakes. The dog could barely lift the paw. The horror that someone could treat an animal this way made Paul utterly dismayed. But whereas he would have become extremely angry a few weeks previously, this time he felt completely drained.

"I have nothing for you," he said. He patted his pockets. "I have nothing more to give."

The dog stretched out, giving him the briefest touch of a warm, dry nose.

Inside the station, a lightly sprung door opened and slammed. The dog looked over Paul's head, then slunk away.

Roza appeared out of the screen door. Her hands were shaking and she was very red in the face.

"Are you ok? You look like you're about to faint."

She didn't meet his eyes. "She's ready for us," she said.

The interviews had become standard and Paul was comfortable in front of the microphone. Elire was lighter than normal in her questioning, sticking to issues that did not tax his mind. He mentioned the escape from Bondsteel, but did not dwell on the matter. Her listeners would have delighted in the news anyway.

After forty-five minutes, she asked Paul if there was anything else he would like to say. Paul read a short prepared statement, pausing to allow Roza to read her translation. He finished by saying that the elections in England were happening the next day and, if he won, Tony Blair would be in power for another four years.

"The British like him because of what he did here in Kosovo. And in eight days, the people of Kosovo will decide who they want to govern them. They must think carefully, but above all, they must vote."

It was a snappy, precise finish. Paul expected Elire to wrap, but she didn't.

She frowned, and keeping Paul firmly in her gaze, leaned forward to her microphone. She spoke for five minutes until Roza began to look horrified. Paul pointed to her. Elire stopped.

Roza translated, but in a much abbreviated form: "One moment please, Zotëri Major, there are some questions our listeners would like to ask. There are some issues that have been reported to us by our friends and we have concerns that are quite justified. Would you be willing to stay a little while longer and talk to us about them? They are important matters. They concern NATO and how NATO is protecting Serbian people in our lands, the lands where our fathers are buried. Would the Major remain for just a few moments more and talk to us, without a script?"

Roza's voice was almost a whisper. She had receded inside herself. For a second he wondered if she shook her head.

"Of course I will stay," Paul said, nudging Roza very gently to egg her on.

She translated, her voice almost inaudible.

Elire nodded. "Tell me," she said. "Is it true what you have been telling us, asking us to hand in our old weapons?"

Paul nodded. He had forgotten to plug this message and was grateful to Elire for reminding him.

"It is true. You do not need these weapons in your houses, above your doors and under your beds," he said. "They are old. The Serbs will not start another war. Milosevic has gone. President Kostunica is trying to build a representative government. And the same is true in Macedonia. There is no need for violence in a stable society."

Roza translated, speaking very slowly. Paul was about to continue when Elire interrupted him. "So you agree you have been telling us to hand in our weapons?"

Roza translated and Paul nodded. "Yes," he said, more firmly. Had it not been clear the first time?

"So why is it," Elire continued, "why is it we hear you are telling Serbian people they have the right to defend their homes? That they have the right to keep their weapons?"

Paul looked at her with disbelief and felt his expression turn to anger. "I never said they could keep their weapons."

Elire looked at him. "You deny it?"

Paul shook his head in frustration, "I said on Gracanica Radio that every home owner should have the right to defend their property if they are robbed…"

He stopped, realising that if he was to be crystal clear, Roza would need time. He nudged her and she translated, sentence by sentence.

"Defending property does not mean keeping guns," he concluded.

Then Elire asked, "But what of the Serbian people who have blood on their hands? Are we not able to defend ourselves from them?"

"Of course you are. Everyone has the same rights."

"And so you say now we can defend ourselves?"

"Yes. But defence does not mean attacking others, attacking the monastery in Gracanica."

"But you said to Serbian people they can do so. We have it, on the radio. You say they can keep their guns and then you say we, the Albanian people, we cannot do this."

Roza translated. Paul felt exasperated. He didn't say that. This was futile.

"Look. I want you to hand in your old weapons. It is not necessary to keep them any more…"

Roza started to translate but the phone rang, an old fashioned device with an American ring tone. Elire answered it, shakily holding the receiver to the microphone so as to broadcast the caller's voice.

Paul tugged Roza gently away from the microphone to whisper in her ear. "This is a trap. I don't know how they got this information. I need to extract and will walk out if I need to…"

Roza nodded. She was as trapped as he was.

"That was one of our listeners," said Elire. "He was a fighter with the heroes in the Kosovo Liberation Army during the victorious war against the Serbian aggressors. He is a man of noble blood, a man of courage, a man who fought for the freedom of Kosovo before NATO came."

She made a dismissive gesture.

"He is asking, Zotëri Major, if NATO will return the weapons he handed in. He says he has changed his mind."

* * *

Paul knocked on the Brigadier's door. It was time to come clean.

"Come."

He walked in, saluted smartly, and stood to attention in the centre of the room. "Sir, I've fucked up."

The Brigadier was behind his desk. Simon was sitting to the left and Blanche to the right. A map of northern Macedonia was pinned to the wall. The three of them must have been discussing the next operation. Paul felt very calm. There were lives at stake and he was, ultimately, a man of integrity.

"I've been pilloried by the media. I think I've somewhat over estimated what I could achieve." His voice cracked.

"Go on, Paul" the Brigadier said.

Paul cleared his throat. "I was trying to get the Serbs to return to vote in the election. They thought I told them, in Gracanica, that they could keep their weapons. I didn't say so, it's just what they wanted to hear. They twisted my words."

"When was this?" Blanche asked. She started flicking through her notebook.

"Monday."

"You're sure?"

Now it looked like he'd fucked up but taken two days to come clean. "I'm sorry, I thought I could step over it, deny that was what I'd said. But it's come back to bite me on the arse."

"Go on," the Brigadier studied him, his arms folded and head tilted to one side.

"Today I had an interview with Radio Black Eagle. I didn't think they would listen to Radio Gracanica. It's a different language for a start…"

"But…"

"But I underestimated them. They had been listening. They caught me good and proper. They asked why I was telling the Serbs to arm and telling them to hand in their weapons. I got flustered. It went badly…"

The three officers looked at one another. Blanche nodded. "Just as I thought," she said.

At that moment Paul wanted to come clean about Roza as well. He wanted the heaviness of it all lifted from his shoulders. He was about to speak when Blanche silenced him.

"This is the Albanians provoking an armed response from the Serb community. That will provide an excuse for yet more sectarian killings. Then all hell will break loose."

"*Could* break loose, Blanche," said the Brigadier. "Could, not will."

Blanche did not respond.

Simon was watching the Brigadier. "This changes nothing. We've made contingency plans. In actual fact, Paul has drawn matters into the open. It has accelerated events, but not changed them. We still have the advantage."

The Brigadier looked at his Chief of Staff and then at Blanche. Both nodded to him.

"Paul, thank you for coming clean," the Brigadier said. "You've done nothing wrong. We've had our eyes on the leader of one of the political parties for some time. We suspect he's got more than the normal links to Albanian organised crime. There's a covert operation to arrest him happening at the moment. You've uncovered the means by which he communicates with his armed factions."

Paul felt suddenly exhausted by the intrigue. This was the first he had heard of it. "You mean…?"

"I mean, Paul, that it was good of you to report in so quickly. Just what I'd expect from an officer."

"So what do you want me to do?" He might not get the sack after all, but his relief was quickly replaced by a deep unease. He was uncertain, and that lack of clarity was unnerving.

Montrose said, "I know that you've been working all hours to promote this election, Paul. You look exhausted. I want you to step back from it all."

Paul frowned. He still wasn't clear.

The Brigadier continued. "The elections are in a few days. There's nothing more you can do. What you've done has been exemplary. But we've only got a few weeks left. Why don't you start planning your handover?"

Paul really didn't know how, but he'd got away with it.

"You have my full confidence, Paul. Well done."

"Thank you, Sir." Paul drew himself up, saluted, and left the office.

You have my full confidence. That's what Prime Ministers said about someone in the cabinet shortly before they sacked them.

Chapter 17

Thursday evening passed quietly enough for Paul to think he had actually got away with the interview. And providing he didn't get caught with Roza, he might have got away with fucking her as well. At dinner, waiting in the scoff queue, Simon even repeated the Brigadier's message. "You've had one bad day, that's all. Don't worry about it. It's a marathon, not a sprint."

After the meal he didn't go back to the office as he usually did, but to his room. Lying on top of the bed, he slept for three hours. Waking was almost painful.

"Jesus Christ," he said, looking at his watch. He had not even taken off his boots. Shaking the heaviness from his eyes, he washed and changed his shirt, then went to the Operations Room to listen to the radio traffic on the brigade net.

The Watchkeeper saw him. "It looks like it might get exciting tonight, Sir. There's a crowd gathering near the football stadium. The foot patrols are saying it's going to kick off."

"Do you know why?"

The Watchkeeper shook her head. "The Chief of Staff says it's just their politicians rattling sabres before the elections."

"Are you prepared? If it gets ugly?"

She was unflappable. "All three infantry battalions have troops stood by in riot gear."

Paul asked, "Is it just in Pristina?"

The Watchkeeper shook her head. "There's a full scale riot in Mitrovica happening right now. The French Brigade were fully stretched and we had to send additional troops. Flew them over in a Chinook."

"How many?"

"The Brigadier said we should send the platoon from Gracanica."

Paul's jaw fell open. "So we've nothing protecting the monastery?"

The Watchkeeper shook her head. "No need. It's quiet down there." She smiled up at him. "You were very cool under pressure, by the way, when you drove through that crowd."

"It's an act," Paul said quickly. "Everything I do is an act. So there's nobody in Gracanica at all?"

The Watchkeeper shook her head. "All quiet."

Paul couldn't help grimacing but didn't want her to notice. "Thank you," he said. "I'll be in my office for the next few hours, if you need me."

At his desk he started up the computer but realised there was little point in planning anything. Whatever he had to say was going to be reactive. He jotted down a few ideas, but then placed his notebook on the corner of his desk and turned on the television, volume off. Thankfully the BBC were not reporting the riots.

What was Nick up to? Where was he?

Back home, the election was taking place. On the screen, a pundit waved his hands at a map, the colours indicating the safe seats and those open to swing voters. People were interviewed on the streets.

The whole escapade seemed suddenly rather pointless.

Nothing surprised him, Paul realised. He understood the news agenda. He could see the truth behind everything. He could read between the lines where they existed, and judge the situation where they did not. He could look at any picture on the television and simply smell the subtext. He could feel the truth, taste it.

And it was all, ultimately, quite boring.

* * *

Brassy laughed as he spoke on the phone. For the first time ever, New Labour had won a second term.

"They're ecstatic, Paul, up in Main Building. I always said this was well within your capabilities. Just get Kosovo on message, I said, and that's exactly what you've done."

Paul leaned back into his chair and placed his boots on the desk, crossing them at the ankles.

Brassy continued. "…now the polls are showing people actively support government policy…"

Paul interjected while he could. "What about Aden Short?"

Brassy was dismissive. "Got buried by other news. A shame, but there you go."

Paul felt a mixture of pain and relief. "So it didn't…"

"Didn't make a single front page, even though the press are desperate to talk about anything other than cows."

"Is that good?"

"I've no idea. All I care about is how we look. And thanks to you in Kosovo and the TA up in Cumbria, we look just rosy. Message Operations at their best, old chum!"

Paul was secretly saddened that Aden got so little mention. "Who got in for Shipley, Colonel?" he said to change the subject.

There was a clicking sound. "Wait one… Labour. Chris Leslie, a majority of six thousand. Do you know him?"

"My Dad does."

"Didn't know you were a red."

"You know my Dad's in the Party."

"Yes, now you mention it. I'd forgotten. But each to his own. Now tell me, what's happening with the trial of those dirty little bastards who did for that bus?"

While he talked, Paul kept glancing up at the ticker-tape on the television. He didn't want to miss anything.

"It's kind of complicated. There've been two trials. The first was made up of civvy judges from EU nations. They said the supporting three men should be released due to lack of evidence. But that never happened, something to do with evidence that the panel never saw."

"Ours?"

"No, American. And it's classified. So then a second trial was made up of military lawyers. They were allowed to see the secret evidence and returned a verdict that all three should be retained in custody."

"So where are they now?"

"In Bondsteel," said Paul.

"And the one who got away?"

"Still on the run. We suspect he's scarpered back to Albania."

"And that was Tomato, the one who pressed the tit?"

"Yes."

"Amazingly incompetent these Yanks, aren't they," Brassy said. "I mean how can you let a man walk out of a secure cell in Bondsteel prison? I gather it's like Fort Knox, or meant to be."

"It is," said Paul. "And it has made the whole country unsettled. My interviews are getting more difficult by the day."

"Of course they are." said Brassy. "Normal form in the run up to an election. People are fractious, that's all."

"I got ambushed last week. I told the Brigadier I was nearly burned."

"Burned? You?" Brassy said, his voice rising in pitch. "Nonsense! You're indestructible."

* * *

The Kosovo election was the next day. A poll conducted by the United Nations showed that it would be a close run thing between the nationalists and the liberals, although regional and minor parties were expected to get a share of seats proportionate to their interests. Paul was worried that voter registration among the Serbs was even lower than for the Roma, who formed a mere two per cent of the population.

Just before midday, Paul and Roza left the offices of the Koha Ditore newspaper. He had been meeting the editor to discuss what the results could mean. He could not hide the fact that he deeply wanted Rugova to win, even if his sole reason for doing so was the fact he had shaken his hand. On such small margins the election seemed to hang.

The editor was an urbane and highly educated man of about thirty. He was equally clear in who he supported, but was astute enough not to state it in case his wishes were not fulfilled.

Outside, Roza said she had to go. "I must meet my brother," she said. Where is Jane?"

"She's just rung to say she's stuck in traffic on Mother Teresa Street. I will walk over to meet her to save her coming round," Paul said.

Roza's eyes widened. She looked at her watch. "Ok. But it would be good if you go now. Don't wait."

Paul didn't know what she meant.

"The traffic," she said. "It is very bad. You should go find her and tell her to turn round. Go back to camp."

Paul nodded. Yes, that was what he was thinking too. He reached out to briefly hold her fingers. She squeezed his, then turned and skipped away down the steps, looking at her watch once again.

He couldn't stop thinking about her. The tour was nearly over. The bomb, the arrest, the escape, the valley. He'd done it all, and done it well. And she'd been with him at every step. Enjoying the sensation of being outside, he ambled along the pedestrianized shopping area taking time to enjoy himself. He thought of her tight, firm little body straddling his, the scent of her skin, and the freckles spattered across her breasts. If she was going to study in England, their relationship might...

When the bomb exploded, it took him a second to realise what had happened.

He saw it before he felt it, a billowing of dust and debris that spat and swelled across the pavement beyond a row of shops. He lifted his elbow to shield his face. The blast knocked him sideways and whipped his skin.

He looked up. The cloud of dust had settled almost as fast as it had risen. People ran. He was forty metres away at most.

Where was Roza? He reached for his mobile. He rang her number. It didn't answer. He stared at the phone, then looked up at the detritus and glass scattered over the street. There was no fire, and no screaming. Just silence.

He must call it in. The Watchkeeper answered.

"It's Major Illingworth. I'm on Garibaldi Street, the pedestrian bit. Eleven-zero-five hours. There's been a bomb, a car bomb. There are casualties. It's outside the, wait…"

He stumbled along the walkway looking for shop signs he could read. The street was a mixture of large windowed residential flats and small businesses.

"The nearest building is the…" He stopped dead. The sign was in English. "It's right outside a place called *The Centre for Peace and Tolerance.*" All his energy sunk. "How fucking droll."

He didn't wait to hear the Watchkeeper reply. He was surprised by how unaffected he felt by the carnage.

The car was once a white saloon. The passenger was dead, his charred and bloody body thrown forward against the dashboard. Rags of clothing hung from his shoulders. Smoke rose from his skin. The fingers had tightened into black fists. Part of the driver's head was missing. The torso slumped against the door, the seatbelt partially covering the missing part of the skull.

A woman with curly blonde hair sat at the road junction. She couldn't stand. She tried to gather oranges from where they had fallen around her. She kept putting them into a plastic bag that had ripped down the side. Whenever she put one in, it fell straight back out and rolled away.

Outside the blast area, a group of men looked at each other, laughing hysterically. They checked their hands and clothes for cuts. Had they been ten yards closer, they would have been killed.

A girl with straight black hair peered out of one the flats above the shops, then withdrew. The windows had shattered.

Two men picked up the woman with curly hair and put her in a wheelchair. Where it came from, Paul did not know. They pushed her away while she kept looking over her shoulder for her shopping. Blood ran from her ears.

A Norwegian soldier approached him, though Paul did not know from where. He saluted and his mouth moved. Paul realised he couldn't hear. He swallowed to clear his throat, and pointed.

"Put up cordons and deal with the injured. There will be people in those flats above as well. Direct any reporters to me."

His voice sounded strange. The soldier nodded. He had very piercing blue eyes. Paul walked towards a lime tree surrounded by a circle of iron railings. He held on to a spar to keep his balance while a dizzy spell struck him.

Police sirens. Cordon in place. Casualties under control. What next?

Roza was running past the shops. She saw him, tall amongst the growing crowd, and sprinted. She had tears in her eyes.

"Paul!"

She flung herself at him. Her arms swept round his chest and held him, held him tighter than he'd ever been held.

"I was afraid. I knew you come this way."

He placed his arms around her, surprised at how far they would reach. He was unsteady, but she held him upright.

"I'm working," he said.

Tears ran down her cheeks. "I am so glad you are safe."

"I was worried about you, too," he said, patting her shoulder. "Did you hear it go off?"

A van arrived carrying UN police of various nationalities. An Italian Carabinieri officer started directing bystanders away from the scene. Another rolled out incident tape. The police commander wore a Royal Ulster Constabulary uniform. A squad of British soldiers arrived on foot, sweating and laden.

Yorkshiremen, noted Paul from their uniforms. They saw what was happening, looked round, and the corporal approached Paul for instructions.

Paul disengaged himself from Roza. "The police have primacy now. Do what that RUC man says," he said, then pulled Roza with him, one large hand on her upper arm.

In the lee of the shops on the other side of the road, she embraced him again. Her chin puckered.

"You rang me first," she said. "After explosion. You rang to see I am ok."

"Yes I did," said Paul.

"You do love me," she said, hiding her face against his chest.

Then without meeting his eyes, she shook herself free and ran away through the crowd.

* * *

"Nick, it's Paul. You've got my number. I thought you'd want to know about the bomb that went off today. Give me a ring. Cheers."

That was the second time. He wasn't going to do it again. If Nick didn't want a source, that was fine. Very soon *The Times* or *Reuters* would send out a replacement for Aden, and Paul would make sure he was properly briefed. Or at the very least, there was a charming Frenchwoman from *Associated Press* who could provide similar access to one of the other wire services.

Paul sat at his desk looking up at the television. The lights were off and the blind drawn in case Roza came round, though he didn't know where he stood with her. The idea of her coming to London filled his chest with lightness. Even though she was so much younger, their bond had been forged in war. If they could survive this, they could survive anything.

He only had a few days left. Then he could sleep. Wake up at eight. Go to bed at ten.

When he'd got back to camp and taken a shower, he found bits of glass in his hair. He had a ringing sensation in his ears for several hours. He should go and see a doctor, but dismissed the idea.

On the TV, Tony Blair waved to a large crowd, still jubilant at his election victory a week before. The bombing was not reported at all. The only foreign news was the killing of a mujahedeen fighter in Northern Afghanistan.

The phone rang.

"Nick?"

"Paul, I see you've dialled my number."

"I thought you'd want to know about the events of this afternoon. Where are you?"

There was a pause, then, "I'm in London. I came here to speak to Alice, Aden's wife."

"He was married?"

"Divorced, of course. Not many relationships last in our game I'm afraid."

You're not the only one, chum, thought Paul. He said, "So did you hear about…"

"I did Paul, and I thank you for thinking of me, but I'm not going to write it up. The BBC will get it from the wire services and the Guardian have appointed a staff reporter to cover while I'm off."

"So you don't need…"

"No Paul, I don't. And to be frank, since you insist on adhering to the official bullshit, I can't rely on what you say."

That stung.

"I *never* lied to you, Nick. You may not like the official lines, but what else can I do?"

Nick scoffed. "You can't pretend you have no role in this. It's the half-lies that perpetuate the madness."

That was too far. "Bollocks! You cannot say we are to blame."

"Can't I? You obviously think that you can deliver peace in the Balkans simply by using the media. How is the reverse not also true?"

Paul didn't know what to say.

"I'm coming back at the end of the week, Paul. I'll meet you, if you like. But don't think it's going to be like before. You lied about the Macedonians. You know you did. And you got away with it, really. But Aden is still dead and NATO are doing nothing about it. They're pretending – you're pretending – that it doesn't matter. I'm sorry, but that will not do."

Nick started coughing. It quickly became a racking, hacking clearing of the lungs.

You'd better stay there, old man, Paul thought. But he would be sad to lose Nick's friendship. "What can I do to help you recognise I'm not a bad guy?"

Nick thanked someone, then gargled deep in his throat. "If you want to prove yourself, Paul," he said, "you can tell me why there is such a veil of secrecy surrounding the trial of the men who bombed that bus. Why is there no trial date? Why is it being held in secret?"

Paul shrugged. "I don't know. That's a UN police matter, not for NATO. We arrested them, but the legal process is outside our jurisdiction."

"Not good enough. I want to know why the men are being held."

"You can demand all you want," Paul said. "But that's still not my responsibility."

"It never is," Nick said, and hung up.

The Guardian, 24 August 2001
Balkan Democracy Marred by Murder of Serbian Politician
Balkans Correspondent

The troubled Balkan region of Kosovo rejoiced last night as the first Kosovo Assembly elections were completed.

"We are newborn!" shouted Bekim Xhaka, a taxi driver, as he honked down the capital Pristina's most famous road, Mother Teresa Street.

Asked about the elections, Kofi Annan, the United Nations Secretary General, said, "The all-inclusive nature of the elections will provide a solid basis for the institutions of Provisional Self-Government."

President Kostunica of Serbia would not comment on the election, but front runner Ibrahim Rugova said that the election victory for his party was "an immediate call for full independence from Serbia".

The future of a democratic and accountable Kosovo was called into question, however, by the murders of Serb politician Zoran Simic and his bodyguard the day before the election. Simic was standing as a representative of the minority Serbian population. Following the incident, Serbian people boycotted the election in vast numbers.

Chapter 18

It was not only Paul coming to the end of his time in Kosovo. The brigade was being replaced by another, and as a result the camp was permanently alive with NCOs shouting, heavy vehicles backing up, and lines of bergens being stacked ready for the next lift to the airport.

"What do you mean she's gone?" Paul said, slumping into his chair. "She didn't say goodbye."

"You were away. She come into interpreters' hut," said Roza. "She say RAF make mistake with the manifest and she have to go or wait another two weeks."

Paul laughed, despite the shock of the news, that would have been an easy choice.

"She told me she respect you very much, Roza said, placing a hand on his shoulder. "She said to give you big kiss."

Paul folded his arms. Seagood's sweet laughter had been one of the highlights of the tour. How she'd panicked when the mob surrounded the Landrover, and yet how quickly she'd recovered. No taller than the spare wheel on the rear door, after the Gracanica incident, when someone honked at her on the motorway, she had this way of slowing down to thirty kilometres an hour and holding that speed no matter what Paul or anyone else did. She'd purse her lips, stick her chin in the air, and fix her hands either side of the steering wheel.

"Nobody honks at Jane Seagood. Nobody."

The memory made him smile. He still felt guilty about telling her off. It was now obvious that Seagood had said nothing to anybody. They'd been tight, the three of them. And he'd almost spoiled it. She had remained true, and that made the hollow inside him even deeper.

He would make a point of writing a letter to her officer commanding – she was based at an RAF station somewhere in Norfolk – to say how reliable she had been. It seemed so paltry a gesture after everything the three of them had been through, but that was military life.

For their final trip to Radio Gracanica, Paul found they had been allocated a signaller from the incoming brigade as their driver. He was thin, spotty, and nervous; only just out of training and on his first operational deployment. He had been told to learn the routes. Paul wondered how long he had had a licence, given how many times he stalled the Landrover.

"Don't look at the women," Paul said. "There's a three-fold increase in road traffic accidents in the summer months."

The boy laughed.

"And the roundabouts are different. You give priority to people coming on, not the ones coming off. In short, drive defensively."

The boy nodded, leaning forward with both hands on the wheel. His rifle was locked in the weapon mount and the magazine was fitted, but he wasn't Seagood.

It was the beginning of the end, Paul thought. His final days.

Looking over his shoulder, he could tell Roza was thinking the same. She was wearing a long sleeved blouse and had pulled the cuffs down over her hands. Knees tight together, she swayed from side to side in the back of the vehicle, her eyes fixed entirely on him. She didn't smile. In fact she didn't make any expression at all. She just looked at him, and he at her.

"Last one, with Stefan," he said. She nodded, but didn't speak.

When they arrived, Gracanica had a deserted feel about it. Some leaves were being blown off the sycamore trees by high winds. They fell across the road giving the light a reddish hue that reminded Paul of home.

Along the monastery wall, a group of old women stood in a line, scrubbing off paint.

"Bollocks," Paul said, shaking his head.

He'd done all he could. He'd proved what Message Operations could do if given the latitude it needed. Despite the ambush by Elire and losing the support of one old codger from the Guardian, the brigade had recovered over a fifteen-hundred rifles. He had illuminated the risks of Albanian extremism, and done everything he could to ensure the Presevo Valley was returned with minimal loss of life. He'd encouraged the Serbs to vote in the elections; encouraged everyone, come to think about it. And the best man had won. Liberalism, rather than nationalism, had gained the majority of seats in the assembly. That seemed important.

Most of all, Kosovo was more peaceful and more stable than it had been when he arrived.

Getting out of the Landrover, he nipped quickly round the back to help Roza out. She was waiting for him and held out her hand. The wind whipped his trousers. Her sneakers were very clean and he was afraid she'd slip on the mud, so guided her round to the gravel path.

"*Faleminderit, Zotëri Major*," she whispered.

"*Nuk ka problem*," he replied.

Stefan leaned against the wall, smoking. He smiled, then scrubbed the cigarette down the masonry.

"What happened to the monastery?" Paul said.

Stefan shrugged and shook his head.

"You know answer," he said. "They come in night. They shoot guns at holy picture. They write words." He gestured as if using a spray can.

"I'm sorry," Paul said. "We are handing over to a new brigade. There will be new soldiers here in a couple of days. They will make sure this does not happen."

Stefan shook his head, looking at his feet.

"I'll speak to the incoming Chief of Staff," Paul insisted. "There were no soldiers here last night because they had to go to Mitrovica. It's impossible to hold every position when you're handing over."

The argument was weak and Paul knew it. Stefan took it with resignation, as if he always knew Paul would let him down.

"Is very bad," he said. "This is why Serbian people do not vote in your elections."

"They weren't my elections, Stefan. They were yours."

But he knew, before he'd finished the sentence, what Stefan would say next.

"They kill him in his car."

Paul glanced at Roza. She was shivering. It was obvious Stefan was not going to invite them inside.

Stefan pointed to the door but shrugged in apology. "No point for this. No power."

That was why everything seemed so desolate. There were no lights anywhere in the village.

"Have you spoken to the UN? You want me to call someone?"

He wanted to leave Stefan in good spirits but it was as if all the woes of Gracanica were being placed at his feet. He'd worked eighteen hour days for the last seven months and could do no more. A power cut was just something the enclave would have to bear.

Stefan shook his head. "It come back. In time, it come back."

"I'm sorry, Stefan. I'd like to thank you for the conversations we've had. And I'd like to wish you the very best for the future."

He held out his hand. If Stefan was not going to take it, that was fine too. They had to stand up, these people. They had to learn for themselves.

Suddenly, Stefan's face changed. He drew back his lips and snarled. "You make us hope, Major. But you don't make it good. You don't make it happen. This worse than no hope."

"Stefan, that's not fair…"

But Stefan had said what he wanted. He turned his back and retreated behind the metal door. And all Paul could do was watch the smelly, skinny little man make the only gesture he could.

* * *

On the penultimate day of the tour, the brigade staff gathered to debrief the management of the elections with a view to capturing any lessons worth learning. Despite the number of people in the room, it was cold because the heating system had failed.

Paul sat quietly in the corner.

The officer commanding the brigade engineering squadron identified that the combat engineering tractors were not able to cross the culvert at a particular grid reference.

The Air Liaison Officer reported that the Chinooks had been grounded because a batch of oil had been sourced from a supplier in Albania, but it had proved to be the wrong sort. A new batch of higher grade oil had been ordered from Germany, so the Chinooks should be back on task with effect from Friday.

The Watchkeeper said she would have preferred more information about the involvement of external agencies. She did not understand the role of the Department for International Development. Representatives of that organisation had turned up at one of the infantry battalions demanding escorts. The infantry battalion had obliged, thinking that the request had been sanctioned by the brigade headquarters. As a result, they did not have resources available for maintaining vehicle patrols through the Serb enclaves. Had they done such patrols, the monastery might not have been defaced once again.

After ninety minutes of scribbling what people said, the Chief of Staff placed his tammy on his head and flicked the hackle with his middle finger.

"That will give the incoming brigade a few pointers," he said. "And it goes without saying that I'd like to thank everyone for their hard work. We've had a good tour, and it has been a pleasure and an honour to serve alongside you."

The Brigadier, who had said almost nothing during the whole meeting, took this moment to stand.

The room fell silent, the staff looking up at the tall, rangy officer with the utmost fondness. Their thoughts were increasingly with home; their children, wives, families, lovers, pets, the partially remembered brickwork of their own front doors. But despite this, their last moments in Kosovo felt like being ripped away from something more meaningful than they had ever done in their lives.

Brigadier Sandy Montrose took the time to look into the eyes of everyone in the room. "I'd like you all to know that what we did here," he said. "The return of the buffer zone, the weapons amnesty, the elections. These things will have strategic implications for the future of Kosovo. We have worked hard. And it has been worth it.

"You all know, of course, that one of those we arrested for the bus bombing, the one we named *Tomato*, has escaped from the American detention facility at Bondsteel. We don't know how it happened, but the Yanks have promised that an investigation is underway. But we should not let their fuckup get in the way of the fact that we also found, located, and interdicted a dangerous extremist cell.

"I have no doubt that the due course of law will prevail." Here, the Brigadier allowed a broad smile to explode across his face. He opened his arms wide. "But that is for the next brigade to worry about."

The room erupted into cheers. Their replacements would arrive that afternoon, and the flight home seemed more real with every passing minute.

It was only as they stood to leave that one officer asked, "About the elections. Does anyone know who won?"

The officers chuckled as they looked from one to another, shaking their heads. They turned to Blanche, but her face told them that asking her was in some way inappropriate.

Paul was at the back. "Rugova," he said. "Doctor Ibrahim Rugova. He's a moderate, the guy we would have wanted to win."

The officers turned to look at him. They nodded, respecting the fact that he had bothered to find out.

The colonel who had asked the question shrugged. "Well, there you go," he said, and the gathering broke into deep guffaws as they left the building.

None of this was real for them, Paul thought, whereas to him it felt like a knot of iron in his belly.

"Paul, would you mind staying behind a minute?" Simon was waiting for the others to leave.

Paul nodded. He had expected to be summoned. The Brigadier owed him a final interview to give him his appraisal. Then he'd find out if he would ever make it into Staff College.

"Sure," he said.

When the room had emptied, Simon suggested they go into his office. Blanche and the Brigadier would join them. Paul stepped sideways round the chairs. He felt nervous, all of a sudden. Why did the conversation require Blanche? Why Simon, for that matter?

Inside his office, Simon faced the Brigadier. "Sir, you said you wanted to see Paul after the debrief?"

"Yes, absolutely. Let's have the discussion now."

Blanche held a folder in one hand and took a seat underneath the window. Simon sat behind his desk and the Brigadier took a chair behind the door, stretching out his legs as he did so.

Paul remained standing in the centre of the room. He looked from one officer to the next. "I'm not clear what's…"

"Sit down, Paul. There's something we want to discuss," the Brigadier said.

This did not bode well. He sat, but remained straight backed.

"So we have the results of the elections?"

Paul nodded. "Yes, Sir. They call Rugova 'Mother Teresa of the Balkans'. Because he's caring of the poor."

"Good. But very little turnout from the Serbs?"

Paul shook his head. "I'm sorry. Almost none. After that politician was blown up, they had no one to vote for."

The Brigadier nodded. "No, I suppose not. And you're leaving us soon?"

"Yes, Sir. Next flight but one."

"And your replacement has been identified?"

"Yes, Sir. Spoke to Colonel Brassy this morning. My replacement can't get out for a few weeks, but I've left him a file."

"And you and I will have a chat about your report before you go?"

"I hope so." Paul was surprised. What was this about then? There was no hint of what the Brigadier was thinking. Would he be recommended for Staff College or not? Did it matter, if Roza was coming to London?

"Paul, I know Simon and Blanche have both asked you, but you've not been romantically involved with your interpreter, have you?"

Paul shook his head. "No Sir."

"Well that's good. Because we now know that it was her that told Radio Black Eagle what you said to the Serbs. We also know that it was her who told certain parties that we pulled the infantry platoon out of Gracanica, leaving the opportunity open for the latest desecration of the monastery. We also know her associates planned the attack on that Serb politician."

Paul's mouth fell open. Blood drained from his face. That could not be. It just could not be. He blinked. It was like having his entire body sucked through the floor, leaving only his skin.

"I can see this is something of a surprise. We've been monitoring her laptop. We think that being so close to you, she was at the heart of... Paul, are you all right?"

His mouth was dry. He sat back, breathing in, breathing out. A ring of red light appeared before his eyes. He felt sick, his stomach threatening to contract. Simon went out of the room and came back with a plastic cup of water from the cooler.

"I'm sorry. I just felt like I was going to puke."

He was shaking so much that he spilled some of the water. His head cleared and he regained control of his voice.

"Sorry, Sir. Must have been a bad bit of bacon, but I'm fine. You were saying. Miss Xhaferi was spying on me. I had no idea, no idea at all..."

"We realised," Simon said. "But we didn't tell you we were watching her in case you gave the game away."

Blanche turned her shoulders towards him. Her voice was clinical. "We were playing her and still are. We're feeding information to her and tracking what others do with it. As an intelligence asset, she's proving wonderfully effective. All the communication corridors are becoming clear. We're currently mapping the third tier of associates, some of whom are in organised crime, and some of whom are members of political parties."

Blanche smiled, her hands on the folder on her knees. She had won. She knew it, and knew he did too.

"I didn't realise..."

What didn't he realise? That Blanche could be so devious? That the Balkans would be so draining?

Or had he known about Roza all along?

"I didn't realise it would be so hard," Paul said.

The other three laughed even though he hadn't intended it as a joke. The Brigadier smiled warmly as he placed the flat of his palms down on his thighs. "That, Paul, is the truth of it, I'm afraid."

PART FIVE

Chapter 19

Paul recovered his car from the long-term car park at RAF Brize Norton. Once he'd jump-started the battery with the Watchkeeper's Volvo, he drove home. Six weeks post-op leave. After that there'd only be a month and then it would be Christmas.

Having so much time to himself felt too open, too free. He had never had to entertain himself for so long. He was back with his parents for a full week before he slept less than nine hours a day. His parents fed him his favourite dinners – fish and chips from the place in town, lamb madras from the takeaway next to the garage – and over time he regained the stone that he didn't know he'd lost.

Earnest and concerned, his parents never asked about his experiences, but he could overhear them talking about him as he lay in bed. He could have saved them from worry, but was too emotionally withered to bother. They wouldn't understand. And the truth was that he didn't actually know what he felt himself.

He had a sense that his tour had been purposeful, that he had worked hard, and that he'd got away with something. But Roza... that was a sore that still festered.

He never even said goodbye. She avoided him in the end.

Alone in the house during daytime, he did not watch the television for several days. But then he found himself drawn back to it. One day he sat for an entire afternoon watching the news channels with the sound off, tracking how stories broke, grew, and faded off the tickertape headlines.

"That's me," he said to himself, his dog resting its head on his thigh. "I'm being pushed aside now."

The next day he went to PC World and bought himself a laptop with the latest operating software. He checked his emails every hour. Nothing had come from Roza, nothing at all, and so he knew he was right.

He knew where his life had to go next, even though the decision meant having to face the fear that he'd failed.

* * *

Dear Roza,

I want you to know that working with you was very special. I really regret not having taken better advantage of the time we had. You are, of course, entitled to your own political opinions. And I wish you, and Kosovo, all fortune in the future. I am certain Rugova will be an inspiration to many. I guess I never thought to put my nation before my family. It seems the wrong way round for me.

My big news is that I've decided to leave the army. The greatest lie I've been peddling for the last few years is that I still enjoy it. It's too hard, emotionally. I don't like being separated from those I love. I can't be devious, and I'm not astute enough to climb the career ladder. Brigadier Montrose gave me a nice send-off, but my report was pretty tepid and to be honest, I think he's right.

After coming home I've realised that everything I was doing was a lie. I don't have the tenacity of people like Simon or Blanche. And everything around me is either copied or fake: the CDs outside the gate; my acting rank; the way the journos crowd over a story and then leave it to rot; the way I peddled lines that meant nothing.

It was bizarre, actually. I got lauded for having brought the Balkans 'on message' but in actual fact the reason the British public thought the Balkans was peaceful was because we couldn't report the news prior to the election. Saying nothing did more good than any fancy statement I produced.

We are all, it seems to me, willing participants in a collective self-deception.

I'm starting to ramble. At the moment it's all just a little raw. I'd really like to see you again, if you are coming to London. But somehow I know that you're not, are you?

With the greatest respect,

Paul

* * *

They'd put everything they owned in the car. Three suitcases, and a sloshing can of petrol that smelled and made Anja's head spin.

"We need something for the journey," Mama said. "We need food."

Tata said he'd go. The village people would give him something, even though they'd asked them to leave.

"No," said Mama, pulling the scarf off her head. "I will show these people I am not afraid."

Anja kicked the seat in front. She was not sorry. She had made no friends, and missed the forest and snow of the hills.

"Why did they not like us, Tata?" she said after Mama had gone.

Tata sat behind the wheel. He looked over and scratched his newly shaven chin. There was something he was not saying. She could feel it.

"The villagers feel we will bring trouble. I have spoken to my brother. We will stay with him in Belgrade. There we will be safe."

"But what about Mama? Will she be safe?"

Tata nodded. "She will be safe, Anja. She is my wife. She is Mrs Cokic and she speaks Serbian almost as well as you do."

"But will she be safe?" Anja repeated.

Tata did not answer. He was looking through the window.

Mama was walking fast towards them. Three teenagers were following her, shouting insults. One of them threw a stone, which caught her on the side of her head.

Tata shouldered against the car door to open it. The seatbelt snagged round him.

"No!"

Anja watched her mother fall. When her head hit the kerbstone, her body lay still. A circular cheese rolled away from her arms, to wobble and finally settle in the gutter.

* * *

Paul had made up his mind. The resignation letter to his regimental headquarters lay on the shelf underneath the mirror in the hall. He was going to set himself free. If he resigned now he'd be out in the spring. In the meantime they'd post him to some dossy administrative job in Colchester, and that would mean easy access to London for job interviews. Not a bad way for it to fall.

It was a Tuesday. He had been for a run round Baildon Moor. The air was clean and the bracken just beginning to wilt. The sky was a bright blue, a royal blue, the blue of cold. He already had three job interviews lined up and was beginning to shape his ideas about what he would do with the next phase of his life. There was a vacancy in London for emergency planners with the fire service. He could do mine clearance in war-torn countries. Or he could work for the UN.

But he'd need a reference. He needed someone to say he wasn't making up all the things he'd put in his CV.

"A reference? Of course old boy!" Brassy boomed. "What you going into? The city? Estate management?"

"I don't know, Colonel. I'm asking in principle."

"Absolutely no worries at all. It'd be a pleasure. My brother left a few years ago and hated it. Thought civvies were wankers, to a man. He did sixteen years and got out with a half pension. He made it good in the end, but it took him a while. He's a fund manager. I'll put you in touch if you like?"

Paul smiled. He could hear the fear that haunted all of them, that one day the pretence would have to end.

"That would be very kind, Brassy," he said.

"No worries, Paul, no worries at all. Listen, about Kosovo. It's a shame you left so soon after the elections. Your successor was a Guardsman – nice chap, but a bit dim. I had to sack him this morning. He'd been shagging his interpreter. Imagine, another one! This time it was an Albanian, Rosie something. But there you go. I need something big to happen now, something to help me 'bury the bad news', as they're saying round Downing Street. Not found it yet, but I will."

The conversation, if that's what it was, had started to tire.

"Brassy, I'll give you a ring in a month, when I'm a bit clearer what I need. Is that all right?"

"Waterford crystal, old chap. Got the Chief on the other line anyway. Got to go. All the hairy breast! Bye! Bye for now!"

The tone hummed. A magpie landed on the wall outside the kitchen window, scattering the pigeons.

Roza. It had taken her no time at all to start shagging his replacement. How dumb was he to have thought it was real? Thankfully, the email was still unsent in his outbox.

What exquisite pain.

Paul took his running kit out of the washing machine and hung it on the line. It was uncommonly warm for September. Opening the fridge, he took out the pork pie and a tub of coleslaw. He spooned the contents onto a plate, grabbed a fork from the drawer, and went through to the lounge to watch the news. After lunch he'd walk into town and post the letter.

He missed it, of course, the sense of being at the centre of world events. But he'd manage. Clicking the remote, he watched the screen shiver into life and out of habit turned down the volume.

Breaking news, the ticker-tape ran. *Second aircraft hits World Trade Centre.* Paul stared at the screen.

This changed everything.

Author's Note

I should first say that this novel is drawn from personal experience, but I have played with the time line and certain facts, such as the timing of the UK election, for dramatic simplicity. No offence is intended by any omissions or fabrications. All the major plot events – the bus bomb, the handover of the buffer zone, the arrest and subsequent escape of the bus bomber, and the shelling of Krivenic – are real, but the press reports and characters are inventions.

To this day, no one has been held to account for the bombing of the Nis express, despite the fact that the chief suspect is known to the UN police. And no one has ever explained why the Former Yugoslav Republic of Macedonia allegedly fired shells at the village of Krivenic, killing APTN producer Kerem Lawton.

I have written this novel not to apportion blame, but to show how secessionist wars are complex, ugly, and brutal. They require courageous political leadership and a dedicated pursuit of the truth, however painful, for the wounds of civil strife to heal. Any comments on the novel would be gratefully received at books@headsailbooks.com.

In this book 'Message Operations' is portrayed as a one man show. In reality, the Information Operations Cell during Operation Agricola 5 comprised a disparate and dedicated team, many of whom I am fortunate to still call friends: Nick Brehaut, Simon Bergman, Neil Tomlin, Laura Bibby, Sarah Holme, Gunnar Wahlin, Silvija Jashari, Jim Fraser, Rolly Rowlands, Asko Tanhuanpaa, David 'Abs' Borley, Gus Gustafson, Nick Jones, and Dicko Dickinson.

For their support in the development of this novel, I would like to thank Catherine Stalker, Gillian Walker, Cherry Moshtar, Cindy Bush, Mimoza Rushiti, Hugh Eaton, John Mazurka, Andrew Jackson, Laura Paduraru, Peter Garrett, Rachel Sargeant, Ogochukwu Nwokedi, Trish McGrath, Maureen Cullen, and especially my wife, Joanne, whom I met four days after returning from Kosovo, in July 2001.

Finally, I would like to pay tribute to Brigadier Hamish Rollo (Late RE), one of the most inspirational leaders I have ever served under. May he rest in peace.

Fergus Smith
September 2016